ADVAN

"Amy Impellizzeri is incredibly talented! She turns the truth topsy-turvy in this sinister and surprising tale of greed, politics, and power. Timely and thought-provoking—this is exactly what psychological suspense is meant to be. A winner in every way."

Hank Phillippi Ryan, nationally bestselling author of *Trust Me*

"Set against the backdrop of Washington politics, fundraising and non-profits, Amy Impellizzeri's *Why We Lie* takes the red hot marital suspense genre and gives it a twist: what if both halves of the couple are lying? A relationship thriller planted firmly in the relationship-optional age, *Why We Lie* asks readers to examine everything they think they know about their partners...and question everything they don't."

Jenny Milchman, *USA Today* bestselling/Mary Higgins Clark award winning author of *Wicked River*

"A labyrinth of subterfuge that will have you turning pages as fast as you can to get to the ending, which is as timely as it is shocking."

Liv Constantine, international bestselling author of *The Last Mrs. Parrish*

"I loved it!"

Barbara Bos, Women's Writers, Women's Books

"Take a brilliant plot concept, populate it with complex and relatable characters, then wrap it all in an intimate writing style that is equal parts 'heart' and 'head' and the result is *Why We Lie*—one of the first truly-great suspense novels of 2019. This is a book that dares to look at the truth behind the art of lying and exposes its value to humanity, society, and individual sanity."

Kristopher Zgorski of BOLO Books

"*Why We Lie* is a timely novel covering current issues surrounding honesty, social media, politics, and work-place culture. Amy Impellizzeri's background as a corporate litigator provides the framework for her novel while her creativity ignites the suspense."

Suzy Approved Reviews

"To thine own self be true, and it must follow, as the night the day, thou canst not then be false to any man."

WILLIAM SHAKESPEARE, *HAMLET*, CIRCA 1603

"Unless you're Oprah, 'Be Yourself' is terrible advice."

ADAM GRANT, *NEW YORK TIMES* OP-ED, JUNE 4, 2016

Amy Impellizzeri

Wyatt-MacKenzie Publishing
DEADWOOD, OREGON

Why We Lie
Amy Impellizzeri

Softcover Edition ISBN: 978-1-948018-35-7
Library of Congress Control Number: 2019932301

Library Edition Hardcover ISBN: 978-1-948018-34-0

Wyatt-MacKenzie Publishing
DEADWOOD, OREGON

Wyatt-MacKenzie Publishing, Inc.
www.WyattMacKenzie.com
Contact us: info@wyattmackenzie.com

DEDICATION

To My Parents, Mike and Kathy Shelley,
The first ones to teach me that it is never ever ok to lie.
I love them anyway …

Prologue

First edition of *The Washington Truth*, dated June 1, 2014
Excerpt from the Op Ed piece, by Nate Essuzare

...Some say launching a newspaper named for the truth is redundant.

Skeptics say the opposite.

I'd suggest that maybe every media outlet these days is trying to balance how much honesty we can all take.

Maybe—hear me out—we can't actually handle *all the truth, all the time.*

Then again, monitoring one's innermost thoughts and feelings sounds a lot like censorship and no one wants to talk about that in a newly launched newspaper. But there *is* research that shows that success—at least in the professional and relationship arena—might require a little discipline, a little monitoring, and yes, a little censorship.

In short, success does not always hinge on telling the truth. Success just might hinge on figuring out what people want you to say. And saying that instead.

But that's not what *The Washington Truth* is setting out to do. So let's all see how successful this new venture turns out to be, shall we?

Chapter 1

(April 2014, A small town in Pennsylvania)

Chelsea traced the letters on the arm of the wooden bench distractedly. Years and layers of BFFs and True Loves Forever and the errant foul word littered the soft wood under her fingers. She had been coming here since she was 12—the arbitrary age her mother deemed her old enough to cross the Route 497 intersection on two wheels without supervision. More recently, she'd been visiting the bench more often. There seemed to be an incessant amount of free time, despite taking as many extra shifts at the diner as she could stand.

The wooden bench hadn't always been there. It was placed near the lake with a memorial plaque one summer—Chelsea couldn't remember which one—and she had watched over time as the bench became a seat for scrawling, carved graffiti but for nothing else. In fact, other than her, Chelsea couldn't remember anyone actually using the memorial as a chair.

Memorial for whom? She wondered suddenly. Chelsea wrenched her head over the back of the bench and studied the weathered plate upside down from her angle.

Agnes Lewis. Beloved Wife, Mother, Grandmother, Great-grandmother, and Friend. 1905-2003.

Chelsea dropped back down in her seat and shuddered, doing the math.

98 years. What must Agnes Lewis have seen and done in 98 years? She had lived over 4 of Chelsea's lifetimes.

Chelsea didn't really think she had it in her to live out *this* lifetime, let alone three more. This is what she told her therapist week in and week out. This was hard. Living these days was almost more than she had energy for anymore.

The guilt and the sadness.

The heaviness.

God, she missed feeling *light*. She missed waking in the morning and still believing the day had *life*.

Her newest therapist, Dr. Flannery, told her to keep a gratitude journal to counteract her increasing hopelessness. He had given her a bright orange notebook with "Be the Sunshine in Your Own Day" scripted across the front in curled, nearly illegible letters. "Write in it daily," he said. "Focus on the life and promise around you."

Chelsea had started using the journal as a mockery. A way to make fun of her clearly inexperienced and joke-of-a-therapist who seemed to represent the upper limits of her meager medical insurance policy. For weeks, Chelsea had been filling the orange notebook with snarky comments and lines–adding scribbles and doodles in the places where gratitude was supposed to lurk. Her therapist seemed to be growing weary when they met last. He told her that maybe she would like to investigate other therapists. He'd given her a list of reputable people in her zip code who took her insurance. She had felt defensive then. She'd gotten back into therapy because she'd started to feel like her mother had given up on her, and now she felt like maybe Dr. Flannery was giving up on her too, so she decided to try a bit harder. If they were going to break up, she wanted to be the one breaking up with him. And she wasn't ready to leave therapy yet. She at least knew that much.

Chelsea had nodded stoically. "I'll use the journal for actual journaling," she'd promised. "Can we maybe meet on Mondays instead of Fridays? I'm less snarky because I'm less tired at the beginning of the week." Dr. Flannery looked skeptical while he agreed. They were scheduled to meet the very next Monday.

Meanwhile, Chelsea wrote in the journal. She journaled about her step-dad and how she hoped he'd start dating soon. How she was rooting for him. She journaled about her new shifts at the diner. And about her mother.

Chelsea had also started journaling about Rafe. Long detailed entries about exactly what he'd done to her.

And not done.

The truth finally. She'd recorded the truth. Although Chelsea had not been sharing those entries with her therapist yet, she felt that the fact she could write it down honestly showed promise. So much so that she wanted to continue with the therapy for the time being.

The writing? It was actually *helping.* It may have been the first thing to do so.

Under the glaring sun, with splintered wood scraping her legs under her too short waitressing skirt, Chelsea finished up the latest entry about her mother. If the journal was a way to keep her mother alive—even this way—it might not be so bad after all.

After so many hours on this bench, today she felt lighter. Maybe this eyesore of a journal would work after all. Maybe she'd get stronger. For real this time. Strong enough to leave town now that Rafe was in jail. Strong enough to move on to a new relationship. Strong enough to start over.

Chelsea pushed up from Agnes Lewis's rotting memorial bench with renewed strength, and thought: *In the future, there will be a time when I will no longer be afraid to tell the truth.*

But even as the thought was forming in her brain, Chelsea suspected she'd have to tell a great many more lies to get to that point.

Chapter 2

(Five years later, April 2019, Washington D.C.)

The television volume at the nurse's station was louder than it needed to be. I was trying to focus but all I could hear was the background noise debating the possibility of war in a small country that I wasn't quite sure I'd ever heard of before. Funny how the bloody mess of the world can become so inconsequential when your small corner of the world starts to cave in on itself.

This wasn't supposed to happen, Jude.

"Mrs. Birch. Do you need water? Are you all right?"

My vision came back into focus and I realized I had nearly fainted.

I reminded myself that I was only looking at pictures of a brain. Not a brain itself.

"Mrs. Birch. Do you need water?" Dr. Drake was repeating himself. As I calmed down, I wondered how much repeating he'd had to do in this meeting. I was losing my sense of time and place. I pinched the skin on my fingers to try to get some feeling back in them. Everything was going numb.

It was not a new feeling. I had been feeling this way—numb and light headed—on and off since the night of the shooting three months earlier. As I'd waited for Jude to come out of surgery on that night, all the lead stories, on every local channel, had basically begun the same way.

Jude Birch, newly sworn-in Congressman, is the apparent victim of stray bullet in gang fight to the death in Anacostia neighborhood. Congressman Birch not expected to make it out of surgery.

But that was nearly three months ago. And Congressman Birch did indeed make it out of surgery, and beyond. As we drove the route to meet Dr. Drake at the hospital earlier that morning, I'd noticed the cherry blossoms were bursting along the trails of the Washington D.C. Mall. It was my favorite time of year—and yet—everything inside me felt dead as I stared hypnotically at the backlit images on Dr. Drake's wall.

This wasn't supposed to happen. I love you, Jude. And that's the truth.

I had been repeating this mantra silently and quite often in the three months since the surgery. During the surgery, the hospital had given us a private room. It turns out that hospital security and confidentiality rivals the best security detail on Capitol Hill, and I should know. Even though Jude was brand new to Capitol Hill at the time of the shooting, I'd already had my fair share of interactions with the illustrious U.S. Capitol Police.

I waited for Jude to come out of surgery while trying to ignore the news reports. I knew they didn't have accurate information about the shooting or Jude's condition. I was the only one who had actually been there, and no one had been permitted to talk to me. The press stayed away from our private hospital room, unbidden and unknowing. And I was left alone with my affirmations and mantras.

After surgery, I kept everyone away. I wanted Jude to myself. I sat with him for days while he was in a medically induced coma, and later, while I waited to see if he would wake from the delicate surgery required to remove a bullet from his brain.

This wasn't supposed to happen.

I repeated the mantra often as I moved through a new routine in our home—a routine that included seemingly incessant physical therapy and occupational therapy for Jude. Round-the-clock care even when I was home. Which I tried to be as often as I could.

In fact, in those early months after the shooting and the surgery, my time with Jude was only interrupted by afternoons of respite care supplied by Jude's best friends, Huck and Finn, that filled me with a gratitude that surpassed anything I had felt from the flood of calls, food deliveries, and other overwhelming support we'd gotten from our D.C. community.

This wasn't supposed to happen.

I had tried to protect Jude, and I'd failed. But now, I was focused on getting him well. And—although he didn't know it yet—getting him out of D.C.

Dr. Drake ignored my inner monologue and pushed onward.

"So, Mrs. Birch."

"Dr. Drake, please call me Aby."

I was forever reminding Dr. Drake of this. He would reluctantly comply before lapsing back into his Mrs. Birch salutations and I'd have to begin the reminders all over again. He never reciprocated by saying—"Sure, call me, Dan." But still I felt ridiculous being called Mrs. Birch after the shooting—like I might turn around and find out my late mother-in-law had been sitting behind me this whole time.

"This is the CT scan we took that first night to get images of the bullet's location before surgery."

That first night.

I had to work hard not to chuckle at the irony. I have a lousy habit of laughing when I am uncomfortably stressed. It was something Jude was always trying to help me through, you know, before the shooting. When appearances seemed to be more important to him. In meetings with Dr. Drake, Jude largely sat mute next to me letting me do all the speaking, a point of regret and relief. It seemed all of my feelings after the shooting became mixed ones. I became aware how much more black and white my world had been previously. Even though I always felt so angrily ambivalent about it.

The grey zone seemed to really emerge after the shooting.

Mrs. Birch, this is the CT scan we took that first night.

Dr. Drake meant, of course, the night we first arrived at

the hospital—the night we first met Dr. Drake—who just so happened to be the on-call neurosurgeon at the university hospital. But I didn't remember it that way. I didn't remember it as the *first night*. I thought of it as the *last night*. The last night of our old lives.

That's why I was sitting in Dr. Drake's office three months later asking him to make sense of the nonsensical for me. By all accounts, Jude was healing. Dr. Drake went so far as to keep saying Jude was healing *nicely*. The therapists who came in and out of our Brookland home in Northeast D.C. said he was making remarkable progress. They said I should be overjoyed. But I didn't feel overjoyed.

I looked at the images Dr. Drake had pinned up on his wall morosely for me and tried desperately to make sense of the coiled shadows. Dr. Drake pressed his finger up against the films backlit on a screen affixed to the wall. His finger grazed the clear lines of the silhouette of a bullet, and I shuddered at the grey and white shadows, thinking again about how close Jude had been to death.

"So again, these are from that first night," Dr. Drake repeated. "And these," Dr. Drake backlit a new second row of films dramatically, "are the pictures we took today."

I tilted my head left as if the images were lopsided and that might help. It didn't.

Even to my layperson's eyes, it looked as if these were two different people's brains. It was more than the fact that the bullet was missing in the second set of films. The shape, the shading, all of it was different in the second set.

"I don't understand. How could his brain have changed *that* much in three months? It doesn't even look like that brain should belong to the same person as that one."

"I couldn't agree with you more, Mrs. Birch. Jude's brain is healing itself in a way we have literally never seen before. He's very lucky, your husband. His prognosis was very grave that first night. But things have really turned around."

That first night.

Here we go again. Why does he keep calling it that?

"What does it mean?"

"We're not sure. It could be fine. It could mean all good things."

"I hear a but, Dr. Drake." Of course there was a but. I had come here for a follow-up appointment that hadn't been scheduled, for more scans and to remind Dr. Drake to call me Aby, and finally, to hear the but.

Jude is acting strangely, Dr. Drake.

That was the best description of symptoms I'd been able to muster. The physical therapists and the occupational therapists kept telling me to be patient. That Jude was making extraordinary progress. But I wasn't sure the progress was in the right direction. And I might even have thought I had overreacted, that I was crazy, if I wasn't sitting with Dr. Drake, looking at the two disparate brain pictures right that moment.

Something was off in Jude's brain.

I knew it. I felt it. And now, with Dr. Drake's help, I could see it.

"It's just that his brain is replacing prefrontal white matter with excessive amounts of grey matter. He seemed to have a higher than average ratio of grey to white to begin with so it appears that his brain is over-compensating. And so of course his multi-layer thought processing has been dramatically affected."

"Dr. Drake, I'm sorry. I know I misled you into thinking that because I'm a fairly intelligent woman that I can handle all this medical mumbo jumbo stuff, but I have absolutely no idea what this means. I'm staring at Jude's brains—brain, I'm sorry, of course, he only has one brain. What's wrong with me? But—even though I'm looking at the same thing you are, and listening so very carefully, still, I can't make sense of this. Are you saying that Jude's brain has changed since his surgery? That's the reason for his—well, his outbursts?"

"Yes, I am."

"Is it like, Tourette's or something?"

"No, not exactly."

"So, what?"

"Aby, Jude has lost the filter of his prefrontal cortex."

"What does that mean?"

"Well, for one thing, it means he can't lie."

"I'm sorry, did you just say he can't lie? Like can't lie down?"

"No, not like that. Jude can't tell an untruth."

"Hell of a problem for a politician," I gave into my natural impulse and laughed uncomfortably. Jude sat quietly next to me, and Dr. Drake didn't join in the laughter either.

"I'm sorry. Dr. Drake, are you actually serious? This is my husband's brain's funny way of healing itself? He's perfectly fine in all ways, except that he can't lie?"

"I'm completely serious, Mrs. Birch."

"Please. I'm begging you. Please call me Aby."

Later when Dr. Drake was done with us, Jude and I sat in the room alone, waiting for a computer print-out summarizing the visit, and I studied the films again.

When the CT technologist came back in to pull down the copies of the films, I greeted her. "It turns out my husband's brain has over-compensated so much that he can no longer lie. This is the reason he's survived his near fatal wound, actually."

She looked at me blankly. "Well, the doctor doesn't share diagnoses with me, ma'am. I just take the pictures."

I nodded, understanding. I took in her colorful scrubs in direct contrast to the doctor's slate grey scrubs that had recently exited the room. I'd learned that in hospital hierarchy, the more decorative the scrubs, the less information you could get from the wearer. Clearly, Jude's diagnosis was above the technologist's pay grade. But she had worked so hard for us. I decided I'd reward her with the inside scoop.

"It turns out he's perfectly fine, except that he can't lie

anymore," I advised the technologist, wanting someone, anyone, to acknowledge the craziness of this new diagnosis.

"Well, I'm glad to hear the Congressman is doing well." The technologist looked anxious to leave.

I let her and then I wondered to myself why I kept saying: "perfectly fine, except."

Because was it really such a bad thing that he couldn't lie?

Was it the worst thing that could have happened? To him? To us?

I leaned far back in my chair with the newly delivered prognosis, waiting for the nurse to come back in.

No. It wasn't the worst thing that had happened. Not by a long shot.

But it might just be the worst thing that could happen *next*.

෴

I left Dr. Drake's office, pushed the down button outside the elevator doors, and stepped inside moments later when the doors opened loudly, all hand in hand with a silent Jude. What had once been a customary act of endearment between us had taken on new significance since the shooting. Jude was easily tired, disoriented even. Outings could be arduous. Medical appointments could be exhausting. I was usually leading him, pushing him, or prodding him along when we went out in public these days. It might have looked like holding hands, but it was more than that. In the elevator, Jude finally broke his silence.

"Is that what Dr. Drake meant, Aby?"

"What do you mean, Jude?" I was distracted on my phone, scrolling through some work emails with my free hand, trying to figure out how many of them could wait until the next day. I was so tired.

"I couldn't really follow what he was saying. But I heard

you talk to the tech. My brain? It's ok, except now I can't lie? That's what the doctor meant?"

"Um hum." I squeezed his hand in mine. "Don't you worry, Jude. That's not such a big deal, is it?" He stared off into space, and I took a few deep breaths to try to quash the rising panic in my throat that wanted to scream out.

Jude's not being able to lie was a *very* big deal.

Dr. Drake's office was in a section of the hospital that had valet parking and after we headed outside the ground level of the building's automatic doors, I handed the valet our claim check and a $5 bill and waited on the curb with Jude for the valet to bring our car around. It took a few minutes, and as I saw our own car pull up, I briefly noticed a black Mercedes pull up to the curb behind our valet. No one got in or out of the Mercedes as it sat there, not even as I helped Jude into the passenger side and then walked around to my side. Something tugged at my subconscious as it noticed that fact.

The valet closed the driver side door for me attentively as I got in. I glanced in the rear view mirror to see the driver of the car behind me, but between the glare and the dark windows of both of our cars, I couldn't make anyone out.

"Are they with you?" I asked the valet gesturing to the Mercedes. The valet glanced back, shook his head quickly, and then said, "Have a nice day, Mrs. Birch," as he pocketed some cash and ran up to greet the next patient exiting the building. This was a hospital and staff used to dealing with high level dignitaries and politicians. Discretion was a way of life. As were kickbacks. I thought about the bills the valet had just pocketed. They could have been a randomly timed coincidence with the arrival of the car behind me, but I didn't think so.

I hadn't asked for any security to follow us to or from Dr. Drake's office that day, given the last-minute nature of the appointment, and now I regretted my carelessness. Jude wasn't warranting round-the-clock security yet. We were still working on that.

Despite everything that had happened in the weeks leading up to the election, the local police had already investigated his shooting in the days and weeks immediately following, and they had resolved that, just as the press had initially reported, he'd been the victim of errant gunfire of some local gang bangers who had a history of shooting up that particular block and who seemed to have gone on the lam shortly after the shooting.

Jude's shooting had become part of the political rhetoric for the D.C. mayor who was constantly begging for more federal resources to erase the gangs and drug lords from the urban landscape of our nation's capital. I didn't really believe that version of the incident, but I had more important things keeping my attention, like Jude's recovery and healing, our future, and now—his brand new bizarre diagnosis.

I sat behind the wheel, still parked on the curb, trying to shake the feeling that the dark car situated behind me was something to be concerned about. I pulled up the block a bit, still within view of the valet station, but trying to get out of the way of it. I stayed close to the curb without pulling into the traffic. The Mercedes behind me mirrored my actions, hugging the curb. I glanced at Jude in the passenger seat, looking tired and worn from the day's activities, but also oblivious. I gave another glance at the valet station. There were enough people, including a hospital security guard, within earshot and view, to empower me to get out and confront the car behind me.

Better to do it now, than to let the car follow me home.

I walked up to the driver side window, which I saw was being lowered to greet me. As if the driver had been expecting me. "Mrs. Birch. Sorry if I startled you. I wanted to check on Jude. He's doing better, yes?"

I couldn't help but gasp.

After all, he was the last person I expected to see. Or to be inquiring about Jude's health.

"Mr. Treese. You *did* startle me. How'd you know I was here? That we were here?" I felt an ominous sense of foreboding. Maybe this confrontation idea was a bad one.

"Listen, Aby. I know we haven't exactly been on the same side of the political table lately."

I stifled another inappropriate laugh as that was an understatement for sure.

"But I have something very important to say to you. Be careful about who you trust. Do you understand what I'm saying to you? Jude's shooting? It might not have been as random as you think it was. Just don't dismiss that possibility, ok? You might want to ask the police to re-open the case. That's all I wanted to say. Goodbye, Aby."

Dominic Treese put the window up, pulled away from the curb and drove around me, leaving me to analyze his warning.

I shuddered as he drove away. After all, he was the man who had tried hard to help Jude's adversary defeat him in the recent Congressional election. Treese was right; we hadn't been on the same side in politics.

Still, I had lots of suspicions about Jude's shooting. And lots of guilt. I couldn't say for sure that Dominic Treese was wrong.

And as I watched him drive away, I wondered exactly what Dominic Treese knew that I didn't.

Chapter 3

Poetically, exactly one year—*to the day*—before I learned that my husband had actually lost his ability to lie, Jude stood in a crowded loft in Northeast in front of 500 paying guests and promised to be honest always. "If elected, it will be my great honor to serve with humility and authenticity."

The blur of the lights of Brookland speeding past was hypnotizing as Jude and I raced along Michigan Avenue on our way from our home to the rented loft space where Jude was scheduled to make his big announcement. He was officially entering a special election added to the fall schedule, to fill a brand new seat in the House of Representatives—a new Congressional representative for the District of Columbia.

Maybe the rest of the country was focused on bigger things, but the buzz leading up to the announcement had been electric in our little circle.

"A formal announcement of the worst kept secret in D.C. since Marilyn Monroe." That's how *The Washington Truth*—a small but earnest press with a cult-like following in D.C.—leading the way for every other larger news outlet—would report it the next day. And everyone who was anyone in D.C. would become part of our days and nights.

We'd been to events like these before. Classic Washington events with politicians and donors and more than enough booze to lubricate both groups. "Two-drink minimum is also a two drink maximum," Jude always sang into my ear when we headed into the room. We'd been auditioning in the D.C. political scene for years, and by then, each event was starting to take on a similar feel to the last one.

Except that night. That night was … *magical*. Because we weren't heading into an event for someone *else* that night.

We were heading into a night that was for Jude. For *us*. Everything we had sacrificed and worked for. All the lines crossed, and boundaries blurred—for *this*. It felt worth it in that moment. It really did.

Jude had been visibly elated as we headed into the Freedom Art loft space rented out by his fundraising committee, which at that point was still him and his two law school roommates doing business as Friends of Jude Birch.

I have to admit, though it runs counter to all I've tried to achieve since first arriving in D.C. years ago, I loved being on Jude's arm as we entered the room that night. I had spent weeks picking out my dress. Business but sexy. Trendy but classic. Appropriate but daring. In the end, after non-stop boutique and designer exclusive shopping, I ultimately decided on something a bit more understated. I picked something from an online shop—an MM.LaFleur design that I admired on the website with a cashmere-like softness when it arrived and peplum pleats that helped me lose no less than 10 pounds in my hips the moment I put it on. No matter that it was an online find. Maybe someone else would be wearing it, but they wouldn't look like this in it, I told myself. And it was black. Not like the latest vividly colored line from the runway that would be recognizable instantly. I paired the dress with my Louboutin heel splurge from the last season ($550 on eBay for "Worn One Time" shoes and an extra $20 for sole guards that I put on every time I went out to try to preserve the distinctive red soles). I was also wearing my favorite necklace: a cascading turquoise and glass bead monstrosity that my mother had bought from a glass blower in Bermuda on her honeymoon with my step-dad, and brought home to me as a "souvenir." I touched the necklace and let the emotion of missing my mother wash over me.

Because it was so powerful—the loss—I only let it enter my consciousness every so often. She would have loved to see me wearing the necklace. She would have loved Jude, too, of course. But she would have hated so much else about my life. I shook off the emotion and sealed my mother out of my brain for the rest of the night. My mother—dead or not—had no place at Jude's campaign event, I told myself.

After we walked into the event, I had to relinquish Jude to the Friends of Jude Birch, while I practiced the role of a Congressman's partner—gabbing and making small talk, and remembering who was who, who was sleeping with whom, and whose wives didn't know about the latter. Jude practically danced around the room flanked by his buddies, Huck and Finn. I caught his eye and smiled. I heard his laugh float across the room. "No, no, those aren't their real names. It's a long story actually."

⌒

Harvey "Huck" Whitman, III and Jude met the first week of law school at George Washington bonding over legal briefs and *Pfalsgraf* (*whatever that was*). A few weeks later, Huck and Jude had agreed to grab beers after class at the Foggy Bottom neighborhood bar where Huck was meeting his roommate, Carl Merrow, IV, a fellow law student, but a year ahead. Legend had it that after about four Guinesses, Jude slapped Harvey "Huck" Whitman, III and Carl on the backs and announced that there was no way he was going to be able to remember their full names, and was going to call the duo Huck and Finn for ease of reference. A new nickname was born, and an unbreakable bond among the trio.

Only days before law school started, Jude was still living with his college girlfriend—a debutante from McClean, Virginia, whose father had bought she and her seemingly soon-to-be fiancé a lovely townhome in Old Town Alexandria, Virginia. The plan was for the couple to live there and for Jude to commute to GW, while Cindy commuted to her internship position on the Hill. The arrangement lasted through the summer between college and law school, at which point Cindy broke up with Jude for not being "intense enough," a quality Jude swore to me in later conversations was not something he had ever promised to be. In fact by law school orientation, he said with a laugh, "I was quite intense. She probably should have held out a few more days."

In truth, he said, Cindy most likely was comparing him (both sexually and intellectually) to the fellow intern from the Hill that she had started sleeping with at some point during the summer (July as best he could figure), and kicked Jude out to make more room for the guy who was going to start sleeping over more often while Jude spent his nights holed up in the law library.

So when Huck and Finn met Jude, Jude was actually crashing on couches of old college fraternity brothers, who were a few years older and had relocated to D.C., and with whom he'd reconnected through Facebook; they were, Jude had to admit, growing bored with their freeloading resident. Since Huck and Finn's roommate had recently exited their extra Foggy Bottom bedroom with three months' rent, a substantial heroin addiction, and also the big screen TV, Jude was invited to move in by Guiness number five for the cost of a TV and no security deposit. The trio of "Huck, Finn and Jude" was born and perhaps they would have moved about the world just the three of them forever, but for that night outside a bar on H Street where I was waiting, as the trio was exiting one night a few years out of law school.

〜

Under the exposed beams of the Freedom Art loft space, I looked at my watch and noticed the time was getting close for Jude to be announced. I caught Huck's eye and waved across the room to him. He was rolling his eyes discreetly to show his disdain for the woman he was stuck in conversation with. I laughed and held my wrist up and pointed to it reminding him visually that it was almost time for the big moment.

"What are you thinking about gorgeous?"

Jude came around the corner then and surprised me as I was surveying the crowd and trying to keep Huck on schedule across the wide plank-floored room. Jude stood behind me and wrapped his arms around the neckline of my dress from behind and rested his head on the top of my head in his signature move. Even with my Louboutin heels, I barely reached Jude's chin. He had to duck down to kiss me and whenever he snuck up behind me like this, he rested his chin on my head in an equally affectionate gesture.

I leaned forward away from Jude's chin to give Huck one more watch-pointing mime signal and then leaned into Jude's backwards embrace. "I was thinking about the night I broke down in front of Little Miss Whiskey's."

"Ah yes," Jude whispered into my hair warming me down to my toes. "If not for that rusty 2001 Hundai, we might not even be standing here today."

I laughed and leaned farther into Jude. "Oh, I have a feeling you'd still be here. But I would have had to *buy* my ticket." Jude spun me around until I was facing him, dizzy from the stilettos, the rosé, and the night. I closed my eyes and felt Jude's lips on each one of my eyelids, another of our paired moves. "Now. Listen up, Aby. Because I might forget to say this tonight and every night after today. Everything I am right now. Everything I'm planning on doing. Everything that is about to happen. It's because of you, Sweetheart. You are my gift. You are my muse. And I couldn't do any of this without you. I love you."

I smiled tentatively up at him. Jude wouldn't forget to say it. He'd say it again and again like he had been saying it so much over the last few weeks. It was beautiful and lovely, and it was starting to get easier to believe. But, still our love felt fragile.

Even then. Before the truth came to light and everything we had both said and done before would need to be examined under a new lens.

But in that sparkling moment in the Freedom Art loft, Jude's words were heady and gratifying. I interrupted the moment anyway. "Oh you. Let's face it. This campaign announcement had been in the works already that night we met on H Street."

Jude smiled and nuzzled my ear. And ignored me. "We need a little reunion in front of Little Miss Whiskey's, you know. I haven't been back there in years."

"Me neither."

When we told the "how we met" story to newcomers in our life, it always started on the corner of H and 11th, on a spring night in 2015. I was standing outside, next to my car parked on the corner, hood up, and a not insignificant amount of smoke bellowing from within. It wasn't long before I found myself on the receiving end of a ride home offer from an incredibly tall, incredibly handsome (but also a little bit drunk) man who pointed to his shorter, less handsome, but apparently sober friend who was actually offered up as the driver for this whole adventure.

The third friend—who turned out to be Finn—was in between—in looks, height, and sobriety.

I had figured out by that time—finally—that I could take care of my own damn self. Which is why I was even there in the first place.

The tall man was persistent as he pointed to his short sober friend. "Meet Huck. He'll drive. He's our designated driver tonight. I'll navigate. We promise to be complete gentlemen."

Something in Jude's eyes made me want to deviate from my script and say yes on sight. Something so clear. After all I'd been through in the last few years before he found me broken down on that corner—literally—I was clear-eyed finally. I liked that I'd found someone else who was clear-eyed as well. Still, I was not naïve. I understood that three handsome frat boys who also happened to be lawyers were still to be turned down when they offered damsels in distress rides. Such boys are a dime a dozen in D.C. and they may be or may not be serial killers, or rapists, or worse—conservatives.

I wasn't going to take that kind of chance outside Little Miss Whiskey's, and I told them so, as I held up my hand and started dialing information for local cab companies.

"Conservatives!" The trio laughed in a way I could already tell they did most things—in unison. "You have us all wrong. Jude Birch here's a *bona fide* District of Columbia born and bred liberal—he's going to run for office one day. Probably even be President of these here United States." Huck slapped Jude on the back and feigned a midwestern accent that didn't exactly match his ambiguously copper-colored skin that I thought at the time might be Indian, might be Middle Eastern, or might be the result of a long summer in the Caribbean. I found out later it was a combination of all of the above. "Jude here" as I started calling him for a short-lived time had a pretty face and too long hair. A couple of years later, after his political aspirations were much more than a pipe dream, when Justin Trudeau rose in fame with our Canadian neighbors to the north, I pointed to him on the television, and said to Jude, "You two could be brothers!"—and Jude had laughed, and said, "Eh? Canadian, hunh?"

But outside Little Miss Whiskey's that night, Jude didn't look like anyone except maybe my next boyfriend. Someone to help facilitate my launch of the next leg of my journey, a short-term fling at best, but one that I was already looking forward to as I leaned on my hunk of junk Hundai trying to look as svelte and cool as possible. I hadn't planned to fall for Jude Birch at first sight, but that's what happened anyway.

The heart wants what the heart wants, my mother always said. She said it every time people asked her how she could have fallen for a poor struggling artist like my step-dad. Those words ended up in her final conversation to me, too, but in a much different, more painful context. Still, something in me bottled up those words and saved them for later. Later came outside Little Miss Whiskey's as it turns out. Standing on the corner of the trendy bar waving away smoke billowing out from under the car hood I'd inherited from her, I remembered that ridiculous quote of hers. I had an urge to call her and apologize for always dismissing it. While the boys argued over who would be able to best diagnose my car troubles, I dialed her old number and let it go to voicemail. She was dead by then, of course, but still I hadn't given up the habit of calling her occasionally.

As I said no to the ride, I smiled and flirted right back while Jude moved about my car pretending he knew what he was doing and sort of pretending to supervise Finn under the dinged-up hood of my car.

Finn looked up from under my hood that I had somehow—incredulously I always claimed when we reminisced about that night—managed to pop open shortly before the boys arrived on the scene, where he was fiddling with the wires underneath. Something about Finn always seemed a little less threatening than the other two. When I found out, much later, that Finn's real name was Carl—I had laughed and said, "Oh! I wouldn't have had any qualms letting a 'Carl' drive me home that night. That makes *perfect* sense." From around the corner of the hood, Finn yelled out, "Radiator hose is busted. You aren't getting home via this car tonight. And you're right, Miss. You should never accept rides from strangers. No matter how good looking they are or whether they are going to be President of the United States one day."

Jude shrugged his shoulders innocently. "Well, let us help you anyway. We can buy you a drink while you're waiting for your cab." He gestured inside, but I ignored him as I tapped on my phone and then shushed him as I spoke into it.

"I need a cab, please, at the corner of 11th and H, northeast. Yes, outside of Little Miss Whiskey's."

I shushed them again.

"No, I broke down, I'm not drunk. Tell the driver I have no plans of throwing up on his pleather upholstery. Please, thanks. Um, Where to?"

As I repeated the dispatcher's question, I looked over at the boys who looked a little too expectantly at the imminent blurting out of my home address. "To Georgetown, please. I'll give the driver the exact address when he gets here."

Jude whistled as I hung up. "Georgetown, hunh? So do you have a nice waterfront condo? Wait, you're not like an undergrad are you? You're legal, right?"

I belly laughed at that one. "Thanks for the compliment. Not an undergrad. I work for a fledgling foundation in town. Let's just leave it at that."

I was admittedly embarrassed under Jude's intense stare. ("Well, she was wrong. you *are* intense, Jude," I had said when he finally fessed up to the reason his previous girlfriend had dumped him for her comrade on the Hill.)

Later—much later—Jude would connect the dots on the timing of my job. Consequences and choices would unravel and unfold, and we'd all be accountable for our mistakes and withheld information.

Later.

But not that night.

That night outside Little Miss Whiskey's when everything was still unknown?

Contrary to what Dr. Drake might say a few years later, *that* was the real first night for me and Jude. Everything that came next stemmed from *that first night*.

⤸

Waiting outside Little Miss Whiskey's for a cab *that first night*, I had to inform the boys a few more times that neither Jude, nor the other two would be driving me home. I'd wait for the cab, and I didn't need them to wait with me, thank you very much. I refused to give them so much as my first name or initials. Certainly not my number no matter how many times Jude asked. I would have relented, of course, if Jude didn't insist I take *his* name and number—which I did with an exaggerated show of begrudging gratitude. When he said, "Seriously—just call me and let me know you got home ok, please," his words were punctuated with a sincerity that I was certain I had never seen in any male's eyes.

Yes, unfortunately, it was his sincerity that hooked me.

I called later that night, and said simply, "Hi, it's me. I made it home."

And I could have sworn I heard a sigh come from Jude as he said, "Thank you for calling. How about lunch tomorrow?"

We agreed quickly on an Ethiopian place on Ninth Street and hung up before I realized I hadn't even given him my name.

⤸

An hour before I arrived at the Ethiopian restaurant, Jude texted me.

I still don't know your name.

Well, I'm not sure our relationship has progressed quite that far, Mr. Birch.

Fair enough. What should I call you at lunch?

I was still pondering when I saw the three dots pop up and then:

The future Mrs. Birch?

Ha ha. Very funny.

Well, you seem like someone who could make a guy forget all before you.

All before you.

I traced the words—the letters—in his text and finally relented.

Sigh. Very romantic, Mr. Birch. Ok, then. At lunch, you can call me Aby.

Aby it is.

Three more dots and a pause. A pause long enough to make me wonder if I was making a fool out of myself, and then he added: *And the future Mrs. Birch, for short.*

〜

At lunch, surrounded by plastic orchids and wood paneling decorated with cheap photographic prints of tourist attractions in the nation's capital, we pretended we were actually getting to know each other. Sharing job descriptions, and the best of each other's families and travel highlights and humanitarian projects.

Jude told me he had lived all his life in the city limits, and for Washington D.C., that was like 1,000 dog years. Even though I was relatively new to D.C., still I knew enough about the town to know that no one was *from* D.C. Mostly, it was a stopping ground for those ambitious enough to walk through its doors. A place for the elite from places outside of D.C. to come to work. To make a difference. And to leave again. But Jude was *from* D.C. and crazy obsessed with advocating for its city schools, its equal voting rights, and countless other measures. He was born into a family of middle class, hard workers; his parents had both been career educators in the District of Columbia school system, before retiring in Florida. But they had not had the opportunity to enjoy retirement as they had died tragically in a car accident the year before Jude started law school.

A proud product of the District of Columbia public school system, Jude had worked and saved and taken out government subsidized loans to put himself through college and then law school within the city limits of his native town. While in law school, he had worked summers interning for the inhouse counsel's office of a notorious construction company, and then leveraged an important recommendation to get a prestigious (and relatively new) spot at the U.S. Attorney's office, where he'd been working on internet privacy and some other high profile cases for the last two years.

I shared only snippets of my life before. I told Jude my mom had been involved in local politics, and that her death was tragic and nothing I wanted to talk any more about. He nodded with empathy. He confessed that the reason he'd been living on frat brothers' couches at the start of law school after leaving his girlfriend's townhouse was that he was struggling with his own grief as well as lack of funds.

I was impressed that other than those brief months living with his Virginia debutante in Old Town Virginia, Jude had never had an address outside of the District of Columbia city limits. He knew where the best Vietnamese food was, had six favorite dive bars in various neighborhoods of the city, knew the best times to jog the Washington monument mall, and where the best community theatre was. But he was far from provincial.

In college, Jude told me, he'd traveled every spring break with Habitat for Humanity to underserved areas of the country, helping build homes and restore communities in crisis. As a D.C. lawyer, he used his charisma to propel fundraisers and to broaden his world view; he used his vacation time to travel to places like Haiti and Honduras on mission trips organized by the local churches.

I sized him up over lunch. Jude had the understated experience and world view of a veteran privileged politician with the drive and courage of a rookie one. And I let him know that his interest in politics was a hurdle for me, not a selling point. "I'm looking to make my own mark on the world. I'm mostly here in D.C. to help underprivileged kids. I'm not really into politics, if you must know."

Jude nodded. "Yes! That's exactly what I'm talking about! I think my place—and the District's place—and indeed the United States' place—in the global picture can only be viewed along a spectrum where educational reform, and under-served *kids*, are the priority. *Not* politics."

By the end of lunch, I told Jude that while I had not planned to get involved in politics when I first came to D.C., he was already making D.C. politics sound sort of unexpectedly interesting to me.

Jude told me he was excited about the journey ahead, and that he was sure he would never lose focus of what really mattered. That he'd be the first politician in history to avoid becoming a cliché and would never forget about the reasons driving him there in the first place.

I wondered how much of the story Jude was feeding me was pure bullshit. *Wasn't this just a politician's lies?*

As our waitress came over to check on us, a note dropped out of her apron's pocket. Jude reached for it and skimmed it, then blushed. I thought it might be a love note. I said as much. "No," he said quietly. "It's a grocery list. Itemized by aisle. Diapers, wipes, baby soap. She's a *mom.*" He said it almost reverently.

When she came back, he handed her back the list, and I noticed he glanced at her ring finger. I did the same. I caught his glance and felt the thought in unison. *Single mom.* He paid the bill, and I asked to leave the tip. I wanted to leave something generous for this sweet waitress who could have been my own mother twenty years earlier. I slipped $20 into the bill folder, and excused myself for a final trip to the ladies' room. As I walked away, I glanced back over my shoulder to see Jude quietly slipping more bills into the folder.

And I realized in that moment: he *believed* this stuff he was saying. And that fact, more than anything he'd actually said that day, made me realize how perfect we might be for each other.

We ended up back in Jude's apartment for dessert. The politics discussion ended there.

His roommates were gone. When I asked where they were, he told me, "We lawyers all usually go into our respective offices on Sundays to get a jump start on the week. I had other plans today," he winked at me.

I told Jude that I'd left Pennsylvania for the best of reasons and the worst of ones.

"There was a guy. I wanted a fresh start. Put it that way."

"Ah. Ok. So tell me about your last boyfriend. The one you left behind."

I weighed the question. Balanced how much I'd decide to tell him. How far I wanted to go back. How truthful I wanted to be. Out came my decision.

"Oh boy, Wilson. Well, you should know he was a lawyer, too."

Jude fake gasped. "No!"

"Don't tease. I swore off lawyers completely after that one. You're lucky we're even sitting here."

"So what was the final death knell? Other than just, you know, the fact that he was a member of the most noblest of professions?"

I gulped down a bite of thawed-but-still-frozen cheesecake and washed it down with some red wine that Jude had opened, before answering. I wondered if this would be a bit too complicated. I dove in anyway.

"Sarbanes Oxley if you must know."

Jude looked at me with his mouth a little open but to his credit, didn't burst out laughing.

"Sarbanes Oxley?"

I nodded. "You know it right? Please, tell me you know the law that was passed for no other purpose than to prevent another Enron in this lifetime. Yes? No? Maybe?"

This time, Jude laughed. "Yes. We lawyers are generally pretty familiar with Sarbanes Oxley. So how did that kill the relationship with Wilson? Do tell."

"Oh, forget it." I waved my hand trying to dismiss the conversation, realizing this was no longer first date stuff. I'd gone too far. But Jude insisted. "What? Tell me."

I decided to go all in.

"He was covering up all sorts of bad stuff with a public tech company he was representing in town. There were a bunch of whistleblowers making a name for themselves in the press, and I finally confronted him."

"And?"

"And, he was pretty dismissive. But I said, come on. It's not one or two—it's dozens now. You need to report the creative bookkeeping that's going on. You're the *lawyer* for God's sake.

"And he had the nerve to reply, 'Right. Which is exactly why I won't be reporting a thing. I have a client confidentiality to uphold. I'm not going to risk disbarment because of a few disgruntled citizens who might not understand that the stock market is a pretty volatile place to put your money.'

"And I said, 'Seriously? You are going to risk disbarment—or worse—if you *don't* report them. That's the point of all the new regulations since the whole Enron debacle. You *have* to come clean. You can't hide behind the lawyer privilege. You're being very obtuse.'"

Jude watched me and when I didn't keep going, he moved me along with his hands. "Yes, come on. Now I'm invested. How did he respond to you calling him obtuse?"

"Well that's the best part. He called me 'adorable.' And then he said, 'A lot of very smart men have been all over these books. How about you just leave it to them? Don't you worry your pretty little head about this stuff.'"

Jude's eyes got big and he opened his mouth in a real gasp. I felt a powerful relief that was distracting. I paused an extra beat before I realized that it was still my turn to talk.

"So. I left town and I never saw him again. And those corporate whistleblowers were somehow quashed. Fired."

"No legal recourse?"

"Nope. A few of them started their own tech company and—from what I heard—they developed an anti-cyber bullying App called *Out The Bullies*.

"Interesting name."

"Well, but as far as I know, they've had their struggles actually getting the app to market. I can't help but wish karma throws them a bone one of these days, you know?"

Jude looked mesmerized. He took my hands in his and said, "Some day I hope to meet Wilson to thank him for being such a complete and utter asshole."

I had told him the story just to get *Out The Bullies* into the conversation. I'd read in the paper about *Out The Bullies* supporting Jude's big internet privacy win, and I wanted to impress him in a way the *real* story about the *real* ex-boyfriend wouldn't.

And yet, his reaction to me being belittled? Dismissed? It was the most intoxicating thing Jude could have done. I couldn't pull away from him after that.

He teased me by pulling me by the hips and saying, "Let's fight about Sarbanes Oxley. You make corporate whistle-blowing so damn sexy."

"Jude!" I playfully slapped him. "Stop it." But I only meant for him to stop talking. And I showed him what I wanted with my hands and mouth.

Afterward, he ran his hands down the length of me and I savored the way his fingers cooled my skin. I kissed him gently and then fiercely until he pulled away. "What's this?" Jude traced a long scar along my outer thigh. One I'd grown so used to already and was so faint, I'd forgotten it could feel foreign to a new touch.

"Just one of my many scars, Jude Birch."

He kissed my scar and I arched my head back toward his distressed wood headboard for round two and wondered if I should be jumping out of that bed and running as fast as I could in some other direction. I said something faintly along those lines as we lay in bed together, exhausted after-ward.

Poor Jude. He could never say in campaign speeches (and to his credit, he didn't bother) that he had a partner who had supported him always. Who had never had a moment's doubt. In truth, I swirled in doubt from that first moment. I never intended to get in very deep with Jude. I had done my research to impress him, and in turn, I wanted information and I wanted to be able to say I knew him. So I could make a fresh start. A real fresh start.

And yet, I was already in deep. From that first date that was the result of so much research and preparation on my part. Still, I was entirely unprepared for how my heart would fall for Jude.

The heart wants what the heart wants.

As we wrapped up our highly successful first date, and made a second one before kissing goodbye outside his apartment as I waited for my cab, I thought about all the lies I'd told in one day.

And wondered how many Jude had told in return.

The Washington Truth, dated February 14, 2016
Excerpt from the Op Ed piece, by Nate Essuzare

...I wonder if we all woke up in a world where no one could lie anymore—whether we would even want to keep living that way?

Imagine—truly imagine what that means.

Everyone wants to believe they default to truth, right? But do you?

Where does your truth punch someone else right in the gut?

I hate your choice of movies.

This meal you spent all day making tastes like burnt rubber.

This piece of art you created isn't all that good.

I don't love you anymore.

In some ways, love is based on the ultimate lie: I will feel this way about you—and only you—forever.

Do we really want to live in a world where this kind of lie no longer exists?

Exactly.

And do you know what I've come to think of as the biggest lie of all?

Charity.

No one really wants to help one another. They do it for the publicity or to attract customers or friends.

Even in the cases of so-called "anonymous" acts of kindness, I think you'll find that they make sure *someone* knows. And if not, well the giver knows. And the giver gets a rush from that act of charity. Same as a shot of alcohol, or a drug hit.

That's right. Giving actually changes your brain chemistry with a release of endorphins similar to that achieved from morphine or heroin. Giving can calm you and relieve stress and anxiety.

Giving acts on your brain just like drugs.

You know what else can give you that same feeling?

Love. In essence, love is an act of charity, too. And an act of selfishness. All everyone's really trying to do as they go around the world loving and giving is get high. For *themselves.*

But you've never heard *that* on a first date, have you?

Chapter 4

Following the 3-month post-surgery appointment with Dr. Drake in which he had shown me the competing CT scan images, and I'd almost fainted in his office, and I had to remind him yet again that I really wanted him to call me "Aby," and not my late mother-in-law's name, I came home to Brookland to the home I now shared with Jude and cried for the first time since the night of the shooting.

I'd cried a lot *that first night.* (Dr. Drake's words, not mine.)

Buckets and buckets of tears into my terrible vending machine coffee and by Jude's bedside while he was unconscious, and into the phone as I called Huck and Finn.

"Aby, we need to be there," Huck had said in his bulldog voice.

"Aby, I want to be there," Finn had said more gently.

"Please, guys. There's nothing for you to do here but wait. I need you to do the practical things I can't possibly do right now. Please. These are the real life things I need you to handle while I sit here and wait."

They had agreed, reluctantly, to carry on the tasks needed to take care of Jude from the outside. I knew how hard these concessions were to make—for both Huck and Finn—which made my gratitude even more enormous.

Within a few hours of the shooting, I had choked out, through tears, instructions for Huck to strategize a press release while I dealt with the medical issues at the hospital— mostly trying to save Jude's life. I made promises to the universe while he fought for his life.

If he lives, I'll tell him everything.

Even if it means he'll leave me.

Just let him live. Please.

I had drowned cup after cup of bad coffee with my tears.

I'd overwhelmed a stranger at the hospital bathroom sink who had the bad timing of being next to me washing her hands while I flooded the sink with my ugly cry tears, trying to collect myself before returning to the waiting room.

And then later that night—or maybe it was early the next morning?—when Jude had made it out of surgery—with a surprisingly optimistic though guarded prognosis, I had been relieved to find myself temporarily out of tears. I'd been able to go about the steps of arranging Jude's care and further press releases and eventually returning to my work at the Foundation with a fair amount of stoicism I could only assume I'd inherited from my own mother and never noticed before inside of me. *Damn her.*

No matter. I was grateful when I could finally stop crying.

The gratitude overwhelmed my nagging feeling of hypocrisy. Because when Jude woke up, finally, I did *not* tell him everything. I told him nothing.

And I kept on waiting.

The day I came home from viewing the new CT scan images with Dr. Drake, the floodgates opened again. I made up an excuse that I had to run to the pharmacy and I left Jude at home—in a rare occasion of being unattended. I drove my car around the block and parked in front of the old Tool & Die Factory Building in our Brookland neighborhood and let the tears flow in deep cathartic rivers.

Months and months of pent up sadness—and yes, guilt—cascaded down my face, streaking my neck and my hands as I tried and failed to catch them all.

I told the universe to leave me alone. I'd handle things in my own time.

Guilt.

That's what drove those tears.

Because while Jude might not be able to lie any more, I still could.

∽

It took some time after the Dr. Drake appointment to settle Jude down for a nap, which I figured he'd need after the exhausting outing to the doctor's office. After I explained again what Dr. Drake had said, about the filter and his new inability to lie, he seemed distressed in a way he hadn't seemed in the last few weeks, and while I thought briefly about calling Huck and Finn for help, I managed to muscle through the rest of the day without placing any calls to them.

I wanted to settle Jude on my own, yes. But mostly, I wasn't ready to give out the news of Jude's condition to his inner circle. I doubted it would affect them the same way it was affecting me. And Jude, of course.

I called into the office to talk business with my boss, but said not a word about Jude's newest diagnosis. *It's none of her business,* I told myself as I deliberately kept vague when Philomena (known as "Mena" in her inner circle) asked perfunctorily, "How's Jude today?"

We left unspoken the elephants between us, she and I.

And I didn't mention Dominic Treese's surprise curbside visit either. I couldn't even imagine forming the words: *Your father paid me and Jude a little visit today.*

〜

After the phone call to Mena Treese, I washed my face and plugged my tear valves by compartmentalizing as I had learned to do so well. I needed to take care of Jude until his caregiver got there. And so I shifted gears deliberately.

I walked into the living room where Jude was sitting.

"Do you need anything, Jude?"

"No. I'm not hungry. And –" Jude looked off into the space behind me as if considering other possible needs. "I'm not cold either. I feel ok. I'm tired from our trek into the hospital and I feel like I'll sleep well tonight."

"Good." I felt a small wave of relief sandwiched by waves and waves of terror. Something was crawling inside my brain despite all my compartmentalizing.

What would happen next? And next? And next? Everything has changed now.

I thought about Dominic Treese's words to me over the lowered Mercedes window.

Jude's shooting? It might not have been as random as you think it was.

Dear Mr. Treese. It turns out I don't think the shooting was random at all.

I reached for the nearest chair arm and lowered myself into it. I looked around the house, making a mental note of some chores that had to be taken care of in the next few days.

A lightbulb out over the dining room table, and we were out of light bulbs. A mantle that hadn't been dusted in close to two weeks and was probably going to induce an asthma attack in an already compromised Jude. A stain that looked like red wine on the arm of the couch, and since I couldn't remember the last time I'd enjoyed a quiet glass of wine, was likely well set and beyond help by this point. It would need strategic covering, rather than cleaning. I glanced over at my favorite photograph resting on a side table, a picture of the majestic boat, *Front Runner*, with the St. Michael's sunset behind her. For me, that photo always represented hope—never more so than recently—so I focused on it for a short while during the silence.

I noticed the pillows on the loveseat across the room were flattened into the corners and needed straightening. Everything else in the room could wait, but for some reason those pillows compelled me to move.

I sighed and pushed myself out of the chair. My feet felt heavy as I walked the short distance to the loveseat. I squeezed and fluffed the pillows until the flamingoes on the fronts of the pillows were restored to their rightful place, facing each other bravely from either side of the sofa.

I've always loved flamingoes. Ever since fifth grade, when

our usually strict and formal teacher, Mrs. Corso, arranged a last minute field trip: a visit to the local zoo with an actual tour guide. I'd been to the zoo with my mom before; I'd seen the flamingoes before. But I'd never seen them the way I did that day. My mom took the day off and signed up to be a chaperone, a move that surprised, embarrassed, and delighted me all at once.

Zoey, our tour guide, was a bright girl with bleached blonde hair and pink lips that matched the exact shade of her fingernails. She led us around to watch the timed feedings at the monkey cages and alligator pens. Some of the more delicate kids in my class looked away as the alligator chomped down on raw chicken. "Ew gross!" Marley Miller had yelled out. Marley Miller thought everything was gross. I had rolled my eyes and kept on watching the alligator feeding.

When we arrived at the section of the zoo called the "Bird Bath," Zoey asked, "So. Does anyone know what color baby flamingoes are?"

I'd stared long and hard at the pink flamingoes and thought about how they kind of matched Zoey's lips and nails. I wondered if she'd ever noticed that, too. I raised my hand. "Pink?"

"Nope!" Zoey looked pleased with herself. And with me, for my wrong answer. So much so I didn't even really mind being wrong.

"Light pink," I offered a second answer without raising my hand again, in direct violation of Mrs. Corso's rules. Mrs. Corso scowled at me, but Zoey looked at me giddily—just as happy with my second wrong answer.

"Nope! See, everyone thinks that. But in reality, flamingoes are born white. Then their diet of shrimp and shellfish turns their coat pink. Within a few years, those flamingoes are no longer white, but the coral color you see here. And everyone sort of forgets that they started out white, and thinks of them as pinkish-colored animals. "

There was some oohing and ahing from the group, including from me. And some snickers and side conversations from some others in the class, warranting some more Mrs. Corso scowls. My mom and I caught each other's glances over the heads of the group and gave each other a quick "Who knew?" expression.

"So you know what that means, don't you?" Zoey had asked.

I didn't raise my hand this time. No one else did either, giving Zoey a chance to execute on what I can only imagine was her favorite part of the tour. "Like your parents and teachers tell you, you really are what you eat!"

I knew Zoey was wrong of course. But I refrained from telling her what I knew to be true—even then. By then my step-dad had converted from town drunk to starving, but still, generous artist. And my once single mom had become one half of a loving couple. And I'd gone from being the girl who never had parents available for back-to-school night to having a mom who could make time to chaperone the school zoo trip.

So I knew then, and I confirmed later on, that the metamorphizing flamingoes were less a testament to good food choices, and more a testament to the fundamental truth that eventually—with enough practice—you can become something entirely different, and no one will even remember what you were before.

I heard myself sighing again as I fluffed the flamingoes and remembered bright and pink Zoey. I looked over at Jude who was still sitting in his original spot, seemingly oblivious to my angst and sadness and nostalgia.

"Do you mind if I go get a hot bath, Jude?"

I started to walk up the stairs while the words hung in the air meant really to be a rhetorical question, but Jude's response stopped me.

"Yes, I do mind. I really don't want to be alone right now. Can you come sit with me?"

I turned and looked at Jude incredulously. *Was he seriously not going to let me bathe when I wanted to anymore?*

After spending the morning in the cold, sterile hospital looking at disgusting films of Jude's old and new brain, all I wanted to do was go up to my modern marble-lined bathroom with the radiant heat under the floor, lock the door, hide, and crawl into a warm, sudsy bath. But Jude continued staring at me as I tried to measure out a way to escape the room, and he pointed to the spot on the couch next to him. His protective head bandage looked fresh and pristine having just been changed at the hospital that morning.

A kind nurse had taught me how to change his bandage before he had come home months earlier, but after trying it on my own his first week home, I had resorted to letting his caregivers do it as part of their weekly duties. Frankly, I couldn't look at the scar on Jude's head without gagging. One day when he was sleeping, the visiting nurse told me that when his hair grew back in, the scar would be less noticeable, and of course with time it would fade. More plastic surgery was possible, too.

"It will never be gone of course. But it will get better," the nurse had said kindly. I hoped she was telling the truth. It made me wonder if the scar on my leg ever disgusted Jude this way. And that made me hate the scar for a whole new host of reasons.

I stared at Jude still pointing at the couch next to him. I focused on the fresh bandage and exhaled audibly.

Jude noticed. "Oh. Do you not want to sit right now?"

"No, it's fine. Of course. If that's what you need. That's what I want, too."

After I lied, I walked over to the couch and sat next to Jude. Our arms touched and the intimacy startled me. I still hadn't gotten completely used to the new intimacy we'd found when Jude got home from the hospital. Of course we hadn't been intimate for weeks while he was holed up in the hospital bed. But we hadn't been intimate for weeks before the shooting either.

Jude didn't seem to remember that.

Before the shooting, Jude had been sleeping in the guest room, and I had been sleeping in our master bedroom—alone—while the space between us grew wider and wider. I hadn't had time to think about that space while Jude lay in the hospital bed fighting for his life.

But later as we returned home, and Jude naturally wanted to sleep in the master bedroom, I would lie next to him, our arms touching again for the first time in months, our breathing in sync, and I would wonder how long it could last. How long before I would have to share what I knew. And what I had been planning.

Each night, lying next to Jude, my mind would spin and jog and keep me up and if by chance I fell asleep, it would quickly wake me up again.

I sat on the couch for an hour with Jude that night instead of taking a bath. I felt the space between us closing in and instead of relief, I felt panic.

"Jude, do you want some dinner yet?" I asked hopefully.

"No," he shook his head and still we sat for what felt like hours more.

Eventually, I lost the energy to even walk upstairs and bathe. I felt like crying all over again, but instead of making up excuses to leave the house and drive around the block again, I lay my head on Jude's shoulder, and silently wondered if I'd ever truly learn to live this way.

How could I live with only truth from here on out?

With so many lies still left between us?

The outcome of the day's Dr. Drake appointment was that Jude now knew he had lost his ability to lie, but other follow- up appointments had revealed more residual effects of the shooting. Migraines. Temporary hearing loss that resolved itself relatively quickly. Memory loss that had not yet resolved itself. And perhaps never would.

Jude seemed to have lost some memories. Not all of

them. Just some. He never talked about the night of the shooting or the weeks leading up to it. I wasn't sure whether he couldn't really remember the night or whether he didn't want to talk about it. And now, with the knowledge that he couldn't lie about any of it, I didn't dare ask.

Contrary to what Mr. Treese had said, I didn't think Jude's shooting was random at all. And that meant that we were both still in danger.

Which is why I'd made a deal to save us both.

The rub was—it required *both* of us to be able to lie.

~

During Jude's session with his evening caregiver, I finally got my hot shower, and returned a few emails. Jude agreed to go to bed a little earlier than usual, and I made up excuses why I had to sleep in the guest room for the first time since the shooting. I was feeling stifled and panicked, but I told him that I was feeling achy and I didn't want to risk getting him sick if I was coming down with something.

"That's a good idea, Aby. I don't want to fight off any germs on top of everything else," he said truthfully and without putting up much of a fight.

I tried not to complicate my feeling of relief that he didn't fight me on the issue, with a feeling of disappointment.

After Jude went to sleep, I paced around the house in the dim light. The house seemed so small *before* with me and Jude filling it up with stuff and papers and bodies and heat. We'd both given up our small apartments to move in together the year before, but our lives expanded quickly in that Brookland house, and it often felt small before the shooting. But now it seemed enormous.

Before I went to bed finally, I doubled back to the alarm panel by the front door to punch in numbers setting the alarm for the evening—the address of Little Miss Whiskey's was still our pin number and alarm code and the prefix to most of our computer and other passcodes as well. Everything started with that night. Even though sometimes, looking back, I felt as though I had lived several entire lifetimes before I met Jude, still everything for me started with Jude.

I headed to the guest room, tucked myself under the covers, and let my mind wander. The wandering led to the boat.

⌒

I first saw the boat in two dimensions. Jude pulled a photograph off the home office printer and handed it to me with a smirk. "Here, put this in a frame. Isn't she gorgeous? I'm going to call it *Front Runner*. What do you think?"

Front Runner was a modest 24-foot Sea Ray Sundancer that Jude had bought at auction shortly after we moved in together. I had thought he was crazy, sinking fifty grand into a boat, but he'd assured me that it was a bargain and a necessary one at that.

"With our crazy life—we need a place to escape to. A place away from D.C. And politics. And campaigns. And our circles. In D.C. politics, there are few places you can really escape to," he had laughed, "but the Chesapeake Bay is certainly one of them."

I had reluctantly given my blessing without actually being asked for it. *Front Runner* didn't seem like such a sound investment, and indeed it meant that weekend getaways were usually spent on the boat or in harbor marinas, where showers were communal and breakfast was all you can eat, instead of the more luxurious accommodations that I would have preferred. But still, I had quickly come to find the Bay was a unique find. Sometimes we went hours with no viable signal and it turned out the salt spraying off the water was good for my skin, and the time on the boat felt like time that was uniquely all our own.

We loved to get on the boat without a plan. We'd travel down the channel and dock at one of the bayside towns, forage for food at nearby cafes and shop for antiques and other trinkets. There was something primal about these weekends. Shopping at farm stands and drinking our coffee from an antique pot plugged into the harbor's electricity rather than braving the nearest Starbucks. It was about finding each other's rhythm. About listening and lying. About loving and eating and shopping and touching. Days and weeks of little physical contact would bubble over underneath the deck of the boat where we'd lay sticky and sweet and salty, licking the long absences off each other hungrily. Marking each other the way only we could. Remembering what we knew about each other that no one else did. Sharing secrets and plans. Even though Jude always described it as escaping *out of* our life for a few blissful days, I thought it felt miraculously like the only time we actually burrowed *into* a real life. There was promise in those weekends.

Promise that I might finally be able to tell Jude the truth. All of it.

It wasn't that I was afraid of revealing the lies. I was afraid of revealing the reasons why.

Most of my lies had been told for reasons of safety, security, and even helping others.

A lot had been told for no reason at all.

One lie had been told because I'd simply broken in half.

But the worst lie? That had been told for the worst reason of all.

Revenge.

⌒

In the guest room, I remembered that July weekend—a few months before the election when my stress and emotions were sky high. The emotions returned just with the memory. I felt my heart speed up and my pulse rocket into my throat.

I almost called out for Jude. I tried breathing, trying some of my tricks from the yoga classes I'd given up after Jude's shooting. I closed my eyes and thought about my happy place: *Front Runner.* A memory surfaced like a warm hug.

In my memory I was dizzy. Whether it was from the third gin and tonic, the restless motion of the boat, or the sex, I couldn't be sure.

Jude was drowsily humming along to Ed Sheeran's "Shape of You" playing in the background, but I put my finger to his lips, because the song was too fast, Jude's humming was too fast, and I was trying to slow my heart and my breathing down to a pace that would match the boat's soft rocking.

We were lying on the deck. Later we'd sleep down below, but we weren't ready to give up the stars yet. They were slowly retreating behind clouds. There would be a storm. That night was dry and warm, but the tilt of the boat was giving a telltale warning about rain and wind the next day, and so we had decided to can our planned trip across the bay to St. Michael's, and stay moored in the channel at Annapolis instead until the storm passed.

Jude and I were on a three-day getaway. No one was expecting us to return emails or weigh in on google documents for at least 48 hours. I had packed a small overnight bag with a cold bottle of Tanqueray and enough limes to constitute an actual food group.

As I lay on Jude my body felt light against his. He'd fallen asleep quickly after I'd shushed his humming and now his chest rose and dropped with a light snore. I'd convinced him to get a couples massage with me earlier in the day before we headed to the boat and his skin smelled musky and faintly of lavender oil. His chest felt like velvet against mine. I stroked him carefully, not wanting to startle him, or disturb him. I wanted him to stay under me so I could rest. Could enjoy him. My body rhythm slowed down and then plateaued with the pace of the boat. It always took a little while for my body to adjust to the boat.

Put your sea legs on, Jude commanded whenever we stepped onboard.

When we stayed in place, instead of taking the boat out for a ride, it tended to take longer for me to put on those sea legs. A ride was out of the question for this small vessel that weekend—the water was promising to be too choppy—the waves lapping against the side of the boat were proof the weather commentator had not been overreacting.

I felt Jude start to rouse underneath me. He stroked my hair and I turned my head up on his chest to see his face.

"Hey," I whispered.

"Hey you. What's a beauty like you doing with a guy like me, hunh?"

My breath caught. Jude was so beautiful. Sometimes I forgot that. In the midst of all the ambition and hard work, and all we were doing and accomplishing together, sometimes I forgot that he was beautiful to look at. He was always self-deprecating, but I knew we weren't a mismatched couple. We were an "of course" couple. If a woman met Jude and even flirted a bit, when I walked in, she would think "of course." And the same with any reasonable man when the situation was reversed. No one would look at either of us and wonder how we "got" the other one. We fit together in the planning room and in the bedroom. But sometimes, in all the complexity of our lives, I could forget just how easy it was to be with Jude. How he knew me. Knew what I needed. Silence or noise. Thai or vegetarian. Chardonnay or beer. Top or bottom.

He knew. And maybe the familiarity would get old one day. But it wasn't old yet.

I raised up and sat on top of Jude curling my legs behind me and caressing his lavender infused chest hairs as I looked over him toward the shore. All was still silent. As were the boats surrounding us. We hadn't noticed anyone getting on the boats. The rich loved to sit on their boats instead of gassing them up and taking them out. But on a night like that night, as a storm rolled in from far out, we were alone with the quietly rocking boats.

Names of boats nearby with descriptions as if they took on the characteristics of their owners.

Ambitious at Bay

Easily Amused

Lazy Lady

I remained seated on Jude and he pulled his hands off me and tucked them under his head, smirking. "You look beautiful in this light. Like a mermaid. Scratch that. Like a sea siren. I'm trapped. Sing to me."

I laughed and crooned along with Ed Sheeran. Jude growled and dropped his head back, tracing my hips deliberately and familiarly with his fingertips. "I've missed you, Baby," Jude was hoarse from hard work and want. I settled into him, matching his want with my rhythm. "I hope old Man Romeo isn't on the Juliet tonight." Jude waved drunkenly over his head toward an august bayliner with *Juliet* scrolled across the white fiberglass in navy letters. "He'll have his binoculars trained on you Miss Thing, for sure. Probably sell the pictures to *People Magazine*."

I laughed and stopped rising and falling on Jude long enough to reach over for my gin and tonic that had been sitting in the cup holder next to the seat cushion above Jude's head. I laughed again at his panicked look that I might be leaving my perch. "Don't worry. I'm not going anywhere. I'm not afraid of Old Man Romeo."

I drained my gin and tonic and pulled a lime piece out with my fingers, biting into its tartness before offering it to Jude who shook his head and pulled me down to him instead. My heart met his and I felt the familiar blending of beats. It was extraordinary how our hearts knew how to do this. Gather up and meld into one beat only. "Aby," Jude murmured. And I nodded. Moments like this were why I kept up the charade. Because it didn't feel *false*. It felt *true*.

I let Jude kiss my citrusy lips tenderly, and then I straightened up again and looked down at Jude with a smile. I bit my lip and tasted gin and Jude and sea salt as I tossed my hair in the direction of the Juliet and reminded him: "Don't joke about that. Nude pictures of us would command a pretty hefty price tag, and you know it."

I laced my words with a tease as I straightened up taller, facing the direction of the Juliet, and sucked in my belly so my ribs and breasts puffed out seductively. I moved my hands down my body from my breasts to my hips, inside my thighs, and landing on Jude's perfect abdomen where I felt him tremble gratifyingly under my touch.

"Aby, We need to be more careful, Sweetheart."

I nodded. He was right, of course. I lay back down on him out of eyesight of Old Man Romeo and anyone else.

"I know. I wouldn't mind some pictures of these days. For posterity sake. We're going to miss these bodies in 50 years. If you can even put up with me for 50 years, Jude Birch."

There was a catch in my voice. Jude might have heard it as fear that Jude would grow sick of me if I changed. Became someone different than I was now. But that wasn't my fear.

Jude untucked one of his hands, reaching up carefully to trace my breast painted silver by the moonlight. I closed my eyes and sighed. Jude untucked the other hand and drew soft proprietary lines down my back, I fell into the boat's rhythm on top of him and moaned and yelled recklessly. Jude didn't shush me.

I started to roll off of him and reached for a discarded robe on the boat deck, but he stopped me. "Let me look at you. Don't get dressed yet."

And I didn't because, "Really," I wondered out loud, "how many more naked years do you think we have left?"

Jude ran his hand down my side softly, as he whispered: "All of them."

And when we lay together afterward, Jude whispered in

my ear. "I'll be happy to put up with you for 50 years and more, Aby. Wild horses couldn't drag us apart."

And I was afraid then, not that I would grow old, and Jude would become sick of me, but rather that Jude wouldn't be there.

That—when all the truths came to light– he'd be gone.

~

I sat up in bed and turned a light on. I reached under the mass of papers for my bright orange journal hidden at the bottom of the drawer. I traced the letters on the cover. "Be the Sunshine in Your Own Day."

In recent years, I'd taken to writing my stories online, in what felt like a much safer, more anonymous venue, but every once in a while, it helped to pull out this ugly book, and write in its pages. It had been five years since my therapist had given it to me in the wake of my mother's death—in another life altogether—and I was still pulling it out and writing in it occasionally. It helped me distinguish what was true and what was not. Now that my mother was no longer here to help me do that.

After a day filled with a bizarre diagnosis and an eerie warning from a man I certainly didn't trust, the memory of being with Jude away from the world out on *Front Runner* helped soothe my agitated spirit. I longed to be with him out at sea—far from the worries and people on land who were trying to hurt both of us. It was part of my plan, in fact. His love for our time on *Front Runner* helped fuel my fervent desire that he'd go along with the seemingly crazy plan I'd cooked up for us.

Some day soon. I scrolled these words at the bottom of the newest passage in the orange journal.

Thinking about it, and indeed, writing about it, helped. And as I drifted off to sleep down the hall from Jude who could no longer lie, I dreamt about rocking boats and limes.

And wild horses.

The Washington Truth, dated August 21, 2017
Excerpt from the Op Ed piece, by Nate Essuzare

....I have a dear friend who has always said people are their truest selves in airports.

I usually ignore her, but sometimes I challenge her.

"Don't you mean Church?"

She laughed hard at that suggestion.

And I realized how ridiculous that answer was anyway.

"How about therapy?" I offered as a consolation prize for my prior ignorance.

"God, no. Airports."

She went on to point out that:

"In an airport, you will see who is helpful. Who is impatient. Who is solo. Who is brave."

I argued that everyone in the airport is actually putting on their best, sweetest, bravest face in case the worst happened, but my friend insisted that fear was exactly what lowered people's resolves and inhibitions.

So then yesterday, for the first time, I realized the flaw in my friend's argument. Because if everyone is the most truthful when they are afraid, when they are really in fear of what is about to happen, when they are facing the unknown—then why in the hell isn't everyone truthful every damn day of their life?

Because God knows, there's nothing more frightening than life.

I called my friend with my aha moment. She dismissed me by saying these were two totally different fears– fear of living and fear of dying.

I conceded her point.

And then I told her I wasn't at all sure which one was worse.

Chapter 5

After the new diagnosis, I felt as though Jude and I were stuck in some sort of odd new dance. I recognized that I was avoiding him, but I tried to deny it. Even to myself.

I shared the caregiving for Jude with trained professionals who came in and out of the house. That Jude's government salary and more importantly, federal insurance benefits, covered so much help, both gratified and embarrassed me.

When the caregivers showed up, I tag-teamed them to head into my office at the Foundation. I was going into work most days each week, and I welcomed the distraction work provided from Jude's condition.

In the weeks just before the shooting, work had provided a necessary distraction from something else altogether—or someone, rather.

Laila Rogers.

⟿

A few months after the car break-down "incident" outside Little Miss Whiskey's, I found myself back at the bar with Jude meeting his friends for real. We were already inseparable by then, he and I. That was *not* part of the plan.

Neither was hanging out with his friends, if I'm being honest. Which I *am*.

Huck and Finn sloshed beer sloppily on our shared table while regaling me with stories about Jude intended to embarrass him, but in truth, all they did was endear him to me. I was falling fast for him. Things moved at rocket speed with Jude. And I knew it was partly because I was simply looking for a safe place to land after the whirlwind life I'd led already. But I didn't let that dissuade me that maybe Jude Birch in fact *was* a safe place to land.

It didn't help that I started to think he'd be exactly the kind of man my mother would want me to end up with. It didn't help that I started to think my mother was in fact *responsible* for us getting together. No, I mean, I still knew my mom was dead and all, but I felt like maybe she had arranged things. Through the universe, you know. Oh, I know what it sounds like. But this is what *I told myself.*

Jude had had a rough couple of years himself, and yet he had landed nicely. He now shared a nice apartment with exposed brick (I can't say for sure why the exposed brick made the apartment seem so much more grown up than it would have been otherwise), with Huck and Finn. Huck and Finn were new associates at a prominent D.C. law firm. Jude had a high profile position at the U.S. Attorney's office in D.C. And there was a third friend from law school, Laila Rogers, who I had trouble sizing up. Even then.

Gorgeous and looking sort of perpetually 25ish, Laila claimed to have worked on both of President Obama's campaigns.

"Campaigns?" I asked incredulously. "Did you just make that word plural?"

Laila laughed me off without actually answering. She had a rigidity in her shoulders that was off-putting.

I offered what I did for a living even though Laila didn't ask.

"So, I'm in fundraising for a local fledgling Foundation. The mission is bringing arts and writing programs to underserved children in the District. Perhaps you've heard of it? Appletreese Foundation?"

Laila looked as if she might choke. I tried to believe I was imagining it. But when she changed the subject, I gave up trying to make conversation with her and mostly observed what was happening at the table.

Finn kept trying to put his arm loosely around Laila and she kept letting him and then shrugging him off. The way he kept at it was more lost puppy dog than assailant so I was surprised when Laila got up to use the restroom at one point, and Jude poked Finn a bit too hard. "Dude. Lay off Laila, already. She's not ok with this. Just leave her alone, ok?"

Finn shrugged, but I noticed he left Laila alone after that. At one point, everyone at the table shushed and pointed to a row of television sets. Donald Trump had just announced his intention to run for President that day. Jude tapped Laila's shoulder and smiled. "I told you," he said cryptically.

"I can't believe it. But then again, I can," she responded even more cryptically, and then mouthed "thank you" before returning to the table conversation.

After that, Laila seemed much more physically relaxed. So much so, that she leaned into Jude for a long hug as we were all leaving. She thought she was whispering, but it wasn't that quiet. I heard pieces of her goodbye to Jude. "She's fine and all. But I hope you know what you're doing. She works for the goddamn Appletreese Foundation for Christ's sake."

Jude laughed, "Oh come on, not for *him*. For Mena. You know that family is the Kevin Bacon of this town. Everyone's connected to them by six degrees or less. Don't hold it against her."

Laila rolled her eyes, leaned in, and whispered something else to him through a laugh. And this time the whispering worked. I couldn't hear her.

I couldn't help myself in the Uber afterward. After all, he'd called Philomena Treese, *Mena*.

"Ok. So humor the new girl. How do you know Mena?"

"Hunh? Oh, you know, the same way everyone knows her. This town is big, but small, you know. We all worked inhouse for her Dad's construction firm when we were still in law school. He gave me a great recommendation for the U.S. Attorney's office. I met her around the office a few times back then."

Mena's Dad, of course, was, and still is, Dominic Treese.

And Mena's Dad's "construction firm" was, and still is, a conglomerate in the city. An enormous mega-successful and mega-profitable company with a legal department the size of a small country. It wasn't surprising that Jude and his buddies might have cut their legal teeth there; I remembered vaguely reading about Jude starting out at Treese Construction at one point.

"Hey. One more question. What were you and Laila high- fiving about the Donald Trump presidential campaign announcement?" Jude became more reserved. "Oh, it's a long story. There was some talk about the Republicans offering up a different businessman candidate altogether. Someone Laila and I know and—well, let's just say, it would have been a terrible decision. We're both pretty relieved he's not actually running."

Then he changed the subject with whiplash speed to talk about a new restaurant we should try out later in the week.

Bored or unsatisfied with the explanation of his connection to Mena, I moved to a different target.

"So. What's the dynamic with Laila? Old girlfriend of one of you guys? Like, I don't know, you, perhaps?" I giggled to make the question more casual, and less stalker-y but I knew it wasn't really working.

Jude did humor me, though.

"Nah. I wouldn't bring an old girlfriend out to meet you at our place, Gorgeous." Jude smiled and pulled my face up for a long sweet kiss in the back of the car.

Our place. There was nothing I didn't love about this guy. Even then.

I pulled away anyway.

"Seriously, though. I don't really feel like she warmed up to me; so if you guys do have that whole faux big brother, little sister thing going, I don't feel like I'm cracking the code."

"Aby. It's fine. Laila's got an edge to her. She's been through ... some stuff. And we've been friends since law school, but honestly, that's all it is. You don't need to impress her any more than you need to impress Huck or Finn. Or me, for that matter.

"Although, for the record, Aby. I'm impressed. I'm very, very impressed.

I didn't pull away that time.

Chapter 6

Although we hadn't been sleeping in the same room at the time of the shooting, after Jude survived, we resumed our old habit of sleeping in the bed next to each other. There was a new intimacy. Jude reached under the covers for my hand each night, something he'd never done before. Each morning I awoke to him curled toward me instead of away.

I felt a loosening in my chest after the shooting. I was less angry with Jude. I was intent that after he finished healing, I'd share with him what I knew. That I'd ask him for the truth, finally. And I'd share my plans—what we'd have to do as a result.

Those plans involved escaping on *Front Runner*. We'd rename it, of course. I thought about new boat names at night as Jude curled up into me and reached for my hand under the covers. After Dr. Drake diagnosed Jude with a diminished pre-frontal cortex filter, I found these small acts all the more endearing—but also a reminder that my plan might not work at all anymore.

A reminder of how much danger we were still in.

⮜

After Dr. Drake's new diagnosis, I focused on work to distract me from more disturbing thoughts. My work was raising money for the Appletreese Foundation. The money I raised went to support writing and arts programs for underprivileged kids. It was work I'd grown so proud of.

It was work I knew I would miss when everything came to light.

At night, after I returned from my office at the Foundation, Jude and I caught up over dinner ordered in. Jude told me what he liked and didn't like about therapy and the newest caregiver. I shared my days with him, too, and though he seemed interested, he also seemed more easily confused and to tire early.

I carefully avoided subjects like our relationship. I avoided discussing the night of the shooting, and the weeks leading up to it.

I didn't talk about the campaign, the election, Laila, or anything else of substance, because I feared—no, I knew—that if I brought up a topic, I better be damn sure I was ready for what would come next.

I could no longer complain about the neighbor not picking up her dog poop anymore.

If I mentioned it, Jude might get up from the dinner table, walk outside, and call to the neighbor, "Hey, Nancy. Could you make sure to clean up after Dutch every day? Aby was just telling me how disgusting it is to see his feces in our yard. She says she feels like throwing the shit right in your face next time she sees you, and even though that's probably an extreme reaction, I'm sure you'll agree, it's understandable under the circumstances."

I could no longer mention that my administrative assistant was wearing an ill-fitting skirt to the office. Or hope for empty compliments anymore.

I chose my clothes carefully each day as I feared one day, Jude would ask me when I got home, "Were you trying to compete with your admin in the too-tight-skirt department? That outfit looks terrible on you."

I realized that I couldn't bring up any topics I didn't want to hear the absolute honest truth about. And sometimes the truth came unsolicited. Like the time Jude spit out my crockpot pot roast back on the plate and said it tasted like it had been cooked in old bath water. I had never made pot roast before. I never made it again after that.

But those occasions were sort of rare. Mostly if I stayed away from troublesome topics, Jude did as well. And as long as I kept him away from the press, no one was asking him questions.

That was a blessing at least. A small one. I didn't let him near the Capitol or out in public. The publicity surrounding the shooting had died down in favor of other news that appealed far outside our D.C. circles.

But still, as the days went by, I wondered how long I could keep quiet about certain things from the recent past.

Like Innovative Media.

And Out The Bullies.

And Laila.

I wondered how long before everything would begin unraveling and then come completely unglued. Of course, the answer came in no time at all. Like a bullet, it came tearing through the walls of our lives. After everything that had happened. How could it not?

⌐

It was late May, about a month after we learned that Jude's prefrontal cortex was overcompensating with excessive grey matter, and I was working from home while a late spring rain tapped relentlessly on the windows. When it stopped, the silence startled me and distracted me enough to stop working and go look for Jude.

I expected to see him in the living room, sitting in his favorite chair, reading. But the living room was empty. A few moments later, I found him sitting on our unmade bed with a small box in his lap. He appeared to have just gotten up. His face held its usual first-thing-in-the-morning confusion, and I realized I had actually been so distracted by work I'd forgotten to come check on him when he woke. My new habit had been to get up much earlier than him. He slept wonderfully after his hospitalization. He'd enjoy long, full nights of sleep while I tossed and turned starting each night—or rather morning—around 3 am, waiting for 5 am which I decided was a more appropriate hour to start the day. Then I got up, showered, had a cup of coffee and spent some time alone with the crossword puzzle each morning before Jude even woke. Around 8 or 9 am, I would hear him moving about the bedroom and that would be the signal to check on Jude. I'd see if he needed anything to get up and get in the shower before his therapists showed up for his occupational and physical therapy. Then I'd either head to my home office for the day, or—several days a week—I'd head to Georgetown to my office at the Foundation, meeting with staff or investors, or reviewing grant proposals, as if our world was still turning the same way it had been at the time of the shooting.

Or rather the way it had been before I made the deal.

I tried unsuccessfully to avoid now one all too familiar phone number. He called several times a week.

We need to talk, Aby.

I can't. Not now. You need to give me more time. I need more time.

More time is not what you need, Aby.

Click.

He'd called the day before. Maybe that was part of my distraction that May Tuesday morning. And Jude hadn't been sleeping quite as well lately, so maybe I wasn't either. Jude was seeming more and more confused lately and I was debating whether I needed a follow-up appointment with Dr. Drake.

On that particular morning, I was also distracted by actual work. Some new studies had come in linking success in Math to the quality and frequency of art programs at elementary school levels, and I had closed my home office door to Skype with the study authors. I'd been excited about their findings, relieved about their airtight process, less enthused about their small sample size, but overall satisfied about the study's place in my quarterly report to the Board. The rain and the call and spiked stress must have provided enough background noise to override my "Jude intuition." The one that usually summoned me from my work inexplicably just at the moment when he was waking so I could talk to him and ward off the early morning confusion that seemed to settle on him as he woke with some scattered memory loss, and sometimes, like on that particular Tuesday morning when he'd rediscovered his "box," some memory *recall.*

When I walked in that morning, Jude was staring at his lap and his hair looked mussed and the sheets had twisted uncomfortably between his legs and the item he was holding. The air in the room felt thick from humidity creeping in from the outside. And maybe from something else. I didn't know yet.

The box in Jude's hands was small and metal and had a padlock hanging on it. He was fiddling with it. I had remembered seeing the box on different occasions in our shared bedroom closet. It had been there since the day we moved in together. Once I had asked Jude about it, and he waved it off. "It's a fire box, with important documents—passports, and such," he'd replied.

I had taken that explanation at face value and hadn't paid much attention to the box in a long time.

Until now.

The look on Jude's face was very focused as he worked the lock, seemingly trying to break into his own fire box, and my gaze shifted back and forth from Jude's face to the locked box.

I was hesitant—tentative—as I asked the question, realizing as soon as it formed, that it was exactly the kind of question I'd been avoiding since the shooting. Certainly since I'd gotten the news about his prefrontal cortex from Dr. Drake. But I asked it anyway.

"Jude, what's in the box?" The room thickened. I gasped, trying to claw at the remaining oxygen in the air.

"Important documents. Like passports and such." I was overwhelmed with relief at the same answer echoed back to me as had been given before the shooting. *He hadn't lied about the box. It was exactly what he always said it was.*

My relief was short lived.

"And I put a letter in here. A few months ago. I think it was right before the shooting, now that I think about it. A letter to you. I hid it from you."

"You hid a letter to me?" I sorted through his words, trying to understand what Jude was saying and measure it against my old assumptions about the box. For years, I had wondered whether Jude was saving love letters from an old girlfriend, mementos from another life before we met, or something worse.

"It's a letter asking you to agree to lie. About everything."

Jude reached into the fire box then. I watched him sort to the bottom and then I watched as he extended his hand out to me from where he sat.

My mind raced.

Was it all in writing?

I stared at Jude as he sat on the bed with his arm outstretched and clinging to a crumpled letter. The letter was the only remaining thing left in the wide empty space between us that morning.

And I reached for it.

The Washington Truth, dated November 2, 2017
Excerpt from the Op Ed piece, by Nate Essuzare

...A new generation of politicians has arrived in Washington D.C.

Washington insiders have noticed that the newest classes of politicians on the Hill have little in common with predecessors other than title.

The prior generation arrived in the nation's capitol fueled by the threat of international terrorism and focused on post 9/11 strategies and protocol.

But the newer generation fears and faces and fights a different threat. A threat much closer to home.

In a world responding to and reacting to domestic violence, gun control debates, #blacklivesmatter mantras and #metoo admissions, the newest generation of politicians is less likely to enter office based on our fears of ISIS, and more likely to enter elected offices based on our fears of *each other.*

Chapter 7

The first time I was ever in a newspaper, Mena Treese thought she was the one who showed me.

She called me into her office the day after Jude's campaign announcement. That wasn't unusual. In addition to everything else, she was technically my boss, after all, and the founder of the Appletreese Foundation. Mena's pointed questions weren't that unusual either. Mena's style was nothing if not direct. I had learned that—and a lot of other things—about Philomena Treese in the time since I'd started a fellowship position with Appletreese Foundation.

By the time of the campaign announcement, Appletreese was no longer, by any definitions, a "fledgling foundation" as I'd described it to Jude that first night outside Little Miss Whiskey's. I had been working for Mena for just about three years by the time of Jude's campaign announcement.

I'd been with Jude even longer.

Even though I made it sound like I had already started the position on the night I met Jude, in truth, my hire date was somewhat later. I was still working on cultivating a position with the Foundation—as I'd long been a fan of the founder and her story.

On that morning after the campaign announcement, Mena had a copy of *The Washington Truth* on her desk, rotated to face me as I walked in. I had caught a glimpse on the newsstand at the Metro station on my way into the office, but hadn't actually bought a copy. I worried that might look a little gauche. I wasn't sure what the new rules were now that Jude's campaign was officially begun.

The front page story was about Jude's campaign announcement, and the cover photo was Jude at the podium at the Freedom Art Loft Space looking handsome as ever, with me off to the side, looking a little broody. I didn't remember feeling broody the night before, and I was surprised to see that the photographer had caught this apparently split second expression. Looking at myself flat on Philomena's desk, I hoped no one else would focus on me, but would focus on the dashing Jude Birch instead.

"Wow, I finally made it into the paper. Sorry it was with Jude, Mena, and not for Foundation business," I reached for it, but stopped as Mena's hand landed on the paper instead. I noticed something I hadn't when I'd walked by the newsstand too quickly earlier that morning.

Laila was in the shot as well. Not far from me. Closer still to Jude.

Aha. Perhaps that explains the broodiness.

Mena tapped the grainy page, and one of her long fingers landed directly on me in the photo. "You ok with all this attention, Aby?"

Much to my dismay, Mena obviously *was* focusing on *me* in all my broodiness. And as her finger now covered me, the only ones I could see on the front page were Laila and Jude. I looked away as my breath caught.

"Sure. Why wouldn't I be?" I challenged her.

Mena raised a golden coffee mug with a Foundation logo that had been resting on the paper, leaving behind a muddy stain, and sipped her coffee without letting go of her gaze at me. I practiced the move in return, lifting my own Styrofoam Metro coffee cup to my lips.

There was something compellingly earthy about the way Philomena Treese navigated her day and her world. The truth was, and is, I admired Philomena Treese—not because she was born wealthy and privileged—but because she never let that get in her way.

"I'm wondering what you'll do to stay above the fray, if you will. There are sacrifices to this kind of public life. I don't want to be melodramatic or anything, but look, there are *dangers* to it as well."

Mena's words spooked me. I tried shaking them off but I know it looked like a shudder to her.

Her voice became gentler. "I'm sorry. I'm not trying to scare you. It's just that, Aby. I know you grew up around all this—but, I've said it before and I'll say it again—it doesn't seem like your world, you know what I mean?"

I nodded. She was right. Sort of.

"Thanks, Mena. I really appreciate your concern. I guess the way I see it is, if I want to be with Jude, I have to accept this. Just as he has to accept everything about me." I picked up her coffee-stained copy of the paper, thanked her and left her office, heading down the hall to my own.

I was proud of my job. So proud of my office with the glossy letters spelling out "Executive Director, Aby Boyle." I had officially gotten the fellowship position a few weeks after meeting Jude, and I had been promoted from an entry level position within a few short months, after proving myself to be a worthwhile fundraiser and development steward for the Foundation. I had surprised everyone, including myself. I couldn't help but think, despite the way I'd gotten the job, my mom would still have been proud.

The truth was I loved the mission of the Foundation. Bringing arts programs, and more importantly *writing* programs for schools that had no equivalent? It felt life-saving to me. It felt important. I poured myself into it, and I was indeed good at it.

When Mena had interviewed me for the initial fellowship position, I'd told her about my mother, and described her as a "pioneering mayor of a rural town in Pennsylvania." My mother would have killed me to hear herself described that way. A small town outside of Harrisburg, I told Mena, with hardly a population worth mentioning. I was vague, too, about the name of the town for obvious reasons.

I explained in only the vaguest of terms how there had been a scandal. About how my mom—who identified closely with single, working women—had continued to work hard for the low income populations in our area until she'd taken her own life, too overwhelmed by the conditions she was living in and observing all around her. These were details I'd left out of my discussions with Jude. Also for obvious reasons.

In my interview, I told Mena, "I've grown up in politics and I've run away from politics. Admittedly not too far, as I've run away to Washington D.C.—a move some might have argued would have little other likely outcome than to land me right where it has. But I'm trying to shed all that, and I feel a connection to you. I feel like we've been on the same course. I mean yours has been on a much more public stage, but still. I feel as though we're kindred spirits."

Mena waved my words away when I said the bit about the "public stage." She was always self-deprecating to a fault. But something in her eyes changed at the "kindred spirits" part. It motivated me to keep going.

"I admire you so much, Philomena. You're the real deal in this town full of unauthentic people."

What happened next was not nearly as spontaneous as I made it sound. "You remind me of a friend of mine. Jude Birch."

"Jude Birch is your friend?" Mena had looked surprised, and I tried not to let it show how much that surprise bothered me.

"He is, indeed. Do you know each other?" I tried to hide my nervousness. Had I overstepped? Had I misread things? *But no.*

"Well, only the way everyone in this town knows him. A darling of the local political scene. Lots of rumors flying around. Not that I pay attention to rumors, but you know."

I nodded. Reassured that she didn't really *know* Jude, I dove in headfirst. "Well, between you and me, Philomena, we're seeing each other. But I'd appreciate your discretion." I leaned in for emphasis.

"Of course," Mena said a bit too enthusiastically, glancing

back down at my resume, which I knew now would matter very little to what was going to happen next.

"I haven't seen a whisper about it in the papers. Good for you. You know something, I think someone with your drive and connections, and your appreciation for being discreet and professional is exactly what we need around here. And please, call me, Mena. All my friends do."

Touchdown.

She offered me the job that day, and I practically hugged myself on the way out, amazed at how beautifully everything had fallen together.

True, I had only met Jude about a few weeks before that interview. And our relationship was brand new. I'd told him I worked for a "fledgling foundation" based solely on wishful thinking that I might soon score an interview with Philomena—make that *Mena* Treese. I was still working on my resume—had been for several months, along with some help, when I met Jude; I was aware, too, that my resume, once finalized, still would tell some very tall tales—and hide a great many truths—that I was going to have trouble backing up when and if I finally got to the interview. I knew if I ever got in the room with Philomena Treese, I'd need a connection to someone in this town to stay in that room.

It had been a relief to distract Philomena from my resume. Pulling out the "Jude Birch" reference at just the right point of the interview had been a stroke of genius on my part. Hell, the whole meeting of Jude Birch and his friends outside Little Miss Whiskey's shortly before the interview with Philomena, make that *Mena*, had been pretty fortuitous.

Well, I guess that's if you consider stalking Jude Birch's public Facebook check-ins and waiting outside for him and his friends on several occasions with a knife and an innocent radiator hose, until it actually happened ..."fortuitous."

Chapter 8

Before the shooting, Mena and I used to take a yoga class together a few times a month at Mindful Me Studio on O Street in Georgetown.

She'd roped me into it pretty much from the first day I started working for her.

"Aby, Do you yoga?"

I shook my head. I wasn't even sure that was a thing. Like, for anyone.

"You have to try it. Come with me at lunchtime. We'll start taking yoga together. I grabbed an extra mat by accident last time I was at the studio. It looked just like mine, only the lotus flower is a little less elaborate. You can have it."

And so it began.

Usually "taking yoga together" consisted of me sitting on my pilfered yoga mat trying hard to focus on my breathing and my abdomen and my fingertips, but ending up only thinking about the unbearably skinny woman next to me who was making sort of grunting sounds as she was breathing.

"Mena, please," I always pleaded.

And in response, she always opened one eye and winked at me.

The thing you really should know is, I liked Mena Treese from the beginning. I wouldn't have lied to her if I didn't.

⤺

At the time I interviewed for the position at Appletreese Foundation, I knew what the world knew about Philomena Treese. Which was everything.

And nothing at all.

I had moved to D.C. a few months after my mom's funeral. Even though I was 22, I was, in fact, running away from home on some level, and I had pointed my Hundai south and driven until it ran out of gas.

True story.

I had my bright orange notebook, a fair amount of therapy under my belt, a new-found love of writing, and a small amount of insurance money that my mom had arranged for me to use to start a "new life." When I got to D.C., I'd ended up answering one of those tear-off ads on a coffee shop bulletin board in Georgetown for a quiet, non-smoking, felony-free roommate (also a true story).

I'd ripped off the ad on my way inside to interview for a job, which I got. Waiting tables was something I was pretty good at. The coffeeshop manager called my old diner boss back home and she had the kindness to give me a glowing recommendation. She'd left out the mud-slinging and slime. Probably more for my mother's sake than mine, but still I was grateful. I also got the roommate gig. So it was a pretty successful first few days in D.C.

Actually it was more than a successful few days, it was a successful *year.*

My roommate thought I was a fellow co-ed and I didn't let her think otherwise.

No, I didn't *lie.* But I didn't *correct her.* My presumptuous roommate's name was Sol and she was a grumpy but well-meaning Social Justice major who didn't resemble her sunny name in either looks or disposition. She spent most of her time at her vegan boyfriend's apartment, and only came home to secretly eat burgers a few times a week with her dark hair hanging in her face as if in shame, and I mostly found her to be a perfect roommate. In fact, she's the one who really helped all the pieces come together in my application for the Appletreese Foundation. I mean, before Jude wrapped the whole thing up with a bow.

It happened one Friday night when Sol came home from

her vegan stud's place and found me staring at a fellowship application for The Appletreese Foundation.

"Really? You're applying for that?"

Sol thought I spent most of my time at class, punctuated by shifts at the coffee shop. In reality, I spent a lot of time at the coffee shop. There was no class for me to go to after all. And one thing I did a lot of at the coffee shop, was write. And read the news. And according to the news, it was reported that Philomena Treese's fellowship program was expected to attract over 500 worthy candidates from inside Washington D.C. and beyond.

Philomena Treese had started the Foundation because of her father. She insisted this in every media interview. Even though, to the outside observer, it appeared to be opposite of the truth.

Dominic Treese—a self-made real estate mogul of modest origins in the Midwest—had moved East when he was 21 and proceeded to make the most of the 1980s real estate market while still somehow staying on the legitimate side of the housing market scandal when the whole thing tanked. By 2009, he was one of the only developers in Washington D.C. with any credibility and he had capitalized on his wealth, investing much of it in a trust fund for his most prized asset, daughter, Philomena, who inherited her work ethic from her father, and her beauty and shrewd sense of patience from her mother, Suzana.

Suzana was a Croatian immigrant who had been a physician in her own country and a prominent activist for the Croatian Forest Research Institute, before meeting Dominic while he was traveling on vacation. Suzana had returned with Dominic to America after a whirlwind love affair and had found herself marginalized in her new country, unable to continue practicing medicine without beginning her education anew, a task she found impossible with a new baby on the way. Alone, without a family or friend support network, and a work-a-holic, largely absent husband, Suzana struggled to regain a sense of self. There were no forests to advocate for or against in her new concrete jungle home in America's capital city.

Suzana assumed a new position in her adopted country, penning a memoir that became an instant best-seller in 2002, *Giving up the Forest for the Treese*, before fading into the background of American immigrant literature.

Unable, or perhaps unwilling (who could know the truth about a woman with a PR team that made some politicians' teams look like a school bake sale committee), to pitch another successful book deal on the heels of the runaway hit of a memoir, Suzana became an ardent benefactor of the arts, working hard to bring a diverse schedule of theatre, author book signings, and traveling art exhibits to the Washington D.C. area. She was often photographed with the lovely Philomena at her side.

In the waiting room at Appletreese Foundation, guests could peruse a coffee table book entitled *Washington D.C. Champions of the Arts* with exactly three photographs of Suzana and Philomena alone in front of traveling Croatian exhibits and one additional photograph of Suzana, Dominic, and Philomena, posing awkwardly in front of the National Gallery of Art in 2009.

Of course, Philomena was photographed in a lot more places than the coffee table composition. By 2014, Philomena was a bit of a media darling, appearing on the society pages with her latest beaus and even once on the cover of Inc. Magazine as the newly anointed social media manager for an up and coming start-up company called Innovative Media that was blossoming both inside and outside the beltway. Innovative Media was heavily invested in by one Dominic Treese who was looking to diversify beyond the world of construction, and his connection to Innovative Media was a point that I later came to suspect Inc. Magazine had emphasized a bit too much for Mena's liking.

I knew all these things, as I had long been a student of

all things Philomena Treese. The D.C. papers loved Philomena and I had a lot of time to read papers alongside my job at the Georgetown coffee café. Thus, I knew all too well that not long before I'd arrived in D.C., two pivotal things had happened in the Treese household.

First, Dominic launched a short-lived campaign for a Maryland Senate seat. Maryland, because the Treese family—while Washington insiders—lived outside the Washington D.C. beltway in an upscale community near the Potomac River in a home handcrafted entirely of reclaimed wood as per Suzana's insistence. Dominic was heard joking at many cocktail parties that while it might look as though Suzana had the final say in his house, the truth was he had built far too many steel buildings in Washington D.C. to actually *live* in one.

Second, the only child of Dominic and Suzana Treese, Philomena, turned 25, and ceremoniously inherited her enormous trust fund.

Which, in a decision that sidelined everyone, she promptly gave away.

In a move both heralded and criticized by D.C. insiders and outsiders, Philomena Treese left her day job as social media manager for Innovative Media and doled out her new inheritance to various grassroots and community organizations throughout Washington D.C., keeping just $30,000, what she called a "reasonable, but admittedly still generous, salary for my first year as a true citizen of this world."

Living modestly in a loft apartment in Georgetown and sharing rent with several grad students from George Washington, throwing off all the trappings of her prior privileged life, Philomena spent her first year as a pauper, working studiously on a business plan and researching investors to support a new project she hoped to get off the ground by the following year: Appletreese Foundation. The buzz about Philomena's project dwarfed the news that Dominic's campaign stalled nearly as quickly as it had started. No one was talking about Dominic anymore, and many thought the reason for the campaign's failure was that simple.

When interviewed by ForbesWoman about why she hadn't simply used her inheritance to start Appletreese Foundation—her labor of love—Philomena scoffed. "What good am I to the world, if I use my family's money to buy a dream? Shouldn't I learn the business from the ground up? Shouldn't I work hard, and fail, and fall down, and live up to my name?"

The Treese name is indeed a sturdy one, the ForbesWoman interviewer had said too quickly.

Philomena had scoffed again. "No. That's not what I mean. That is not my name. That is my father's name, and now my mother's, and I borrow it gratefully. My name is Philomena. It is my own. And at its root, it means strength."

It means strength.

On my phone in the coffee shop.

Late at night trying to falling asleep.

On my earbuds while walking to work.

I had listened to Philomena's interview on YouTube countless times, enamored by the naivete and the brazen attitude. Philomena—*Mena*—had a grace and fortitude that seemed so genuine, so impenetrable, that I wanted to reach right through the screen and grab some of it. While lots of other women were fascinated with the Kardashians, studying what they wore, and trying to emulate them in many ways—swearing that band of young women had it all, I was studying and emulating Philomena Treese. For me, who had never really had anything, I wasn't nearly as fascinated by the wealthy working-to-have-it all-Kardashian set, as I was with the woman who had it all from the beginning, and gave it away.

I studied Philomena alongside lots of other topics, like Enron, Sarbanes Oxley, and grant-writing for non-profits. I was self-made and self-taught. Like Philomena Treese. All those hours of studying made me think we might have a lot in common.

When Sol caught me with my pipe dream on the screen in front of me, I tried to shut down the computer quickly, but it was too late. "Good for you. And why the hell not? You have the commitment and dedication," she had said rashly.

I wondered briefly what had convinced her of these facts, before realizing she actually thought I had no free time, instead of *all free time.*

Sol kept on with the pep talk.

"And besides, I think Philomena Treese is the real deal. I think she's looking for people with fresh ideas—not the usual Washington insiders who, let's face it, will be filling these applications out by the hundreds."

I shrugged and was about to close out my screen and dismiss the whole idea as a far-fetched fantasy, when Sol threw me one last lifeline. "You know, my advisor was talking about this very fellowship in class last week. He has some interesting ideas about what an application should look like to stand out. He was trying to talk me into applying, but I have zero interest. I can introduce you two if you'd like. Maybe he can give you some good ideas. Help your application stand out from the rest? It couldn't hurt after all, right?"

Sol was on her way to the meat drawer of our refrigerator. I knew I had limited time before she grew weary of her attempt to help me. I jumped in feet first. "That would be great. Yes, please could you put us in touch?"

"Ok. Give me your school email address; I'll do a virtual intro."

"Oh, great. Actually, my school email is acting all wonky. Some spam I opened by accident is eating up all my emails. I'm using my Gmail right now." I jotted it down and handed it to Sol, waiting for the other shoe to drop. But instead, Sol shrugged. "Sure. I'll send him an email tonight and copy you."

It couldn't hurt, after all. Right?

I stared at the open application on the screen with its taunting banner across the top, "Your application is 7% complete." I'd filled in little more than a few perfunctory fields: name, age, address. I could definitely use Sol's advisor's help in making this application stand out.

I sat in front of the screen for about an hour, but only did a little more typing and then saved the application at 8% (I'd added my Gmail address and a compelling mission statement), and closed out. Before heading to bed, I checked my phone and saw the copy of the email Sol had sent along to her advisor.

Her advisor had already responded. *Sure, I'd love to meet your friend. Have her stop by during my office hours tomorrow.*

The advisor's so-called office hours were only two hours of the day and they happened to fall just before my shift at the coffee shop. I arrived early, worried I'd stand out or get lost. After a lot of consideration for my "look," I dressed in a comfortable plum-colored wrap dress and a messy bun that would transition from student to coffee shop waitress with relative ease. The offices were well marked, and I realized quickly there had been no need to arrive so early. I also realized quickly that the advisor's meager office hours were no exaggeration. He wasn't there yet. There was a single uncomfortable looking chair situated outside the advisor's locked door, and I plopped down in it. Turns out it wasn't only uncomfortable-*looking.* While I waited, I scrolled through my phone self-consciously and tried not to focus on how ridiculously underworked Sol's advisor was, and focused instead on how overworked I hoped to soon be.

A disheveled-looking man clothed mostly in tweed and clichés arrived right on time. He reached out a hand to me. "Ms. Boyle. Pleasure to meet you. Professor Tarragon, like the spice." I was glad Sol had prepared me for this as he apparently started every new encounter the same way. I laughed in my rehearsed way.

Before leaving for class that morning, Sol had warned,

"He's corny, but otherwise totally great. You'll love him." I doubted the last bit was true, but I was quickly seeing that everything else she said about him was true. He was indeed warm and instantly likeable.

"Come in, sit down. No need to sit out in the hall anymore. I have indeed arrived!" He bellowed, and gestured me inside. I followed him into his office, which seemed to be furnished mostly with piles of bound manuscripts and books. In one corner, a lamp with the university seal was set atop a pile, and in another corner, a round slate was placed on top of a tall stack of books and actually seemed to function as a table. Professor Tarragon picked up a piece of paper from the "table" and read from it. "So. Sol told me a little bit about you here in this email. But why don't you tell me your story?"

I marveled at the concept of printing out an email to refer to it later instead of simply pulling it up on his phone, but Professor Tarragon seemed intent on human interaction. He sat in his chair by a desk flanked by two more stacks of books and papers and put his feet up on a third nearby stack situated slightly lower than the desk itself. He stared at me, waiting for me to comply and tell him my story.

I had obviously given this a fair amount of thought or I wouldn't have even followed through on Sol's introduction.

I launched right into it.

"Philomena Treese and I are kindred spirits. I just know it. I, too, have a passion for bringing change to underprivileged kids. I'd like to think I inherited the legacy from my mother."

He sat back and peered at me over his glasses. "How do you mean?"

"My mother—she was a legend in our small town in Pennsylvania. You know, like the local mayor, before she died."

I did that air quotes thing, but in hindsight I realize Professor Tarragon missed the gesture.

"She was always helping everyone. Kids. Recovering

addicts. Single mothers were her passion. She had been a single mom for some time and fought some serious demons in her lifetime—addiction, depression—all behind the scenes, with only me for a witness. Then she met my step-father, and things turned around for her."

"But she died young?"

"Yes—she—" I was about to say she succumbed to cancer. But I halted on the words. It was so hard to say it out loud. It was so very hard. I wiped tears from my eyes. My voice caught and I couldn't say all I wanted to say. Professor Tarragon filled in the missing words, and surprise and grief prevented me from correcting him quickly enough. Our conversation quickly started to look like MadLibs gone wrong, with empty spaces provided by me and the all-wrong words provided by him.

"Say no more, your mother sounds like she had quite the life of public service."

"Yes, she did."

"And you are the daughter of a single mom turned pioneering local Mayor," Professor Tarragon supplied.

"Yes, sort of—well, not—"

He waved me off. "And she took her own life. You're having trouble talking about it. I get that. But it's ok."

"Oh! That's not—she died last year—"

Tarragon started scribbling things down on a notepad in front of him. I felt a little out of control. The story was evolving so quickly. Too quickly. I took a breath while he continued writing. I thought about starting over. But it struck me that Professor Tarragon looked like me. The way he was scribbling words down on a page. Maybe they weren't the truth, but did it really matter? If they were just words on a page? That had been my process for "writing therapy" ever since Dr. Flannery gave me the orange notebook the year before.

I sat still while Tarragon wrote, and I thought about how badly I wanted to work with Philomena Treese. Learn from her.

"I really want to craft a compelling story based on the best parts of my past, for my application. Does that make sense?"

Tarragon looked positively rapt.

"Perfect sense. You're a wise young woman. Wise beyond your years. No doubt from the startling things you've had to witness."

"So, again, I know it's a long shot, but I'd be grateful for any words of wisdom you have to share. I really want to make the best possible impression with Ms. Treese." I knew I was laying it on thick, but I felt my time was limited. Tarragon's office hours were only two hours long after all. I handed Tarragon the resume I'd been working on, along with a red pen.

He smoothed it out on the desk in front of him, and started marking it up hungrily.

"Come here. Look." Tarragon waved me around to his side of the desk and invited me to look at my own resume over his shoulder. His tweed jacket smelled musty at that angle. Dust from the piles of books was working its way up my nostrils, too. I tried not to sneeze as I read the notes in the margins and the sentence inserts over his shoulder.

Some of the red words lined up with the story I'd just shared; most didn't. Tarragon seemed to be endorsing the "embellished resume means to an end" philosophy. I weighed the harm with the benefit. If my words had moved him to craft this tale, what might they do to Philomena Treese?

In truth, my mother was a pioneering do-gooder who had never run for political office. She certainly didn't take her own life. She fought for it. She wanted me to carry out her legacy of doing good. There had indeed been a scandal, but it was all completely of my own doing. My mother wanted me to move on from it, but I was still having trouble doing so. Despite running away from home. Despite landing on my feet in Georgetown.

But this red-lined document? As I stared over Professor Tarragon's shoulder, I couldn't help but think it might get me through the door to the next leg of my journey.

I took my marked-up resume and thanked Tarragon as I squeezed out of a narrow aisle in his office between the dusty piles, careful not to turn my back on him.

Or to look a gift horse in the mouth.

The Washington Truth, dated November 15, 2017
Excerpt from the Op Ed piece, by Nate Essuzare

…"Fake it 'til you make it."

Arthur Smith, a leading career counselor had these words of advice for a standing-room-only crowd of transitioning professionals.

The attendees—composed largely of former executives aged 39-55 of some of the leading companies around the nation's capital—heard advice about resume building, networking, and tips on beefing up their LinkedIn accounts during the day-long conference hosted at the Mandarin Hotel on Maryland Avenue.

"What do you mean?" A female attendee asked when called upon by Mr. Smith after the lunch break. "What do you mean when you say 'Fake it 'Til You Make It.' Do you mean we should lie on our resumes? Do you mean we should pretend we are something we are not?"

Mr. Smith leaned forward away from the microphone hooked up to his hotel-sponsored podium and said simply, "Honestly? You've been away from the workplace for a number of years taking care of your family and other things that are important to you, right? You don't have a very marketable resume but you do have something those employers need more than line items on a resume. You're here, right? That means you have the hunger, the passion, to make this thing work for the next leg of your journey.

So here's what I mean when I say: Fake it 'til you make it. I mean that you should say whatever the hell you need to get your next job, and then let your actions—your innate talent—speak louder than any words."

I sat in the back of that room, observing the shock and quiet nods. The woman next to me leaned over, and asked, "Do you believe in all this?"

And I replied, "Absolutely."

Chapter 9

I was working on that application for a few months, even after my meeting with Professor Tarragon, trying to get up the nerve to submit a resume with more compelling fiction than a New York Times best-seller list. And maybe I'd have let the deadline for applying to the Appletreese Foundation pass me by, if the universe hadn't sent me a sign by sending Philomena and her gorgeous mother into my coffee shop one day.

I was thrilled to see them. It was as if they'd stepped right off the pages of the free newspapers provided by the coffee shop that often littered the tables after the morning crowd.

The coffee shop owner had this idea that if you provided free newspapers, people would stay off their phones, and if people stayed off their phones, they'd drink more coffee and buy more overpriced muffins. It seemed a fairly logical straight line way of thinking as the coffee shop had been in business over seven years. That was a long time in coffee shop life. Who was I to argue?

I smiled brightly at Philomena and her mother as I took their order at a small, round, high-top table where they were both huddled over a free left-behind copy of *The Washington Truth*. I heard Philomena say, "He really is something. God, I admire him so much. He's got those Innovative Media folks jumping through lots of hoops. That's for sure." After they ordered, I told them their scones would be on the house. I don't think either of them looked me directly in the eye.

They didn't look at my nametag so they could thank me by name. They didn't ask me any questions about myself, or give me a chance to lie about taking classes at Georgetown. They didn't even give me a chance to regale them with a colorful story about my mother. (The coffee shop patrons used to *love* those.)

They didn't even give me a chance to tell them all about the application and resume I was working on with the help of Sol's advisor.

They merely took their free scones, nodded a distracted thanks in unison, and waltzed past me and then out of the shop as if I didn't matter. As if I didn't exist.

I felt deflated and gave up any idea of actually submitting that fellowship application if I even achieved 100% completion.

Who was I kidding?

The streams of people who came through the shop and talked to me and listened to me and flirted with me didn't change a thing. Notable people were always coming through the shop on their way to somewhere important, and I had convinced myself I was someone worth talking to along the journey. Worth knowing. The way my mother was. But the truth was—I was no one to Philomena Treese. Or to Suzana Treese. Or anyone else in town for that matter.

I had left my past behind in Pennsylvania. But I hadn't left *me* behind.

I was licking my wounds and cleaning up the Treese's table when I saw the discarded newspaper they'd been sharing and discussing. It was folded inside out with an article about the impressive Jude Birch and his recent internet privacy win.

I repeated what Philomena and her mother had done. I studied the picture of Jude Birch coming out of the courtroom, and read the article accompanying the photo.

My mood perked up and I got an idea then. I googled a few phrases, like Sarbanes Oxley and whistleblowing. I googled a few companies. Did a little surface-level research: enough to come up with a half-cocked plan that I figured just might work.

A plan that resulted in me meeting Jude, Huck, and Finn

a short while later.

Not long after I met Jude, I got a cheap tattoo on my wrist. The scrolls of my tattoo weren't always visible at all angles. One of the hazards of having paid for a cheap tattoo was that it wasn't exactly centered on my wrist and I could barely see it without turning my wrist inward at a bizarre angle. But when I did see it, it still took my breath away.

A-B-Y.

"Your name," Jude had said perfunctorily, and maybe even a little bit quizzically, the first time he noticed it—only a few weeks after we started dating.

What he didn't know is that he'd given me the idea for that tattoo. And for the name itself.

That day, while I was in a cab on my way to meet him at the Ethiopian restaurant, I was thinking that Jude Birch was only going to be my way into Appletreese Foundation—maybe even a fun one-night stand. He'd texted me—flirting—but something more:

I still don't know your name.

Well, I'm not sure our relationship has progressed quite that far, Mr. Birch.

Fair enough. What should I call you at lunch?

Three dots popped up and then:

The future Mrs. Birch?

Ha ha. Very funny.

Well, you seem like someone who could make a guy forget all before you.

All before you.

I had traced the letters. All before you. A.B.Y.

There had been something in those words—a hope I hadn't felt since my mother was alive. A hope that maybe I could put the past behind me. That the past would really be something I, too, could forget. Something that would stop defining *me*.

The fresh start I was hoping for seemed within my reach. And before I knew it, and partly because of Jude Birch, let's face it, I'd gotten the position at Appletreese, and Jude Birch had my heart. I got the tattoo as a reminder.

While Jude always thought Aby was my name, it was really my mantra.

All Before You. Doesn't Matter.

All Before You. Is Forgotten.

All Before You. Doesn't Define You.

After I got the position at Appletreese, and fell hard for the rising star politician, and committed to helping him get elected to an office he desperately wanted, I was like a baby flamingo. I'd eaten the shrimp. I'd become something new.

And the problem wasn't that the past was always insisting on being remembered.

The problem wasn't that I'd lied. After all, everyone lies.

The problem was why.

The Washington Truth, dated December 1, 2017
Excerpt from the Op Ed piece, by Nate Essuzare

....Jude Birch of the U.S. Attorney's Office, and lead counsel on the case of *United States, ex rel. v. Innovative Media, d/b/a LessThan* seems like the canary who caught the mouse these days. His pioneering victory from 2015 was just upheld on appeal.

Several parties filed "amicus briefs" in support of Birch's position and against Innovative Media, including a small but mighty start-up company founded by a self-proclaimed band of corporate whistleblowers said to be gaining steam (and downloads!) with their newest app, *Out The Bullies*. Experts predict *Out The Bullies* will have Innovative Media's market share diminished before too long.

(By the way, for those interested in the legal mumbo jumbo, amicus briefs are basically supporting briefs from other parties who don't have skin in this particular game, but could be affected by the case on appeal.)

Birch says he is very gratified by the win on appeal, which upheld the federal judge's 2015 decision to impose substantial fines against Innovative Media, the parent company responsible for the controversial app, LessThan. The fines were levied against Innovative Media for being in violation of the Children's Online Privacy Protection Rule (lovingly referred to around here as "COPPA"). COPPA has some mighty restrictions about how much information can be collected and shared by an app that is targeted to children under the age of 13—something Innovative Media claimed it did not do. Because Innovative Media claimed that its website is strictly a "teens-only" app, with particular focus on helping high school age kids get into college, they argued there was no problem with collecting very specific personal information from its purchasers, including school information and the like.

Birch disagreed, and at oral argument, said the app was "practically targeted at youths from the womb. LessThan's 'Disney-like' themes, fonts, music and animation only served to reinforce this point."

According to Innovative Media, at stake is a substantial fine with about seven zero's in it, as well as a slippery slope of government intrusion.

On the other side of the appeal, at stake is Counselor Jude Birch's reputation—which some already say is earning him attention in the political arena. Ironically, Birch started his legal career by interning in-house at Treese, Inc., the famous (infamous?) conglomerate started by Dominic Treese—a well-known and hefty investor in Innovative Media.

It seems Birch is comfortable breaking ties with his one-time mentor. Something that seems to be on trend in this town lately. (Hell, even Treese's own daughter broke ties with the construction giant, abandoning her trust fund to start her new venture, Appletreese Foundation.)

I've got my eye on this colorful cast of characters. Stay tuned.

Chapter 10

Shortly after we started seeing each other in 2015, fresh off Jude's *Innovative Media* victory at the trial level (it would be another 18 months or so before the appeal was upheld), he started traveling to law schools in and around the beltway, to give a primer on the case. It was originally supposed to be a "law school" circuit, but Jude was so charismatic and dynamic, that word got out, and he started getting invited to high schools and even local elementary schools. He would warn the kids about giving too much away to the internet. He became a pseudo-motivational speaker in D.C. and even beyond, some of his speeches going viral on YouTube thanks to the lax cell phone policies in a few of the schools he was invited to.

His most popular talk, entitled "Why You Matter," was actually a commencement speech at his own high school alma mater in D.C. that had gone viral with four million views in just under a month. By late 2017 Jude was a home-town hero—a prominent member of the U.S. Attorney's office in the District of Columbia who was an advocate for entre-preneurs, D.C.'s statehood, eradicating homelessness, and rational gun control, and who, apparently by accident, I eventually learned, because his boss was too busy working on immigration cases, was still the lead counsel of record on one of the most high-profile internet privacy cases of recent years. Jude had become something of an anomaly in Washington D.C. A political insider who was beloved both within and outside of D.C.

And me? Well, I was starting to wrap my head around a future in D.C. politics. After all, Jude was certainly cut out for that life and I loved him. So for many reasons, the answer was just that easy.

And so because of that, I simply ignored all the other reasons.

⌒

It wasn't that surprising to me that by the time the decision became ours to make about whether Jude should begin a bona fide campaign, the decision was a relatively quick one. It was much more surprising—when I stopped to think about it, which I rarely did—how successful Appletreese Foundation was becoming, and how big a part of all that I was.

In fact, in late 2017, when we first heard the musings that, due to population boons inside Washington D.C., a new Congressional at-large delegate position was going to be created for the first time in American history, and a Special Election would be held for the position in Fall of 2018, Jude and I were at an awards dinner in Georgetown. Appletreese was the recipient of a humanitarian award and I was accepting on the Foundation's behalf. I was gearing up to speak when someone leaned across me at the table and stage whispered to Jude, "Have you heard the big news? They're certifying a new delegate seat. Might be the perfect chance for a young man with political aspirations to get his feet good and wet in this city."

I was right at that moment being introduced by the Georgetown President, so when Jude looked at me and said, "Wow. You hear that? Sounds official, now. What do you think? What if I actually pursued it?" I had whispered "Go for it!" more out of expediency and nerves than true commitment to the decision.

But that had apparently been all he needed to hear. We'd never talked about it in what ifs or maybes again after that night. On the way home that night, Jude was on the phone in the car with Huck and Finn, future campaign advisors extraordinaire, fully believing—or at least saying he did—that

I had given him my full blessing on a night that was supposed to be mine.

While he animatedly discussed campaign logistics, I held my heavy crystal humanitarian award, and when Jude asked me, "You don't mind if we go straight home instead of out for a celebratory drink like we planned, do you? I have some work to do. Phone calls to make?" I shook my head. "Of course not, Jude."

"Thanks to you, Sweetheart," he'd tapped my knee that was propping up my brand new crystal hardware. "I would never have the guts to do this, but for you, Baby."

I had stifled that little queasiness that tried to make its way up as I realized that Jude hadn't congratulated me on the award or complimented my acceptance speech. He'd given me credit instead for a decision to run for the At-Large seat. All the credit. I was supposed to be comforted by that fact, I supposed.

Still, there was a little piece of me that wondered if Jude was hell-bent on giving me all the credit for the decision, wouldn't there be the possibility ... if anything went wrong ... that he'd also want to give me all of the blame?

⌒

We kept our separate residences during Jude's rise to fame, but not for Jude's lack of trying. Sol had graduated and moved out while I was still working on my application for Appletreese Foundation, an application that I actually submitted under my new name of Aby Boyle. Actually, Sol had left town altogether to work for Teach America, and we hadn't kept in touch. She didn't even know that I'd gotten the fellowship with Appletreese. If she read about it, she'd perhaps wondered fleetingly who in the hell Aby Boyle was, and perhaps she'd be sorry that Aby had swooped in and stolen the position out from under Chelsea Boyle. Ditto for Professor Tarragon.

I'd kept the apartment I'd once shared with Sol, but since I'd gotten the position at Appletreese Foundation soon after Sol left, there was no need for me to advertise for my own felony-free non-smoking roommate.

I kept my driver's license and lease in my actual name. Since Jude and Philomena Treese had no reason to look at either one, I was able to transition to Aby Boyle out in the world. The bookkeeper at Appletreese had looked at my social security card and driver's license to get my paperwork in order when I started work, but she didn't make a big deal of the fact that my checks were to be made payable to Chelsea Boyle, but my business cards were to be ordered with Aby Boyle on them.

"Aby's my middle name," I told her. "But it's the only name I go by anymore." She was overworked and tired, running the books for a non-profit on a shoestring budget. She nodded at my explanation. She didn't care. Mena had hired me. Mena had vouched for me. It was Mena's company. That was enough.

Jude was always asking me to give up my apartment and move in with him, but I held tightly to my own space. Shortly after that Georgetown awards dinner, when Jude claimed I helped him decide to join the political fray, Jude also bought a Brookland craftsman house for nearly $700,000. It was turnkey, and he asked me to move in and help him decorate it. "It's time. Come on. Let's move in together." It was my last holdout—my last vestige of protection—keeping my own space. Jude didn't understand how monumental it was that I agreed to give that up and move in with him. It meant that someday I'd have to tell him who I really was. And what I'd done to get there.

"A brand new life." That's what Jude had promised as he carried me across the threshold on the day of closing on the craftsman. I had enjoyed the romance of the act, but hated the words that accompanied it and what they meant.

After all, I had a "brand new life." I didn't need yet

another one.

It hadn't mattered to me in the beginning that our relationship had started with lies. When guilt crept in, I pushed it back out with the truth: All relationships are built with lies, some big, some small.

I like your friends. I'll never be jealous. I love to go to concerts, watch football, give up my side of the bed.

All relationships start with lies.

Especially the lies we tell ourselves.

When I ran away from my old life, I was trying so hard to stop lying that I avoided relationships altogether.

But falling in love with Jude changed everything and so as the years went by, I wished for a world where there'd be no more lies.

But you know what they say.

Be careful what you wish for.

The Washington Truth, dated April 1, 2018
Excerpt from the Op Ed piece, by Nate Essuzare

...As Jude Birch puts the pieces in motion to run for the At-Large position, some have argued it should not exactly be a coveted position. The fact remains that it is a non-voting position with very little actual current power. Others argue that if Jude could secure the pioneering position, and maybe even succeed in his quest to obtain statehood for D.C., the power shift would be great indeed. After all, the D.C. delegate cannot vote on final legislation, but he can sponsor legislation, propose amendments to legislation and even vote on those amendments. Many speculate that it could be a stepping stone to a long, illustrious career in politics in much more prominent positions—including a Supreme Court nod or a Vice-Presidential bid down the road, and then, well, who knows?

Given this projected trajectory, what do we think about

putting a young man in power who hasn't exactly proven himself yet?

Or has he already proven himself in ways the public doesn't know about?

What will we learn about Jude Birch as this campaign proceeds?

Chapter 11

Here's the truth.

It drove me crazy that Laila Rogers was one of Jude's first phone calls that night after the Georgetown Awards dinner, along with Huck and Finn. He told her he wanted a meeting. To talk about becoming his campaign manager.

"I know her from the early days of practicing law, Sweetheart. I trust her," he said on that occasion and on several ones afterward.

But dear God, the way she made the hairs on the back of my neck stand up, I didn't know if he was right to trust her. And I even wondered if maybe he was lying about trusting her.

I sure didn't.

It was Laila who got to be Jude's liaison to the world whenever anything good happened with the campaign or otherwise. In fact, it was Laila who wrote the press release about Jude's landmark internet privacy case being upheld on appeal. It turned out to be a very big deal, for the campaign that we were still putting together at the time (months before the official announcement at the Freedom Art Loft space), and for Jude personally. As he explained to me, it would now become "precedent" in other internet privacy litigation—a rapidly growing field in the law.

"Meaning what exactly, Jude?"

"Meaning other parties can use it when they are trying to win their own cases. They can point to this case, and say, Dear Court, it's already been decided. You have to decide this way, too."

"Hunh, sounds like a lazy person's way of getting out of work, if you ask me."

Jude had laughed then, and said I had a way of keeping

him humble, and happy. And that made me happy, too.

And I grabbed onto that word "precedent," which seemed to mean something I could actually relate to, namely—*if I say it's true, it's true.*

⌐

In campaign meetings, I struggled against any reaction to Laila that might be viewed as intimidation, even though Laila was, of course, intimidating. Laila used ridiculous words like "moreover" and "nevertheless" and "whomever" and she winked at *whomever* was speaking, as long as he was male. At first I thought it was a tic, but eventually I came to realize it was an intentional and cultivated gesture meant to put male speakers off-balance while at the same time rewarding them for saying interesting things. Laila had never once winked at me. And I know for a fact I said lots of interesting things. She always wore black, and she smelled distinctly of almonds. People were often complimenting her perfume, but I found her scent cloying.

"I absolutely love your perceptive eye, Aby," Laila replied—with no wink—to my comment a few months in, that the campaign seemed to be focusing on the wrong demographics, bringing in donors and fundraisers who actually lived outside of D.C. city limits, like the affluent Maryland and Virginia suburbs.

"I'm just concerned that it's time to refocus on how and when a white lawyer with some degree of privilege named Jude Birch is actually going to switch gears and speak to the issues important to the economically and racially diverse voters actually *living in D.C.*," I had said moments before Laila responded with the "perceptive eye" comment and moved on to a discussion of the catering for the next campaign event. I was dismissed.

But then, Laila suggested, "You know, Jude. We are going to need to start working on your education narrative. We're going to really step it up and add some details to the website about your commitment to improving the inner city schools."

Jude nodded violently as if that was the most brilliant thing he'd heard all day. I couldn't stop myself. I had to remind him the issue pivot was *my* idea. "Good. You agree with me. I'll work on the education narrative. That's right up my alley." Laila looked at me blankly. I stepped further into her trap. "Because of my work with the Appletreese Foundation, obviously."

"Whoa." Laila actually put a hand out in front of her like I was physically charging at her or something. Which for the record, I was not.

"We need to be very careful, Aby, to separate Appletreese from Jude's campaign. Let's not forget, Appletreese launched on the back of seed money from Innovative Media."

Innovative Media.

Laila threw that name around like kryptonite whenever we were all together. And it seemed to really work on Jude.

"Listen to this," Laila put her hand up yet again and proceeded to read from a recent issue of *The Washington Truth.*

**The Washington Truth, dated June 15, 2018,
Excerpt from the Op Ed piece, by Nate Essuzare**

...Jude's adversary in the Special Election is one Kylie Rutter, a candidate who is openly backed by Innovative Media, a developer of one of the most downloaded social media apps in the last three years, and sworn enemy of Jude Birch, who won a landmark case resulting in an eight-figure fine against the company for failing to comply with COPPA rules. LessThan has substantially revamped its information collection practices, and it continues to be extremely popular with children and teens (and adults!) alike.

LessThan reports over 100 million installs in 2017 alone, the year the fine was upheld by the District of Columbia Court of Appeals, and is used by tens of millions of teens to measure themselves and friends against celebs and the "popular kids"—ostensibly to improve their appearance and grades and social status. It even boasts the ability to enhance college applications with concrete improvement suggestions that will give an edge against the very real competition of the college application pool.

In reality, however, many claim that LessThan has been responsible for dozens of cyber-bullying related suicides in 2016 and 2017, and breaking the spirits of millions more.

In 2016 and 2017, Innovative Media spent millions supporting the campaigns of several politicians across the country. And, given their investment in ads supporting Kylie Rutter's campaign, they clearly view the new seat in D.C. as an important one. With the COPPA case resolved on appeal, and not in their favor, some have asked why Innovative Media continues in such a public spotlight. But insiders say Innovative Media is working hard to ensure tech development-friendly legislation. With Net Neutrality under fire by the FCC, Innovative Media is worried that their particular form of controversial, but highly profitable app, LessThan, could be on the chopping block in the near future, and they are highly interested in making sure bought politicians are in positions of power. Put simply, they have the money to keep paying off their fines. But the money evaporates if their app is actually taken off the market.

On the other side of the ballot, Jude Birch has not yet articulated a clear position on Net Neutrality, but he has repeatedly noted his disdain for the concept of LessThan, including in the lengthy court battle he waged against their parent from the U.S. Attorney's office.

Of course, it is impossible to ignore that Birch started

out as a lawyer working inhouse for one of Innovative Media's biggest investors, Dominic Treese. And similarly hard to ignore that Birch's girlfriend, Aby Boyle, helps run a Foundation headed up by Treese's daughter, and which was practically launched with Innovative Media money.

The webs in D.C. are tangled ones, and though Jude Birch runs on a platform that promises to untangle those webs and keep everything open and transparent, there are some of us who have, from the beginning, questioned what that really means.

Chapter 12

After Laila finished reading from *The Washington Truth*, I rolled my eyes and looked at Jude. He wasn't jumping in to correct her fast enough. So I had to. "Oh, come on. Neither Mena nor Appletreese has ever been beholden to any donors, and certainly not donors whose money was spent years ago now." I slipped into party line mode as I did so often where the Foundation was at stake. "When Innovative Media donated that money, it was for tech support to the inner city schools. Appletreese provided one-on-one technology resources, including iPads and chrome books to students who had never before had access to working computers. That money has nothing to do with that loathsome app, LessThan, and it was used to do good work. Maybe the only good work Innovative Media has ever done. Let's not trivialize that fact. And similarly, let's not exaggerate their connection to the good work that's currently being done by the Foundation—which is now supported annually by *hundreds* of corporate donors, big and small."

Jude finally found his voice. "Yes, of course. Laila, let's drop this whole Innovative Media seed money thing once and for all. I don't want to buy into that propaganda 'The Washington So-Called Truth' is spewing along with others. You know they're just trying to bait me. I won't have it. I want to prep talking points for the Town Hall meeting next week ..." And with that the two of them were embroiled distractedly into another strategy session. I excused myself loudly, and needlessly, from the room.

I returned after a walk around the block with three lattes to go, feeling hyped about the imminent caffeine. In the hallway outside the strategy room, I reached for the door handle, but at the sound of the loud voices on the other side,

I stopped with my hand on the doorknob and the drink carrier perched awkwardly on my knee. I was afraid to move, afraid the doorknob would turn loose in my hand and I'd be thrust into the fight that was blowing up on the other side.

I heard Jude yelling but his words were hard to make out because Laila was interrupting him, repeating over and over. "That's a lie."

Jude gave up trying to make his point when Laila switched off her one-line script with a loud hiss: "Are you kidding me, Jude?"

"Laila, it's been years, for God's sake. What do you want me to say? I'm sorry? Haven't I apologized over and over again? I have tried to make it up to you. I gave you this job. Do you know what a wedge having you in this position has put between me and Aby?"

I felt all the air leave my chest and rush to my head.

What was Jude apologizing for? Were my suspicions correct? Laila and Jude *did* have a history together that seemed to include much more than law school and political strategizing.

I let go of the doorknob in my hand and it squeaked softly. The occupants inside didn't seem to notice, or if they did, they didn't let it disrupt them.

Laila kept on hissing. "You didn't give me anything, Jude Birch. Don't you even dare. I earned this position on my own merit, and if you want to see a wedge between you and your girlfriend, then let me have a few moments alone with her to tell her the truth. I suspect, knowing Aby the little that I do, it won't just be me who's no longer accepting your apology at that point."

I backed away from the door and walked backward down the hallway, lattes spilling out over my arms. I didn't want to hear any more. I didn't want to know about the relationship Laila and Jude had before we met. Or maybe it overlapped with our relationship? Maybe Jude had broken up with Laila for me? Regardless, their relationship had not ended amicably. It had ended due to something so terrible, that Laila was using it as blackmail against Jude—to get this job I knew she wasn't really qualified for. And to put a distance between him and me. A distance further exacerbated by the lies I was still perpetuating about my own past. How could I expect Jude to be honest with me? And yet I wanted to trust him so badly. I wanted a relationship that moved forward in truth. My heart was a jumble of hypocrisy and jealousy and pain.

I ran out of the building, and jumped into my car, throwing it in drive and then park again, as I realized there was a huge crack in my windshield that hadn't been there earlier that morning. I laid my head on the steering wheel in frustration and startled myself when the horn buzzed loud and low beneath my chin.

I lifted my head and threw the car in drive again and drove straight home where I retreated to the guest room, refusing to come out even when Jude got home later that night. From the guest bed, I heard him come into the house, and pad down the hallway to the bedroom. I heard his hand pause on the doorknob, and then I heard the decision to turn it, rather than abandon it, as I had earlier that day on the other side of a door from he and Laila. I heard him whisper quietly into the darkness I was cocooned in, "Sweetheart—are you awake?"

And in the silence that followed, I thought about that crack in my windshield and how it probably started out as a small and totally reparable chip, but I'd ignored it so long, it had started to spider out until the whole damn thing was now impossible to fix.

The Washington Truth, dated July 1, 2018
Excerpt from the Op Ed piece, by Nate Essuzare

....The news, they say has become all fiction.
That's too kind.

What they really mean, is that it has become all lies.

But that's not fair. The media voice may just be the one place devoid of filters these days. In life, everyone is tempering their words and their actions with exaggerated courtesy, with a misguided sense that the truth is too difficult to handle, too difficult to stomach.

Political correctness, they call it. And it's advocated for.

What an odd turn of events. Since when did politics become the barometer for what is true, for what is correct?

Since when did the media become the enemy?

Chapter 13

When I was a kid back in Pennsylvania, my mom, my step-dad and I would go to the local arts fest every year. I'd wait for it to come to town, even though in hindsight it was a silly thing to pine for. We'd get up early and always beat the traffic. We'd wind through the makeshift fields-turned-parking lots stacked against each other until we ended up close to the entrance. We'd walk back through the early bird exhibitors to a place I later learned was the favorite and perennial spot of Kane, my step-dad; it was near an oak tree that was downwind of the funnel cake stands and upwind of a thick lilac bush. There was an old stump with swirled signs of life decorating its top, even though it was long dead. Kane used the old stump as a stool and set up everything around it for the day. Easels, a folding table of canvases, paints and brushes.

I looked forward to this familiar routine every single year.

The first time Kane told me about the Art Festival, it went like this: "Come on, I want to take you and your mom and walk the grounds a bit before I'm scheduled to paint."

"Scheduled to paint? What does that mean?"

My mom grabbed his arm and beamed, like she had just been selected homecoming queen. "Didn't you know? Kane's on the schedule as a live oil painter. He creates a piece of art before a small crowd and sells it to the highest bidder."

"Really?"

From what I knew about my step-dad, even in those early days, he didn't seem like someone who would jump on board such a commercial trope. Sell his art to the highest bidders? I told him so.

He simply smiled at me. Maybe he didn't want me to

know the truth. I'm not sure why not. But my mom jumped in and answered for him. "Oh, he doesn't keep the money. It's for charity. It's for the art fund in the local school district."

Of course it was.

Kane had been around since I was about eight. What I'd understood was that he'd pretty much been the town drunk who'd run off his first wife and children. After years of recovery and relapse, he'd finally gotten his life back on track, but his first wife and kids, now grown with kids of their own, wanted nothing to do with him. They'd moved across the country, and advised him every year when he called on birthdays and such, to basically "stay the hell away."

At first, some people in town said my mom was crazy for taking a chance on Kane, but she always smiled and said, "The heart wants what the heart wants." Eventually people forgot who Kane had been, or maybe they just showed it less. I never really had to take a chance on Kane, as I'd never known him in his town drunk days, and in my world, he was a good guy who loved my mom and donated money to the art fund in the local school district.

My mom was a recovering alcoholic as well, who had lost a baby daddy and a preschool teaching job when I was still very young. As the years went by, I forgot all about those years. I just knew her as my mom, diner waitress extraordinaire, and dispenser of kindness and advice everywhere she went.

So when Kane wanted me to go with him to the Arts Festival the year I turned 10, I went. And every year afterward, until my mom was too sick to go. After I moved to D.C., Kane and I didn't keep in touch, something I felt badly about, but I thought about him when the last week of July came around each year—the traditional week of the Arts Festival back home. I hoped he was still going. Still selling his art to the highest bidder. Still sober.

When I was a kid, I'd circle the opening day of the Arts

Festival on my calendar and look forward to it for weeks prior like it was the prom or something. When the morning arrived, my mom, Kane, and I would climb into the pick-up truck at 8 am sharp. Always the same departure time. No debating it or trying to change it or trying to sleep in that day. It was understood and I went along with it. After I climbed into the truck, I'd always give the same backward glance at the canvases and painting supplies cluttering the back seat.

Blank canvases.

Later on, those canvases would really become my best memory from those summers.

⌣

I shared a pared-down version of the story of Kane and the pick-up truck and the blank canvases with Mena one day after Yoga class, before I could filter myself. Our yogi had finished the class by asking us to focus on a pure and happy childhood memory.

"Take the first thing that comes to mind, and strip away its layers until you are left with only its essence. That essence? Keep hold of that. Use that when you are trying to meditate. Focus."

I'd thought the whole thing was sort of hokey, but nevertheless, I kept thinking about those damn canvases in the back seat of the pick-up truck year after year. My poses felt effortless for the first time since I'd started the class.

The yogi must have sensed I was on the verge of a breakthrough. She came up to me after class. She was wearing a thin salmon-colored tee shirt with "OHM" on the front; her white-grey hair pulled off her lined face in a pony tail that made her look younger than her years. She put her cold hands on my shoulders for a moment and then released me. The touch was unexpected but not unwelcome. I stood still, while she spoke to me in a thick unidentifiable accent.

"What is it that you need, Aby?"

I was struck with the realization that no one had ever asked me that question. I stood looking at her, bubbling over. Raw from the words she had spoken out loud. I held my breath, afraid that I'd say something I didn't mean. Or worse—something that I did. I felt the tingly feeling of emotions coursing too close to the surface, as if the slightest touch, scratch, or bump would pierce my skin and let them all ooze out.

"I don't know," I said honestly.

She nodded, as if I had gotten the answer right, and I felt some relief in that. "Keep showing up, Aby. Don't give up on yourself. Keep fighting for you." I nodded earnestly in return.

Later, over a glass of pinot and chef salads at the café across from the yoga studio, I told Mena about the blank canvases. I think the yogi had pierced me open after all.

Mena nodded and returned the favor by telling me that when she was a child, her most vivid memories revolved around the times she and Suzana frequented a Maryland soup kitchen. She told me they spent every Thanksgiving (and a few other Saturdays per year) there. Her father never came. He was always too busy working or something else.

Mena hated this custom.

They'd leave their house early in the morning, dressed unassumingly and let the press follow them to the Franklin Street Soup Kitchen.

There they'd meet with some other hard-working volunteers who probably had actual families waiting for them at home but still had chosen to come to Franklin Street on Thanksgiving morning. In Mena's mind, this constituted actual sacrifice while her and her mother's holiday plans at the Soup Kitchen seemed more designed to cover up the fact that they didn't have anywhere else to be.

While they waited for the doors to open to the public, Mena (and her mother) would head to the back of the kitchen and take some inventory so that Suzana would know what to have her staff send over the following week. As Mena counted and made notes on a clipboard, Suzana would routinely stack the soup broths on top of each other with the labels facing outward. Mena always noticed that Suzana wasn't alphabetizing them as she did at home. It was conspicuous, her mother's need for things to line up, she told me.

In their home, Mena reported that gourmet jars of soups and exotic creamy sauces purchased at full list price, without any coupons, from a gourmet kitchen store in town, lined the shelves of an immaculate well-stocked pantry. As she watched her mother's hands twisting and turning the jars in the soup kitchen every Thanksgiving, Mena imagined that Suzana was likely congratulating herself inwardly for resisting alphabetizing, but Mena didn't share her mother's pride in the restraint. Mena felt even the resistance was—itself— an act of ridiculousness.

"Who else would even think about putting the cans of soup in proper order while waiting for the doors of a soup kitchen to open?" I shook my head wondering when this story was going to get, you know, *happy*.

As it turned out, Franklin Street wasn't an ordinary soup kitchen, Mena told me further. The press had confirmed Mena's suspicions about the Franklin Street Soup Kitchen by writing up numerous stories about it. Sometimes the press would profile the actual patrons of the soup kitchen, but more often, thanks—Mena suspected—to the highly paid publicist Suzana kept on her payroll—the stories were about Suzana's pioneering efforts, and the pilot program she was trying to inspire with it. At Franklin Street, Suzana had advocated for the needy hungry families to come in and cook for themselves. Pots were lined up on the counters and before they could eat, vegetables would be sliced and diced, meat would be browned, and containers of soup broth would be dumped into industrial-sized pots to be boiled and stirred by people who would not have had a hot meal in several days, perhaps longer. It felt like a taunt, a tease to Mena, but her mother insisted that this was how to really help people. By not providing a fiction that the world would continue to provide for them. To not pretend the world would keep on preparing soup *for* them.

From Mena's point of view, she told me, there seemed a soft whiff of well-meaning intention underneath a back note of patronizing condescension, masked by rancid self-righteousness.

"I hate that my mother has always worked so hard to turn everything into a learning life lesson—even for hungry people."

"Dear God, Mena," I said when she was done. "I don't think you've done the exercise correctly. You can't strip that memory down to any happy essence. You have to try again."

"You weren't listening, Aby. It *is* a happy memory from my childhood. One of the best. I love coming back to it."

"Hunh?"

"I was surrounded by food, and not eating one. Single. Bite."

I noticed then that Mena hadn't eaten her salad, just pushed it around with a fork as she told me the story. And I realized I'd never seen Philomena eat in front of me—not once in all the time I'd known her.

And I nodded while I thought: *well, I suppose demons come in all shapes and sizes and flavors, no?*

Chapter 14

The first time I met Suzana Treese, other than that half-hearted meeting in the coffee shop that Mena never once bothered to remember again in my presence, and that I never bothered to remind her about, was a night that Mena and I were working late at the office. We had a grant proposal due the following day and we were pulling an all nighter, trying make sure to dot every i and cross every t. Literally.

Mena was a brilliant woman but a terrible writer, and her brain seemed to work too fast for her hands so she was always typing things that didn't make sense. We sat next to each other on side-by-side laptops editing the same google document and it was a mostly an exercise in frustration.

Suzana arrived with lattes and granola bars around 11 pm and while she should have been a welcome sight at that point, I remember feeling annoyed. Even when she reached into her purse and pulled out a handful of small creamers that were actually alcoholic. "Here you go loves, a little Rum Chata to get the brain juices flowing."

Mena snatched the latte and creamers from her mother's hand hungrily and waved off the granola bars.

"Thanks, Mom."

"Thanks, Mrs. Treese."

"Oh, Aby, Suzana, please. I know we've just met, but I feel like we're old friends. Mena adores you, so that means I do, too."

Her words sounded genuine and warm, and her body language matched. She sat down on the sofa across from the laptops, and took off her expensive looking cardigan, revealing long toned arms, and gestured to Mena.

"Why don't you print out a copy? I'll help you guys proof. You must be exhausted. I'm sure you could use another set of eyes."

Mena looked relieved to have her mother there. I wondered if my annoyance was fueled by competition.

I'm here, helping. Why are you so relieved your mom is here?

But it was more than that. It wasn't garden variety competition. It was jealousy. The kind of green-colored emotion I wasn't used to feeling. Especially where mothers were concerned. The emotion stung with realization as I watched the gentle interactions between Mena and Suzana that night. It was more than missing my Mom. I did that every minute of every day. Another thought hit me with a pang, as Suzana marked up the proposal and made some quality insights that probably would differentiate our proposal from the rest.

Oh my God, I'm jealous that Mena forgives her mom.

Mena hated her mother's controlling nature, her self-righteousness, and her hypocritical dependence on the lifestyle Dominic Treese provided. Yet, she forgave her anew every time she was with her. I'd seen them interacting comfortably in the coffee shop that day, and again that night as we worked on the grant proposal together. It couldn't be a coincidence. Mena seemed to genuinely forgive her mother's shortcomings. And for this, I was jealous.

At her funeral, I stood up and talked about how amazing my mother was. I'd loved how she worked early and late shifts so that she was there every day when I got off the school bus. She'd make celery logs with peanut butter and raisins and tease me that I was eating ants on a log as I gobbled them up.

She saved up for weeks to take me dress shopping for dances and clothes shopping when each new season of school struck. She helped volunteer at school as much as she could, and made homemade cupcakes for my birthday—never store bought. She helped with homework—she was a whiz at Math and always read my summer reading selections along with me so we could discuss them.

After the funeral, Kane suggested I get back into counseling, so I did. I went to a counselor who supposedly specialized in grief management. Apparently that's a thing and I was willing to have my grief managed. I even signed up for some local grief support groups.

But I stopped going when I discovered something troubling about all my grief-stricken comrades. People in grief change history. They tell stories about their loved ones that simply can't be believed. They remember them as superheroes. They remember them as perfect people who never made any mistakes, who never did anything wrong, and who they would trade places with to have back on this earth. In other words, people in mourning lie.

And that made me doubt my own recollection of my mother. Maybe she wasn't as perfect as I remembered. I hated that. I picked at the doubt until it became an open wound.

After all, she did betray me one critical time. She didn't believe me when it came to Rafe Wilson.

And she'd tried taking away the one thing I was so good at: lying.

⌇

I can't remember the first lie I told.

But I remember the first lie my mom caught me in. I was five years old. I'd just started school, and it was "Bring Your Dad to School Day," a notion I've come to understand is as outdated as bikinis in the Miss America Contest.

My mother agreed.

When I brought home the paper announcing the upcoming event, she marched right into school with a litany of questions for the teacher.

Didn't everyone's family look different these days? Two moms or one single dad and Grandmas raising babies? Why were we still pretending that families all looked the same? And that square-shaped families could be smashed into round-shaped holes with silly things like "Bring Your Dad to School Day?"

The teacher, instead of apologizing for the trauma that might have been caused to me, nodded politely, sent my mom home and then called her in the following week to tell her I'd been stealing the school supplies of the girl next to me and blaming it on another little boy who didn't even sit in our row.

I think it's important to point out that the little boy I'd accused of stealing the stuff had a very handsome, impressive father that he'd brought to school on the "Bring Your Dad to School Day" that went forward despite my mom's best efforts.

So did the little girl whose stuff I stole.

At the follow-up conference, I remember that my mother had tried to explain to perky Miss Jenner that I was simply acting out, and that this had to be "normal" behavior. But Miss Jenner shook her head sternly. "I assure you, Ms. Boyle, there's nothing normal about this."

I wanted my mother to fight for me. To tell Miss Jenner to take her little version of "normal" and shove it, but instead, my mother nodded and took a piece of paper from Miss Jenner that had the name and number of a child psychologist, Dr. Hugh Filbert, who could fit me in sometime over the next two to four months.

Dr. Filbert thought maybe I had ADHD and prescribed some medicine that my mom was supposed to sprinkle on my applesauce. I wouldn't eat it, and to this day, I can't even look at applesauce without gagging. My mom gave up on the medicine and on Dr. Filbert in pretty short order. In return, I worked on keeping the lies to a minimum, and life ebbed and flowed. Kane came into our lives a few years later. He brought with him a type of stability that soothed the edges on both of us. It became easier and easier not to lie anymore.

Until my mom was diagnosed with cancer when I was in high school.

Three weeks after my mom sat me down to tell me she had a disease that was going to kill her, she sat me down again to ask whether I'd eaten the last of the special brown rice cereal she'd bought as part of her macro cancer diet. Someone had left the empty box tipped over in the pantry.

I remained steadfast. "I am telling you, Mother. I did not eat the cereal. You are going to have to ask Kane."

"I did ask Kane. Even though he hates the brown rice cereal and would rather eat maggots, his words, not mine, still I asked him, and he confirmed that he did not eat the cereal."

"Then you must have eaten it and forgotten." We stared at each other icily.

"Why are you doing this, Chelsea?" Her expression turned to fear. I hated that I'd caused that, but I couldn't back down.

"Because I didn't eat the cereal."

My mom arranged for me to get back in therapy right away. This time it was Dr. York. Dr. York didn't want to talk about ADHD and medication, so I paid a little more attention to her.

She had an idea for me. She advocated that I take up a new form of physical exercise as an outlet for my frustration and anger. She said the emotions I was feeling were understandable for a girl my age who'd just learned her mother has cancer.

I liked her words; I just didn't feel much like exercising. I didn't feel much like doing anything. But then one day, after a brutal day of chemo, when my mom was sick and spent on the bathroom floor, I laced up old sneakers with no arches left and worn soles, dug out of the bottom of my closet, and yelled into the bathroom, where my mother was heaving, and Kane was rubbing her back in small circles the way she liked, "Bye guys! I'm headed out for a run!"

I had no plan. My legs took me out of our residential neighborhood to the town square, along Walnut, Filbert, and eventually to Canal Street. I got a side stitch outside a motorcycle shop on Canal Street, and stopped to catch my breath and rub my side. The adrenaline and the fresh air running through my body helped me forget about brown rice cereal, chemo, and my mom's death sentence.

I was flushed and still massaging my side on the sidewalk, when a boy came out of the shop about my age. He was wearing a dark, worn tee-shirt and ripped jeans. He smelled of gasoline, musky cologne, and faintly of bleach. I recognized him from school, although we didn't have any classes together, but I was pretty sure he was in my grade. He smiled at me and time stopped for a moment as I studied his dimples.

"You ok?" He broke the silence first.

Presumably because I was still sucking wind and trying to catch my breath. I silently nodded in response.

"Want some water?"

I nodded again.

He waved me inside the shop, and I followed him into a room that smelled like him, only bigger. It was set up like a lounge with leather couches and chairs, and beyond it was an open garage lined with motorcycles in various stages of repair and disrepair. But no people. No customers and no other workers. "You the only one here?" I found my breath. I wasn't nervous. I just wondered.

"Yeah. The shop's actually closed today."

"Ah, it's Sunday." I got my bearings and remembered my mother had been scheduled for chemo on Sunday because she was an emergent case.

The ramifications of that hit me for the first time as I thought: *Her prognosis must be so much worse than she has even let on.*

I giggled inappropriately at the thought, and then caught the boy looking at me funny, as he asked, "What's so funny?"

"Oh, nothing. I just—nothing. Thanks for the water offer." I smiled up at him reminding him.

"Oh, that's right." He motioned for me to take a seat on the lounge chair and he walked around a counter where I caught a glimpse of a small refrigerator stationed out of reach of patrons. I blushed to think that he was reaching into the employee private stash to get me some water. I hoped vaguely that he wouldn't get in trouble for raiding the employee frig.

"Do you want regular water? Or Gatorade? You look like you could use a little electrolyte replenishing." I smiled at him. He reddened and I liked that. He pushed a misbehaved clump of hair out of his eye nervously while he waited for my answer.

"Electrolytes it is. Got any orange?"

"Yes!" He looked surprised as he responded enthusiastically. "That's actually my favorite flavor, so I always keep plenty in the frig."

"Really? No one ever likes orange. I feel like a freak whenever I ask for it."

He came back around the counter and handed me an orange Gatorade bottle. "Not a freak," he assured.

"Thanks," I took the bottle from him, feeling a little jolt after I purposely let our fingers touch. "I'm Chelsea Boyle. We go to the same school."

Right after I said it, I looked down, mortified that he might not have ever noticed me and now I'd admitted that *I* had noticed *him*.

"I know you, Chelsea," he said familiarly.

"Oh." I looked back up at him startled.

"You handed me a water at field day last year?"

"Oh!" I said again, but this time, with recognition. The year before, the freshmen had been in charge of concessions at the school-wide field day. Demi, the most popular girl in the class, and stereotypical mean girl, and her Posse (who actually called themselves that as if they were trying to cast for a Grease sequel or something) had made sure that I had been relegated to the worst position possible—the grill stand.

The grill stand was terrible because it turned everyone into a hot, sweaty mess, and also because it meant you had to be supervised by the parent volunteers helping out for the day. Demi and her Posse worked the snow cone maker which was darling and delicious and required no parental supervision at all, so the freshman girls tied their tee shirts in midriff-baring knots, flirted mercilessly with the older boys, and cemented their place among the cool kids.

It wasn't a particularly happy memory for me, but there had been that one bright light. A boy had come up to the grill, looked me in the eye and asked me for a water. Even though there was a water stand nearby manned by some football players moonlighting as freshman volunteers, still he'd asked *me* for a water.

I had allowed myself a moment's daydream that day that the boy had seen me across the crowded football field, littered with cheerleaders and other pretty girls, and had sought me out. But he had nodded a quick thanks and run off back to his group, and the moment passed, and I hadn't given the whole encounter a second thought until the day of that run. And if asked, I would have bet real money he didn't either.

But he did.

He had.

I remembered his name. I had asked one of the parents standing nearby, a clueless dad, who didn't care why I was asking, but looked over his shoulder while flipping a burger, and told me nonchalantly.

"Rafe Wilson," I breathed his name out loud emerging from the memory of the moment I'd first learned it.

"Yep, that's me. I guess that's why you decided to make a pit stop here? Finally, get me to repay the favor?"

His mouth turned up in a playful smirk, but I was sure he was serious. I was mortified.

"No. What? I didn't stop here on purpose. I didn't even know you work here. I mean, not that if I knew you worked here, I'd have stopped. Not that I wouldn't have stopped either. I just—"

I gulped my Gatorade to get myself to shut up.

"Relax! I'm just teasing. But did you really not know this was my family's place? I mean the name, didn't—"

I looked out the window at the sign I hadn't noticed before.

"Wilson Choppers."

I laughed at myself. "Oh! I'm so stupid. I didn't even pay attention to the sign. I got a side stitch, and stopped. And you appeared out of nowhere with your Gatorade and your cute smile, and oh!"

I slapped my hand over my mouth.

This was not like me at all. Why was I behaving like this?

Vomiting up honesty like a chemo patient?

The truth was, Rafe arrived in my life at a critical time. And he gave me a new reason to stop lying.

I think that's why my mom liked him so much.

But it wasn't long before he gave me a whole new set of reasons to lie.

Still, it wasn't his fault my mom died not believing me anymore.

That's on me.

Chapter 15

Looking back, I'm surprised we could ever manage a full breath during the campaign.

Jude's campaign was all work from Day One.

Kylie Rutter's numbers continued to improve in those last few months before the Special Election. The compressed schedule of the Special Election was both a blessing and curse. I was glad to know there was an end date coming, but it was also nerve-wracking to have our entire lives twisted up in something that felt like a Talladega race track.

I was busy with work at the Foundation. Grant writing was a special talent of mine, since it required so much creativity and storytelling, and let's face it—I am great at that. Mena handed over to me all the new proposals to draft for her review. It was a lot to balance during the campaign, but I loved the added responsibility and the way I was connected to the kids who came in and out of the Foundation. I felt like I was an integral part of the change Jude was always talking about in campaign speeches. I felt like we were part of the same team. And he was so earnest and honest, I felt like it was rubbing off on me a bit.

What? I did.

Nevertheless, there was no doubt that Jude was on the side of ethics and fair play. And as Huck and Finn said one night around the campaign table, ethics and fair play don't win campaigns.

"I'm sorry, Jude, but there it is. You might have to get your hands dirty a little. You might have to let Laila dig up a little dirt on Kylie Rutter. You might have to smear her a little."

Jude kept shaking his head and insisting, "No way. I'm not playing that game. We keep doing what we're doing. We play fair. We let them burn out. Don't believe the numbers. The people of Washington D.C. don't want to be bought by Innovative Media. I hear it every time I go to a new school to talk."

"Jude. School children can't vote. Sad but true," Laila piped in from the other end of the campaign table. I sat silently, because I actually agreed with Laila (and Huck and Finn) but I didn't want to say any of that out loud. Better to be the supportive girlfriend and to let the others be the bearers of bad news.

We drove home from that particular meeting—Jude and I—in silence. The takeaway was that there was a real chance Jude was going to lose and I felt the tension in the subsequent late-night meetings. Innovative Media's stream of money seemed endless. New billboards in support of Kylie Rutter were springing up on every mile marker of the beltway. Video spots that were trendy and yet professional were popping up on social media channels several times a day.

It was an endless struggle to keep up.

We all felt it.

Jude had his drive and commitment going for him. Kylie had the drive of an entire corporation going for her. I started to daydream about concession speeches and Plan Bs. I made plans for long trips on the boat on which we'd lick our wounds and regroup. I waited for Jude to catch up.

Instead he started doubling down on campaign meetings. I'd join him and Laila in the campaign office at the end of the day after I'd left my office at Appletreese, but gradually my presence felt like more and more of a formality.

I hadn't yet asked Jude about the conversation I'd overheard in the conference room when Laila accused him of lying and of something else terrible that I couldn't quite imagine. Part of me wanted to ask him about it. Part of me wanted to know the truth. And a final part of me wanted to know nothing at all.

Two months before the election, I caught Laila and Jude

sitting on the same side of the table and I thought about all the times I wanted to sit on the same side as Jude at a restaurant. Rest our hands on each other's knees. Smell his cologne while I was ordering a burger.

"Sit here," I'd pat my side every time we sat down, but Jude would always shift away from me. To the other side.

"That's weird. It's awkward to sit on the same side of the table."

How many times had he said that? But now he was sitting on the same side with Laila and they could have put their hands on each other's knees and smelled each other's cologne if they wanted to. They could have shared a burger from the same plate because they were so close. But they weren't sitting at a restaurant, I reminded myself. There were no menus or burgers. They were sitting in a conference room in a warehouse—a makeshift political center. *This is where everything happens,* Jude was always reminding me.

He had said it while waving his arms around when I first came to see the space—the day we came to sign the lease agreement and pay the security deposit. *This is where everything happens.* I had believed him and I had been happy for him. I hadn't realized what everything was.

I cleared my throat and Jude and Laila both looked up at me. Their expressions struck me. Not guilt. Or even anger. *Hunger,* I thought. They looked hungry. And I wondered if I should tell them to order a burger to share after all.

"Honey, sit down." Jude waved at the seat across from Laila and him and I was tempted to pull up a chair right next to Jude instead. While I was still standing, he went on, "We've been talking about some things you aren't going to be happy about."

I took the chair across from the duo reluctantly. "What kinds of things?"

"Money." Laila jumped in without hesitation to utter the first words she'd spoken since I had walked into the room. "Specifically this."

Laila handed me back a check that had been made out to the campaign by Mena. I had told her she didn't need to do it, but she insisted. It was a generous amount, so I was confused when Laila pressed it back into my hand, and said, "This isn't going to work."

I looked directly at Jude with challenge in my eyes. I dared him to speak and yet, I promised with my eyes that I was likely to be unhappy about whatever it was he was going to say. "Be very careful, Jude."

He nodded, and looked like he was choosing his words carefully. "I know, but Sweetheart, you need to hear this."

I looked at Laila and she said, "Make no mistake, Aby. The campaign is indeed running out of money."

I knew that was true, but I took the opportunity to make a little dig at Laila anyway. "Laila, I thought you knew how to keep this campaign running on a shoestring budget. We talked about that when you first started." I looked back at Jude as I said it, hoping for his support as I criticized Laila.

Laila chuckled without winking, breathing her almond scent across the table at me. "Honey, clearly you are not cut out for a political campaign if you think money is only a topic at the beginning of a campaign."

My head whipped and I locked in on Laila. "Are you kidding me right now? Don't patronize me, Laila. How many campaigns have you actually run? Besides Jude's? Which you appear to be running into the ground."

"Sweetheart," Jude said it softly and hypnotically, trying to soften the tone of rebuke. The consummate politician, soothing and dispensing diplomacy like it was a chocolate, while sitting on the same side of the table as his campaign manager. I got angry about the seating arrangements again, and even angrier that I was letting such juvenile things bother me at a time like this.

"It's fine, Jude. These are testy times, and I wouldn't be a very good manager if I couldn't take a little criticism here and there, would I? Aby's right. This campaign has cost a lot more than you and I ever estimated at its infancy." Laila was self-deprecating. But still—I felt scolded.

And indignant about her choice of words.

At its infancy? You and I? Was she kidding?

Laila had entered at the campaign's teenage years—not its infancy. Its infancy were the days Jude and I lay in bed planning and scheming and plotting how we'd be better than all this. How Jude would make a difference and I would use my experience through the Foundation in education and development to make his campaign one of integrity. A success. Jude would use his charm and smarts and gorgeous smile to help me get ahead and do good as well. We'd beat the odds. We'd succeed. And we'd do it together. Honestly.

And now here was Laila sitting on the same side of the table as Jude claiming to have been part of this thing since its *infancy*?

I rolled my eyes childishly, and immediately caught Jude's disappointed expression. He'd caught me rolling my eyes. And that meant that Laila won yet again.

I tried a more conciliatory expression. "Ok, I'm listening. What did you want to talk about? Surely you're not expecting me to ask my boss for even more money?"

"No!" Laila answered too quickly and too emphatically. My red flags were hurrying up the flagpole.

She settled in a moment, "We don't want any money coming from Appletreese or the Treese family at all for that matter. Hasn't Jude discussed that with you?"

"That's what we're doing now, Laila."

I was disappointed that the moment in which Jude seemed to be annoyed with and chastising Laila, coincided with a moment I realized he'd been keeping something from me that he'd only been sharing with Laila. The moment was ruined and I wasn't able to enjoy it nearly as much as I wanted.

Laila ignored Jude's tone and kept right on talking with her haughty voice.

"We do, however, have options from a new company called *Out The Bullies*. They've set up a super PAC with a half a million dollars and they want to use it to produce ads supporting Jude. They want to counteract the Innovative Media ads for Kylie Rutter. You yourself have a connection to *Out the Bullies*, yes?"

"How did you find out all this?" I looked at Jude with doubt and accusation firing in my eyes.

"Aby, you and Jude *pay* me to find this stuff out."

Oh so now we're all one big happy team and she works for us. I let the skepticism wash over me while I tried to wrap my head around what Laila was saying.

I had brought up *Out The Bullies* to Jude on our first date as a point of connection after I'd read an article in *The Washington Truth* forecasting that *Out The Bullies* would be filing an amicus brief in the seminal case Jude was litigating. I didn't know any more about them than Google had provided at the time, and now my lies were coming back to bite me.

But I let my indignance overwhelm my guilt in the moment. Why would Jude have shared that information with Laila? And why on earth would Jude be thinking about aligning himself with an internet company?

One other question plagued me. That's the one I actually asked aloud.

"*Out The Bullies*? Haven't they been having trouble getting their product to market? Where'd they get the money suddenly?"

Laila smirked. "Oh, they have money. And they want to donate to Jude. As I said, Aby, you and Jude *pay* me to find this stuff out."

I stared at Laila, willing her to disappear.

⤿

"Jude, please. Why can't we?"

I had spent the first part of our ride home in silence.

Jude had respected my decision with silence on his part. When we got home, I had exploded with accusations, first accusing Jude of keeping the newly discovered information about *Out The Bullies* from me and causing the shocking confrontation ("Honey, I promise you, she had dropped all of this on *me* moments before you walked into the conference room."), and embarrassingly of having a crush on her. ("Oh Sweetheart, you're being ridiculous, now.")

Then I repeated a familiar plead: "Jude, please. Can't we finally get rid of Laila?"

"You know we can't. I know you hate her—and the way she handled things today was reprehensible. But we pay her for information and strategy—not tact. And she's truly what we need. She's got her finger on the pulse of all the key demographics right now: Hispanic, single mothers. She balances out the input from Huck and Finn. She's got a great female perspective. I need that."

I winced. "*I'm* a woman, Jude."

"Baby, stop,"

"Ugh. I know. She makes me crazy. She's turned me into this person. I don't even know who I am. I'm whiny and childish." Alone with Jude in our own home without Laila present, I was feeling more in control of my emotions and my own narrative. More in control of Jude.

Until he reminded me that he needed Laila because she was a woman. "Ok. Let's stop talking politics tonight. For one night. Please." I offered up a conversation stopper.

"I totally agree."

"You do?" I had said the words, but not meant them. Jude rarely took his campaign hat off.

"Yes, I do. Why don't we go upstairs, and take a long bath and turn our phones off and unplug for the night. I think the world can function on its own for a little while, don't you?"

"Why yes, Mr. Birch, I do." I felt a tightness in my chest start to dissipate as Jude reached over on the sofa and caressed my knee the way he might if we were sitting on the same side of the table, which for all intents and purposes, right then, we were.

❧

A few hours later, I was sitting on the side of the bathtub wrapped in a towel. "I guess I'm still having trouble wrapping my head around *Out The Bullies* showing up with money to burn all of a sudden. Is Laila suggesting I reach out to someone there? I didn't know any of those whistleblowers. I thought that was clear when I told you about Rafe."

Jude looked up at me confused. "I thought you said the lawyer boyfriend's name was Wilson? As in basketballs?"

Damn his memory.

I covered my blurt with a cough. "Wilson. Yes. Wrong ex-boyfriend. Sue me, Counselor."

I batted my eyes trying to distract him from my mistake. And then I reminded him he was the one at fault, not me. "I never should have shared that story with you, by the way. And you shouldn't have shared it with her."

I tried to hide my nervousness. I'd made the whole thing up. I'd inserted Rafe Wilson (by last name only) into the tall tale on my first date with Jude for no other reason than to malign Rafe. I never expected to be having a follow-up discussion about that lie years later. Jude's anger at "Wilson's" dismissal of me had told me all I needed to know about Jude on our first date. And I'd fallen hard. The rest was history.

But it was a history I might not escape from. After all, I'd opened myself up vulnerably. Would Laila want me to call some imaginary contact at *Out The Bullies*? I didn't have any.

"The bottom line is, I don't have any contacts over at *Out The Bullies* that I can call."

Of course, I *did* know more about *Out The Bullies* than I was letting on, but I couldn't share that information with Jude or Laila either.

"No one wants you to call anyone," Jude said, reaching over and pulling my phone out of my hand. He needn't have. I wasn't about to call anyone.

He continued. "We don't want to compromise the campaign right now. If *Out the Bullies* is going to do this legally, they have to do it on their own, without any cooperation from the candidate himself. Besides, I'm not even sure green lighting support by *Out the Bullies* is the way to go yet."

It was me and not Jude who had broken the promise to unplug for the night by bringing my phone into the bathroom to charge it. It pinged a few times with messages and reminders from my day job before I stepped out of the bathtub to turn it off.

But not before I started scrolling through for a quick message check. Which led Jude to climb out of the tub and use the time to check his own messages on the phone by the bed and just like that, the unplugged time was over. We met up again in bed, damp and naked with our phones fully charged and loaded with new information. New questions.

Jude traced the scar along my thigh subconsciously as we lay side by side in bed reading campaign memos and the newest propaganda mailings via email from Kylie Rutter.

Jude stopped tracing me, and shook his phone at me with two hands. "Did you know LessThan is reporting nearly 100 million daily users currently? That puts it in the same game with Snapchat, Instagram, and Facebook. This app is poised to become a household name in no time."

"I know, it's crazy."

Jude shook his head with disgust. "I don't understand how an app called 'LessThan' could have obtained such popularity—in such a short timeframe."

"Jude, forget about the ridiculous name. LessThan promises to actually *improve* their appearance and grades and social status. Kids and *even their parents* are buying into the app's ability to give them a competitive edge in the college process."

"Parents? Come on. Who does that? Would your parents have done something like that?"

My sad expression betrayed me. Jude reached over and smoothed my still wet hair apologetically. "I know you hate to talk about your mom. I'm sorry." I shook my head, sealing off further conversation about my past the way I always did. The way Jude always let me.

I searched my memory for something to change the direction of the conversation. "Remember those crazy parents at 'High Top?'"

Jude slapped his forehead. "Of course!"

"You want to know who's buying LessThan? That's who."

⌒

On the eve of the campaign announcement, Jude and I had been having a late-night working dinner at a D.C. bar when we stumbled upon a 15-year high school reunion. A bunch of seeming grown-ups acting like fools, stumbling and slurring as they toasted to their long-gone days at some prep school in Maryland. They'd all met up to celebrate and gloat and compare. Jude and I eavesdropped on them, until we couldn't help but chime in.

"So, I overheard you say it was your 15-year reunion. Did you have a nice turn out?" Jude asked by way of an icebreaker.

"Yeah, about half. I think that's pretty good for a 15-year reunion. Supposedly attendance at these things picks up a bit after everyone's kids are old enough to stay home without a babysitter, you know?"

I nodded and huddled into Jude, oddly disconcerted that my confidence seemed gone in this crowd. At the Foundation, I was present and engaged with donors and our large constituent of children and their working-class families. But this group? They didn't feel comfortable or familiar at all.

I listened to the conversation from the periphery. They

asked what we did for a living, and Jude answered for both of us. Not exactly accurately, I might note.

"Oh wow, politics!"

They gave us some fleeting enthusiasm for the upcoming campaign announcement. Fleeting. After all, this was D.C. Everyone was involved with politics or knew someone who was.

"Kids?" We shook our heads in unison. Most of the couples were passing around pictures of children in various ages and various costumes—little league uniforms, soccer shin guards, and dance tutus.

"Susan is taking Portuguese this year. My friend has an au pair from Brazil, so we're paying her for some lessons—we're loving how that's going to look on her college application."

"I'm sorry. Susan is how old, again?" I asked. I was having trouble keeping up. And none of these couples looked old enough to have college-aged kids.

"Nine."

"Wait. Did you say nine?"

"Yes. She's nine." Susan's mom nodded aggressively. "You'd be shocked how important this stuff is at this age already."

"I would. I really would," I replied honestly.

A perky man and his even more perky-looking wife got up at the end of the table and started a round of goodbyes.

"Already?" they were asked.

"We have to leave early. Jeremy has a travel hockey game four hours away tomorrow. Puck drop at 8 am."

"My god. That means you have to leave at—"

"Yeah—probably by 2 am at the latest. We won't sleep. We'll go home, pay the sitter, and put the kids right in the car where they can keep sleeping while we drive."

"You're not worried about driving through the night?" I directed my question to the mom.

"No way," she said animatedly. "It's like a high for us—

these travel weekends. We caravan and the families—we all like, really support each other, you know. It's one big extended family. It's amazing."

Are you on meth? I thought but didn't say out loud. I raised my eyebrows at Jude, and we laughed about these caricatures all the way home. Without children of our own, they seemed a world away from us. They didn't feel like the people Jude was getting ready to represent, but after reading the LessThan literature, I realized we were being naïve.

෴

"God. This is so ugly. I'm poring over these reports and I can't find an Achilles heel."

"Jude, why did you tell Laila about my connection to *Out The Bullies*? I'm not comfortable with you sharing our pillow talk with her. And by the way—I don't actually know anyone over there, for the record. I know *of them*. That was the point of that story I shared with you way back when."

"Oh yes, Sarbanes Oxley." I chuckled along with Jude at our long-standing inside joke, but quickly sobered, "No, come on, Jude, tell me why you thought it was ok to share that with her?"

"Aby, I didn't. She came up with *Out The Bullies* on her own. Her own research. I swear to you. What you and I talk about *here* is off limits out *there*." Jude reached for me and I let him trace all of me and cover me and devour me, but the entire time I was thinking:

Is Jude really telling the truth? Is Laila really digging stuff up on her own?

And if so, what else does Laila know?

Chapter 16

I woke early the next morning to head into the Foundation.

Jude was already up and he handed me my favorite travel mug of coffee, milk already stirred in as I headed out the door. I stopped for a quick kiss and a question.

"Ok, Jude, now that you've slept on it. How *do* you feel about taking the *Out The Bullies* money? Assuming everything Laila is saying is true. Assuming you're about to lose if you don't."

He kept stirring his own coffee and didn't look up at me. So I put my mug down and lifted his face to me. "Look at me, Jude. Laila says they are your last chance. Your last shot to winning this election, and arguably your last shot to politics in this town at all. No one else is lining up with big bank accounts, you know."

"Oh, Aby, I don't know. I don't want Innovative Media to win. And yet, I don't want to make that decision for the campaign."

And maybe I heard something that wasn't there, but I thought I heard that he'd rather someone else make the decision for him.

⌒

Whenever the campaign proved to be too intense, I threw myself into my work. That day was no exception.

I surveyed my large bulletin board filled with brightly colored post-its. All part of a mock up for the annual fundraiser I had planned for the Foundation.

Our after-school programs were working on the third Annual "Pay it Forward" project with me. On the board, the post-its would each be replaced with a similarly brightly colored envelope with a small note inside from one of the students or staff members. The envelopes were numbered 1 through 550, and would bring in $150,000 in just one night.

For me, it was my most anticipated fundraiser all year. It was easy and fun, and allowed me some fun time with the kids, too, as I worked with representatives of the Foundation's after-school workshops to secure notes from the kids with pay it forward promises that would be added to each of the envelopes.

Donors made a choice to grab an envelope—any envelope at all—numbered 1 through 550—and donate that amount to the Foundation at a complimentary black-tie cocktail hour that served up cheap wine, pigs in a blanket, and gratitude. The $3 donor ate and drank alongside the $462 donor. There was something tremendously comforting about equalizing everyone's generosity.

The envelopes were filled with promises to pay the generosity forward, including baking cookies for the local fire fighters and helping moms with dishes. These hope-filled envelopes were bartered for donations that went to help the Foundation meet its budget every year, and even a little surplus that was usually earmarked for after-school activities or workshops for the single moms of the group.

I stood in front of my board mock-up and thought about the Foundation's population—the children that I helped fund programming for. I rearranged post-its on one quadrant of the Board that would house the envelopes that came in through Corelle's group, and I smiled.

Corelle was a success story, a "graduate" of one of the first after-school programs sponsored by the Foundation. Now she was a high school senior, had recently turned 18, and was leading one of the younger groups on her own. I'd noticed that she had a special relatability with the kids in her group and I'd asked her if she had ever considered teaching or social work. She'd shaken off the suggestions at first.

"I'm too ugly to get kids to listen to me," she said. I'd taken her by the shoulders then and demanded she tell me who had ever put such a ridiculous idea in her head.

She'd shrugged it off. "Ah, Don't worry about me, Miss Aby. I'm just having a bad day."

But I'd watched her a little more carefully after that. And her group had turned in the most beautiful pay it forward envelopes and promises.

I liked to believe I knew our after-school groups inside and out. But that wasn't true. I knew bits and pieces. I knew them as they came here, participated in programming here. Stepped outside of their comfort zones to come to the Foundation's programming. But I didn't know who they were before they came to the Foundation. I was always pretending the past didn't matter. That you only needed to keep your eyes facing forward. I said that to every new donor group that passed through the Foundation doors.

The past doesn't matter.

The only thing that matters now are the choices you make from here on out.

I turned away from my mock-up board, took out a key and unlocked a drawer on the right-hand side of my desk. I'd asked Mena for a desk with a locking drawer "for those times I need to store a last-minute donor or vendor check after bank hours." She'd agreed without questioning and I'd gratefully begun storing a few documents in the drawer that I didn't feel comfortable leaving in the home I now shared with Jude.

A photo of my mother, Madelyn Boyle, and her obituary printed in the local paper from back home was at the top of the pile.

Beloved local waitress, affectionately nicknamed the "Mayor of Little River" lost her battle with cancer on January 4, 2014. Thousands show up to mourn the woman who was known for her small acts of kindnesses throughout town.

"When Madelyn found out my husband lost his job, miraculously

my electric bill was paid the following month."

"When I joined AA, Madelyn served me free coffee every night from 7 pm-11 pm for a month, and talked to me in between her other tables to distract me while I'd jones for a real nightcap."

"She was a fairy godmother."

Jude and Mena knew the version of my story that included a mother involved in local politics. I felt that was a modest stretching of the truth, not a full-on lie.

But the story that my mother had taken her own life, after a scandal—that was blatant lie, fabricated in Sol's advisor's office while he tried to come up with a creative version of my meager resume to ultimately present to Mena, and I was too hungry and too grief-stricken to correct him.

Somewhere I'd read a story advising to fake it until you make it. And I thought, if I wanted to be like my mother—truly like her—and carry on her legacy of goodness, I was going to have to leave behind my sordid dark past, and move the hell on. Ever since I arrived in D.C. on one tank of gas, and read the story about Philomena Treese's mission, I thought my mother had sort of led me there.

Here.

And I stuck to that story ever since. So much so, that occasionally, I had to take out the truth and look it in the eye. The real truth was that my mother had fought a battle against cancer with every ounce of her strength, with every intention of staying on this earth as long as possible for one reason and one reason alone: to keep me from lying again.

My mother's face looked up at me from the obituary and I stared at her uncomfortably for a few minutes before locking her back in the drawer and turning back to my fundraiser's mock-up board.

"The past doesn't matter." I said aloud.

And then I whispered a half-hearted apology to my mother into the air.

Because the truth? The truth was I knew I would keep perpetuating that lie given the chance.

〜

When I got home that night, it was late, and Jude was already home from the day's campaign strategy session with Laila.

I apologized again for my bad behavior the day before.

"I don't know why I was so jealous of Laila, Jude. It's silly when I think about it. I've never been insecure with you. Why was I being so insecure? I'm sorry."

"You weren't being silly, Aby."

"I wasn't?"

"Of course not. She's beautiful and smart and ambitious. And she's helping me. She's focused on one goal—helping me achieve something I want so damn badly. Your jealousy is completely understandable."

I sunk low into one of the flamingo pillows, my eyes welling up with tears, no longer feeling on the same side of Jude's table at all.

"My God, Jude. Really? What about me? What am I even doing here if you feel all those things about Laila?"

"Well you're all those things, too, Aby. Smart and beautiful and ambitious. But in a different way. In a way that doesn't revolve around me. And that's why even though I need Laila for this election, I *love* you, Aby. You're my life. You're my future. I need Laila to win this election. But I need you forever."

"Oh," I conceded with gratitude.

"So don't ask me to get rid of Laila again, ok? At least not for the duration of this election."

"And afterward?"

"Aby, come on. I've known Laila since law school. She's good people. Don't ask me to abandon my friends because you're feeling jealous. Isn't this all a little too *High School Musical* for you?" Jude winked at me and I nodded a concession and excused myself for bed, wishing that maybe Jude could have lied. Just a little bit.

Lying in bed waiting for Jude to come up, I scrolled through my emails relating to the Pay It Forward fundraiser. I loved that project. It was full of authenticity and the kids got behind it with earnestness. They were vested in it and that's what made it so successful. I felt warmed by the imminent success of the fundraiser and my role in it. Something about the warm fuzzy glow I was feeling made me draft an email to Laila that I figured I'd never send.

Thanks for all your hard work. The Out The Bullies angle is definitely interesting. I look forward to brainstorming more about it with you.

And then, before, I could stop myself, I hit send.

⤻

The next day, Laila summoned me—and just me—to a meeting..

Aby, I really need to talk to you. Woman to woman. Can you meet me at Pete's Diner in Southeast after work today?

Pete's Diner was a no-frills place near Capitol Hill, nowhere near my Georgetown office. I thought Laila probably wanted to meet in between some meetings or work-related research. Still the invitation to a place so out of the way for me seemed presumptuous.

I didn't really want to meet Laila without Jude, or outside the campaign office, but calling him to tell on Laila felt like just that: "telling on her." And I decided to be the bigger person.

I can't be there until 6:30. Will that work?

Yes.

Ten minutes into the meeting, things already felt hostile. "Aby, listen. We need more money. Plain and simple."

"So now you suddenly want my Boss's tainted money? Why the change of heart?"

I looked down at my coffee instead of meeting Laila's cold gaze. I irrationally hoped Laila would leave while I was still looking down, and that I would not have to bother saying another word to her that day or any other day, for that matter.

"I absolutely do not want a dime from Philomena Treese. No. I got your email. You're right. It's time to green light *Out The Bullies.*"

I winced. In some ways, this was all predictable. I hadn't suggested we take *Out The Bullies* money in my email—or green light their super-PAC spending, but I was thinking it. And now Laila was making me backpedal with her direct confrontation.

"I'm still not sure, Laila. And more importantly, Jude's not sure."

"Aby, it's this or Jude will lose. Rutter and Innovative Media are outspending us on every front. They will win at this pace. Did you hear me? Jude will lose. They will win."

I looked up from my thick diner coffee, startled by Laila's frankness and by the fact that I wasn't able to conjure her disappearance by staring intently at floating coffee grinds.

I was unsettled by more than the mere fact that Laila had asked me to meet with her. It wasn't altogether unheard of for a campaign manager to want to talk with her client's partner, but I was uncomfortable with the fact that Laila needed to meet in person. And only with me. Most of our communication up to that point had taken place through Jude. Or while Jude was also in the room. It made me uncomfortable—this clandestine meeting that Laila had arranged. It made me feel dishonest agreeing to meet with her. And now, not long into the actual meeting, Laila had me feeling like an accomplice to something gruesome. I thought about asking her.

What was it?

What happened between you and Jude to make you so angry?

But the words stuck in my throat. I drank more coffee trying to wash them down. Pete's Diner was not unfamiliar to me. In fact, we had been in this very booth—all three of us—the day Laila agreed to run Jude's campaign nearly a year earlier. Jude had included me in the initial meetings; insisted that I be included, and I was grateful for that. I *wanted* Jude to have this newly created seat. I was surprised at how badly I wanted it. Sometimes I wondered how much my mother's legacy played into all this. If my mother was somehow divining this path, or whether it was less supernatural, and more selfish. But regardless, I wanted Jude to run. And I wanted him to win. There was no point in wanting one without the other. Laila had talked about money at that initial meeting, too, of course.

"How will you pay for this campaign?"

I knew what Laila was really asking was: *How will you pay for me?*

"Jude has lots of pledged support already," I had jumped in.

"We have sources. And we're not afraid to ask for money."

"Yes, neither am I," Laila had replied. "Then again, we can try this on a shoestring budget. That might be refreshing."

In the end, it had felt as though Laila was doing the interviewing. We had practically begged her to run Jude's campaign. Well, Jude had, at any rate.

"Please, Laila, we need you on the team. We can't do this without you."

I didn't agree then, and later, I certainly wished we were doing this without Laila. Wished we had at least tried. And now I was back at Pete's Diner, and I didn't feel any more in control of Laila than I had at that first meeting.

"How does *Out The Bullies* even fit into the picture here without making Jude look like a hypocrite, Laila?" I was asking a sincere question. Jude had established early on that his high-profile internet privacy victory would be part of his platform. In fact, Jude was running on a platform that included—among other progressive points—a tough stance against cyber-bullying and legislation to protect its victims.

Laila leaned in hungrily. "Well that's just it, Aby. They've finally gotten their app to market, and it's doing incredibly well in beta. And it's precisely on point with Jude's platform."

I felt nervous sweat drip down my armpits and down my sides.

"How so?"

"*Out The Bullies* has trademarked an app used to identify and "out" cyber-bullies through anonymous posts in which victims can choose to be identified only by their chosen "username." The anonymous posts are voted up and down in the home page newsfeed (similar to Reddit), but unlike Reddit, users can pay to "boost" posts outing certain notorious bullies they want to make sure appear on the home page. Certain celebrities have come forward in the beta stage to "boost" posts detailing bullying by Hollywood insiders, raising the profile of both the app, and the bullies themselves. There's money here. They want to spend it on ads supporting Jude and outing Innovative Media as the real bullies here."

I rubbed my temples. *I know about the beta app.* I tried to keep my mouth closed tightly to keep from conceding this point to Laila. But one thing occurred to me as I heard Laila talk.

"Isn't it a problem, Laila, that *Out The Bullies* is playing on the vulnerabilities of bullying victims? And trying to make a tremendous amount of money in the process?"

She shook her head. "You're overthinking things."

"I don't know about this, Laila. It feels like we're merely getting into bed with another bad guy if we let them support Jude's campaign. If you ask me, it sounds like *Out The Bullies* is itself a controversial app that is as much a form of bullying as the traditional social media apps, including Innovative Media's LessThan. Why would we align with them?"

"Oh, Aby. Sometimes the end truly does justify the means. Don't you believe that Jude's the good guy?"

"Of course I do."

"Then we need to let them do this. We need to let them broadcast their ads outing Innovative Media as the real bullies in this campaign. Their support and money can make the difference between winning and losing if you can only convince Jude. They want to make sure we are on board with this before they run the ads. They want an appearance of a united front even though they can't communicate with the candidate himself. That's why I wanted to meet only with you today. Without Jude."

Of course. Federal campaign finance laws were such that *Out The Bullies* could spend whatever they wanted. As long as it was clear they were working separately from the candidate himself. What they were offering to do was exactly what Innovative Media was doing for Kylie Rutter—helping the campaign through a super PAC that would buy ads and broadcast compelling messages in support of Jude and against Kylie Rutter. They could spend as much as they wanted. Jude couldn't stop them. But it wouldn't be worth it to them if Jude was going to come out and publicly denounce the company. He wasn't technically allowed to green light their proposal, but that's what they were looking for before agreeing to spend the money. Jude would have to be convinced.

But first Laila would have to finish convincing me. I was nervous that I'd somehow sullied the campaign with my own actions. Actions I wasn't ready to reveal to Laila. Or anyone else for that matter.

"But why Jude? Why does *Out The Bullies* suddenly want to be on his team?"

"It's not Jude, Aby. It's strategic. They're trying to raise the price of this campaign."

"I don't understand."

Laila looked frustrated at the amount of explaining I required. "They know Jude has sworn to keep going after Innovative Media and *Out The Bullies* also knows that Innovative Media has a lot to lose if Jude is in any position of power, local or otherwise. *Out The Bullies* is hoping if they inject more money into this campaign, Innovative Media, and more specifically, their key investor, Dominic Treese, will keep spending. And the more money spent on the campaign, the less money they have for product development."

My heart—and my conscience—sank.

"Oh no. Are you telling me, *Out The Bullies* doesn't even care if Jude wins or not? They just want to trap Innovative Media into gambling even more money against him?"

"Bingo."

I shook my head aggressively and confidently. I didn't summon *Out The Bullies* with my carelessness. They were in this because of greed. "There's got to be another way. We can't play this game."

Laila shook her head. "There's not, Aby. It doesn't matter whether or not *Out The Bullies* thinks Jude can win or not. *I* think he can. But only with their infusion of money. We're out of choices at this point. And if Jude is going to win, he needs to green-light this."

"Frankly, Laila, I'm sort of disappointed with your concession of defeat. We're paying you a lot of money to find other ways than selling out."

I sat up a little taller. I was pleasantly surprised to learn I could stand up to Laila. If pressed prior to that coffee meeting that day, I might have said I didn't think I could do that. I reveled in the moment until Laila snapped me out of it with frank words.

"No, Aby. You don't pay me a *lot* of money and you don't pay me to find other ways. You pay me exactly what I deserve and you pay me to help Jude win. If that means thinking like the enemy, then by God, I'll do it. The only way Jude is going to beat Innovative Media and that snake of an investor, Dominic Treese, is by green-lighting *Out The Bullies* to spend that super PAC money *now*."

I felt slapped by Laila and sat back sharply in my seat. Laila seemed more interested in beating Innovative Media than Jude's actual adversary—Kylie Rutter—in that moment. In fact, Kylie's name had not been mentioned since I sat down at Pete's Diner.

Laila seemed to realize her overstepping. "I'm sorry, Aby. I'm trying to be honest with you here." She sat back deeply in the booth, and I thought I saw a flicker of unraveling in her eyes. Laila always seemed so confident, so measured. Seeing her waver on the edge of confidence and discovering my own surprising responses empowered me, even if—as I was a bit ashamed to realize—Laila's wavering was in connection with the current viability of Jude's campaign.

I felt something softening in me. "So you really think our last resort here is *Out The Bullies*? Regardless of the reason they are offering their support?"

"I do." Laila leaned forward as if trying to grab hold physically of my weakening resolve. "And, Aby, the truth is, it's their super PAC—they don't need our green light to run the ads they've been preparing. Legally, we are not supposed to know anything about this. But they've reached out because they want to make sure Jude won't come forward and disavow their support. They're a tech company and he hasn't been so friendly to those in the past."

"And it doesn't bother you that if they run those ads, we will be owned by another tech company?"

"What if I told you I didn't care?"

I stared at Laila, wondering how she had gotten so cynical. Did it really come with the job?

Laila didn't bother repeating what she'd been repeating nearly daily in the conference room. She didn't have to. It already rang like a mantra in my brain.

$100,000. Per week. That's what we need to be earning to keep this campaign alive.

It made my fundraising efforts at the Foundation seem paltry by comparison. Laila ordered billboards and events and print ads and mailings to the super-voters and digital ads with some sort of algorithm that made my head spin.

It seemed as though anyone who had ever been registered to vote in D.C. was somehow targeted by a digital ad when they signed on to like their grandchildren's back-to-school photos, dog selfies, and instagrammed food plates. The fundraised money had been flying out the window. And we needed more. And fast.

"Aby, the election is only a month away, and Jude can't lose to Kylie Rutter."

The money spent to date was already obscene. But according to Laila, if Jude lost this Special Election, he'd also lose the momentum to forge a political career. Laila claimed this was an all or nothing opportunity. And the media supported her claims. Jude had to emerge from this election victorious. There would be no second chances. No one would take another chance on him, and his road to the Supreme Court—or the White House—would quite possibly be over. Everything Jude had said he'd wanted—since the night I'd met him outside Little Miss Whiskey's—would be over.

And what would that mean for Jude and me? In some ways, our whole relationship was built planning for this moment. What would be left if all that was stripped away? We'd be left to rediscover each other—who we were without the campaign and all its trappings.

I wasn't sure I was ready for that.

Laila had been persuasive throughout the campaign, but no time more than that coffee meeting. I felt a sense of panic. I agreed we would have to green-light *Out The Bullies* and let them know we would not stand in their way.

Laila had nodded with a sense of relief dripping from her shoulders. "There is no other way to keep Jude's campaign afloat," she kept saying. "If you really want to guarantee a win at this point. After all Jude's and your hard work, this is the last option to make this work."

I softened finally at Laila's last words.

What would be the big deal about letting Out The Bullies spend their own money to defeat Innovative Media? Why had I been swayed by Jude to be tied to the principle of the thing?

I pushed the thought out of my mind as I repeated my agreement with Laila. Laila nodded aggressively. "In my extensive experience, the candidate who spends *more smartly* wins. It's that simple."

Laila stood up and put her hand out to shake on it. "So, you'll tell Jude this is what we decided?"

I tried to smoothe down the feeling of being manipulated.

I didn't want to agree to this on behalf of Jude. But I also didn't want to concede that Jude and I wouldn't have a united front on this decision once I told him my reasons. I didn't want to know the details about Laila's history with Jude, but I wanted to prove to her that I was his future.

I shook her hand wondering, *What has Laila made me agree to?*

And I thought to myself as Laila walked out of the diner, leaving me with a cold cup of coffee and the bill: *It's so easy to blur the lines. When will it stop?*

Chapter 17

Monica Landsberry called me at the Appletreese office three days after the first *Out The Bullies* ad ran on every cable news channel. Her voice was too shrill and I held the phone away from my ear as she shouted into it.

"Aby Boyle? This is Monica Landsberry with *The Washington Truth*."

I nearly hung up after she identified herself.

I never handled press inquiries at the Foundation directly. Those were all filtered through my assistant or the media director or Mena directly. Never me. I handled donors and kids. No media.

"I'm sorry. You were directed to the wrong person. I'm going to pass you back to our Media Director, who will be more than happy to help you. Thanks so much for calling." I had my finger on the transfer button, when Monica yelled out to interrupt my thoughts.

"No. Aby! Don't transfer me. I have information Jude needs to win the election."

"What are you talking about?" My hand froze on the phone's transfer button.

Monica continued talking quickly as if she was trying to beat a buzzer. "I know that you collaborated with *Out the Bullies* to run those ads. I know you are aligning yourself against Innovative Media. And most of all, Aby, I know how to help."

I tried to contain my surprise—my horror, really.

"You can't be with *The Washington Truth*. I read *The Washington Truth*. I've never heard of you. You sound like you're from some rag or scandal blog that needs website traffic instead."

"You're wrong. I'm a veteran reporter here with all the clout and respectability you need to win this election."

"Then why have I never heard of you? I get a Daily Digest email from *The Washington Truth*. I've never heard or seen your name."

In truth, I didn't know all *The Washington Truth* reporters. I knew Op Ed pieces were routinely published by a Nate Essuzare, who didn't seem to have any linked bio, and who I suspected was writing under some kind of alias. Other reporters were long-time career writers with pedigrees that included stints at the *Washington Post*, the *Baltimore Sun*, *The Capital Gazette*, and more. That I hadn't heard of Monica Landsberry meant very little, but I pretended it meant a lot, because I was frightened of her words.

"Aby, listen to me. I've been working behind the scenes on a very important exposé for months now." She paused, seemingly catching her breath for the first time since I'd answered the phone. "Don't hang up. I'm taking a real risk here. And I wouldn't have come out to you if I didn't know that you fully support the *Out The Bullies* ads.

I gulped. How could Monica know that? We had watched those ads together, Jude, Laila, and me. He had watched in stunned silence, and turned to both of us with a look of uncertainty.

"It's their money, Jude. They can spend it however they like. And if they want to call out Innovative Media and Kylie Rutter as bullies, then you are to let them." Laila was firm and direct with him.

"We should prepare a press release notifying the public that those ads were not made by our campaign."

"Jude. You're acting like a child. Those ads say exactly who paid for them, as per federal law, and we are now done having this conversation."

Jude hadn't asked any more questions, and I hadn't told him about Laila and my coffee meeting. So how in the hell did Monica seem to know about it? Monica seized on my stunned silence.

"Aby—you've done the right thing. Aligning with *Out The*

Bullies. And I know you're ambivalent about it. But I've been working on an exposé of Innovative Media for six months now. It's about to hit the press, and we are going to break it. Ahead of *Washington Post*, or CNN, or Fox News. We have the story, we have inside info, and I'm going to time the story to go to press within days of Jude's election for maximum exposure. I very much want Jude to benefit from this. We're on the same side, Aby. I want the good guy to win here, too."

I shook my head at the phone and put my face in my hands. When had the line blurred so entirely between news and politics? When I was younger, my mother and Kane and I would watch the evening news together, and the news seemed more bona fide. But was I wrong? Had it always been this slanted? Agendas and SuperPACS and election fixing? Was it always like this and I hadn't realized?

"I don't know what you're talking about. All the relevant campaign finance reports will be filed pursuant to law, and you'll have ample opportunity to review them at that time. And respectfully, Ms. Landsberry, all media inquiries have to go through the campaign's media director, Ms. Laila—"

"Aby, please. Listen to me. I know you're working closely with Laila Rogers. And I know how much you trust her."

I felt my spine straighten. This Monica Landsberry didn't know so much after all if she thought I *trusted* Laila Rogers.

Monica powered on. "But she has her own agenda for wanting to quash Innovative Media and it has nothing to do with the LessThan app or anything you think you're working for or against right now. I can't tell you much more than that now. But it's going to be part of my exposé'. It will help bring down Innovative Media, just not the way you're thinking."

I choked on the startling words coming from the other end of the line. I held the phone away from my face and stared at it like it was a weapon.

"Who *are* you?"

I told you. I'm a relentless investigator for the truth. But we are on the same side here. And don't worry about Jude. He's not going to be surprised about anything in the exposé. But *you* might be, Aby. And I'd like to make sure to get you a little more up to date about some of the competing agendas."

"Why are you telling me all this? What are you up to?"

"I'm not going to lie to you, Aby. We need you."

"We?"

"Me and *Out The Bullies*. They are fully cooperating on this exposé. And when this all comes to light, Innovative Media will be crushed, along with their supporters, and those on the side of *Out of Bullies*—on the *right* side—will have some great publicity courtesy of *The Washington Truth*, and moi.

"This is ridiculous. I should call the authorities and report this entire conversation."

Monica laughed. More of a whimsical chuckle than an ominous laugh, but still, it made me feel uncomfortable. "I'm not doing anything illegal, Aby."

"I don't understand. What is it that you want from me?"

"We have a mole. A former employee of Innovative Media left with some pilfered subscriber lists. I have a contact who'll give them to us but only if you come get them directly. He doesn't trust us, apparently. He trusts you. The future wife of a politician. He says you and Jude strike him as the real deal. And he'll only give the lists to you directly. He says if we can get you to go pick up the lists, he'll know we mean what we say. That we really are all on the same side—and we are, Aby. Bottom line—he'll trust *us,* if *you* trust us."

"But there's the rub. I *don't* trust you."

"I know. It's ok. You don't have to."

I laughed, and noted that it sounded much less whimsical and more ominous than Monica's laugh.

"So why in God's name would I go do this ridiculous thing you're asking me to do?"

"Aby, you're our last hope at making sure all this comes together before the election."

"What if I don't care about this piece you seem to care so desperately about?"

Monica sighed loudly. And I heard a subtle change—a thickness—in her voice when she spoke again.

"Well, that's the thing, Aby. I do care desperately about this. This is like a do or die career piece for me. This may be the last time I ever have such a perfect storm of events and contacts converge for any story like this. And I can't blow it."

"Ok? So, good luck to you. I still don't know how you're going to convince me this is worth the risk for me. I have a foundation to run. Philomena Treese would not want me becoming embroiled in this story. And frankly, I don't want to become embroiled in this story."

"Aby, does Jude know about ChelseaCat?"

I shook off the chill that had landed on my shoulders and asked, "What are you saying, Monica?"

"I'm just asking you a question, Aby. Just a very simple question."

Chapter 18

After I hung up on her, it only took 24 hours for Monica Landsberry to call back. That was—coincidentally—the amount of time it had taken me to decide that I would probably do anything Monica asked of me.

The election was less than a month away. I had managed to keep my past remarkably under the radar all this time. I didn't want to blow it now. It might ruin everything for Jude.

Monica insisted she didn't want to dredge up the past—or my old sins—in the piece on *Out The Bullies*. But it was my old sins she was calling on to get my help.

"I think your boss might be interested in how little of your resume is fact versus fiction, don't you? You're working with these kids and you have absolutely no qualifications at all."

"I am indeed qualified, I beg your pardon. No fancy over-priced college degree could substitute for the training I've gotten right here in the field. You can question a lot of things but not my commitment to getting resources to these kids. I'm not providing counseling or social work. I'm raising cold hard cash and I think Philomena Treese knows my worth even if you don't, Ms. Landsberry."

"Fair enough. But Philomena Treese would be embarrassed if she knew just how much you had duped her. You have to admit that. And you also have to admit you have no idea how she might react if she is embarrassed. How that might result in you losing your job, or worse."

The only thing that I could think of losing that would be worse than my job, would be Jude. I shuddered at the thought, realizing that was probably what she was insinuating.

"Listen, Aby. This doesn't have to be a pissing match. I

just need the subscriber lists."

"But why? How will that help you get any info on LessThan or Innovative Media?"

There was a pause. Monica had stopped speaking so quickly; clearly the balance of power had shifted in our conversation. I had less. She had more.

"We have identified a very active participant on the *Out The Bullies* Beta Blog, named Corelle."

"Did you say Corelle?" I was stalling. I knew exactly what she'd said.

"On the *Out The Bullies* Blog, she goes by SassyCorelle—one word—and she has a bully she has outed mysteriously named "Donny" in her posts. A commenter who goes by the handle @IAmDonny is all over the LessThan app measuring up hapless victims to celebrities and the local socialite crowd, including SassyCorelle, but we cannot identify who Donny is."

"Ok. I agree this all sounds horrible, but I'm not sure I'm following your urgency here."

"Aby, I need to identify the mysterious 'Donny' in Correllle's posts. We want to out *Donny* in this piece. We want to shine a light on those who are using the Innovative Media's LessThan app to hurt real people. Not the theoretical masses, the way every fluff piece has done up until now. Corelle is one of the single most active new users on the *Out The Bullies* beta Blog. And based on information we've gotten from Corelle, we have reason to believe this 'Donny' is actually a prominent member of the D.C. community. Outing Corelle's bully could really be the linchpin in this whole exposé. But we can't seem to trace Donny through *Out The Bullies*. So we need those original subscriber lists from Innovative Media—hopefully Donny wasn't very careful about covering up her footprint. From our conversations with Corelle, Donny seems to be a she."

"Wait. You've spoken to Corelle about this?"

"Yes, we've spoken with Corelle. She won't give us her

permission to use her posts, but we don't need it. They are in the public domain. She has never identified her bully as anyone other than Donny, but we think it's a high profile person, and we think you can help us track Donny down."

I found myself wavering on my earlier decision to help Monica at all costs.

"Why on earth would I be able to do that?"

"Aby, we know you know Corelle. You can help us."

"I explained to you already—I'm not a social worker or a counselor. I help raise money for arts and writing programs in the local schools. I help ensure these kids have the transportation they need to actually show up for those programs. That's what I do. I don't track down bullies or aliases or anything like that.

"And besides—if it's the young woman I'm thinking of — do you know what a stubborn, fierce young woman she is? She has her own mind. Thank God. In some small part, that's what these programs are fueling—confidence and self-esteem for all these kids, especially the young girls. That's why I do what I do. Why on earth would you think I have some powers of persuasion with Corelle? Or if I did, why would I manipulate her that way?"

"I understand what you're saying, but we want to help Corelle and the millions of others like her who are being tortured by and not helped by LessThan. We think you can help us do that by tracking down the Innovative Media subscriber list."

"But if Corelle doesn't want to help you identify Donny, why on earth would I want to?"

Monica's voice got significantly lower. "Here's where this all gets a little tricky, Aby. Corelle is playing with us a little bit. She's a teen. It's forgivable and understandable. She seems to like the attention. At first she denied even writing on the blog, but once we told her we knew it was her, she relented a bit."

"But she doesn't want to be part of this?"

Monica dismissed me. "We won't be using her real name. She likes the idea of being part of this whole exposé, but she won't give us the identity of Donny, but—well, ok. Here, let me play something for you. We taped an interview with Corelle. With her permission, of course."

I sucked in a gulp of air. Before I could exhale or hang up on Monica, or yell for her to stop, a familiar voice was coming through the other side.

Hi, Monica. What's up?

Corelle, it's ok with you if we record you? We want to make sure we keep things straight for the story and make sure you're comfortable with the direction we are going with this piece.

Yeah, that's ok with me.

So, we want to publish some of your pieces. We are not going to identify you by anything other than your handle, SassyCorelle. Your posts are all public, so that should be fine. And you'll be, you know, famous. And doing something really good. Helping to bring down that terrible app, LessThan. You want to help me and Out The Bullies do that, don't you?

I'll be famous?

Corelle's voice was so thin. She sounded sad but eager. I pressed the phone closer to my ear.

SassyCorelle will be a hero.

Listen, I told you before, it's not me. I'm not on the Out The Bullies app. I know someone plugged my name into LessThan, but I try to stay far away from that app, too.

Corelle, we've been all through this. The information on Out The Bullies is specific to Appletreese's afterschool programs. It's either you or someone else using your name who goes to Appletreese.

No way. No one would use my name around this place. They know better.

Right. Corelle, so we're on the same page. And we want to take down LessThan. We're on the same page about that, right?

Well, I hate that freaking company. And that app pretty much ruined any chances I have at surviving high school. All my friends have dropped me. My boyfriend dropped me. I'm not even going to prom now. All because that bitch plugged my name into a stupid app and shared the results with everyone. And she thinks she's the shit because of her mom, but—oh forget it. I'm not telling you anymore about her.

Donny, right?

Yeah, that's right.

So who is Donny? Can you tell us Corelle? Can you tell us who you think it is, at least?

No, I know the whole thing about Out The Bullies is to literally out your bullies and make them pay. But real life doesn't work the way all those Disney Channel movies do. You don't out the bully and turn cool and popular again. The opposite happens. You out the bully and all their friends turn on you and make the whole thing even worse. No offense, but you're not worth me making my life even harder. This is why I didn't do the outing of Donny myself. Someone else is doing it for me.

There was a pause of silence and I pressed the phone harder to my ear, afraid I was missing something and then—

Sorry you're going to have to do your piece without Donny's real name. Unless—

Unless what?

Well, I mean, there have to be records somewhere, right? I mean, someone must know who it is that plugged my name into LessThan. If you could somehow get hold of the Innovative Media records and see who plugged my name into the LessThan app, and then find out how many others she plugged into the app, you can pin the snitching on someone other than me. My hands would be clean. God knows, she's got to have plenty of other enemies. Probably even the person who's using my name on Out The Bullies.

So, how would we do that without Donny's real identity?

Come on. Aren't you the investigative reporter? Why are you asking me for ideas? If this was an episode on Netflix, you'd have an idea, a new source, and Donny's identity by now. Reporters are so much cooler on television.

Ok, so Corelle. If we somehow get our hands on Innovative Media's subscriber list, and if we connect the dots between your bully and one of those subscribers, you're ok with us outing Donny ourselves, right?

Well, I want the piece to be clear that I didn't give you the identity. That you tracked it down with your brilliant detective work. I don't want to be labeled a rat at the end of this piece, or I'll be worse off than I am now.

You're incredibly brave and inspirational, Corelle. You're not so bad off.

Well, you're not me, right? So trust me, my life ain't that great right now.

"Aby. Aby?"

It took a few repetitions before I realized real-life Monica was speaking to me again—and not taped Monica who had just been talking with Corelle on the other end of the line.

I had known for a while that Corelle was indeed being bullied on LessThan. By some mean girl going by Donny. On both LessThan and *Out The Bullies*. And according to the conversation I'd just heard, Donny had an important mother.

Who could she be?

I remembered again Monica's threat from the day before: "Aby, does Jude know about ChelseaCat?"

How on earth did Monica find that out? And what exactly did she know?

"Aby?"

"Yes, I'm still here."

"So Aby, will you help us?"

Above me, in my office at Appletreese, a ceiling fan spun out a rhythmic beat and skip pattern that I had never noticed before. I turned my eyes upward to watch it. I'd never noticed how loud it was, or how it looked to be spinning too fast. Like it might start breaking apart—spinning off its hub at any minute.

Whir. Spin. Skip. Whir. Spin. Skip. I heard the pattern in my head and then felt myself mumble it as I stared.

"Aby?"

Monica brought me back to her and away from the ceiling fan. I stared into the phone as if I might see her in there. Then I lied, "I already said yes."

⌒

The address I was looking for was on a residential street in Southwest. I passed a long row of connected homes with stone faces of varying colors, shades, and sizes, and similarly diverse populations crowding the various porches. The houses looked as if they might have been grand at one time, and the people on the street looked as if they knew that. They looked hopeful about such a state of grandness again. They were talking over railings of porches and yelling to children out of view—and most likely out of earshot, too. The noise of the block was happy and busy, and I wanted to curl up into it.

The Brookland neighborhood where Jude and I lived was not nearly as busy. In fact, in the time that Jude and I had been there, we had yet to meet a single neighbor. We joked that every house on the block must contain young working kidless couples, or martians, as the yards were meticulous and not littered with a single frisbee, football, or bicycle.

But this block was much more alive. Grandmothers and mothers with their charges were wiping dripping popsicles from sticky necks. Lovers were wrapped up on porch steps whispering to each other. Teenagers were sneaking cigarettes and who knows what else, between the porches where the decor and furniture and accessories marked certain houses as homes and certain houses at businesses and certain houses as abandoned.

I scanned for house numbers—hidden in a different place on every single unit as if it was a game, a puzzle to engage passersby. After I located 2302, I realized I would have to cross over to the opposite side of the street to 2319— my intended destination.

I walked past a row of homes, continuing on to my destination, hoping that I really was on the right path. There were wrought iron-scroll adornments on the upper facades of every other home. There were bay windows the size of Priuses jutting out from the front of several of the homes. When I reached the next block, I noticed 2317 had graffiti art lining the porch floor where wicker furniture might have been a more aesthetically pleasing option. The house numbered 2321 had mismatched furniture in a porch front collage with about 25 plant holders containing plants in varying sizes and degrees of health.

Flanked by these two mismatched scenes, I headed up the steps to 2319 and knocked with feigned confidence on the door several times before noticing the doorbell, which I finally pressed. A man arrived at the door so quickly after I pressed the buzzer, I was certain he'd been watching me, waiting for me to get it right. I felt self-conscious, and out of place in a way I had not felt out on the street walking the city blocks it took to get there. I looked around quickly to try to gage if I was as conspicuous as I felt.

"Yes?" A skinny young man with greasy hair and a five o'clock shadow answered the door. He was about my age or maybe 10 years older or younger. It was hard to tell.

"I'm looking for Gary." The sound of my shaky voice and not his expression made me realize—incredibly, for the first time—how little I had thought this entire venture through, after hanging up with Monica the day before.

I pressed on.

"Monica sent me."

The greasy young man laughed a little like I had told a very funny joke. I stood as stoically as I could muster with his eyes on me and the remnant of his laughter still in the air.

"Did she now? And did she give you the secret handshake? And the password?"

I deflated on the welcome mat of 2319. "Oh. No. She

didn't. But maybe if you call her, she'll vouch for me. I don't know why she didn't give me a password when we spoke."

"Maybe because there isn't one." This time, the young man's laugh had a twinge of sinisterism in it, but I ignored it as I tried to feel indignant over having been tricked and used. By so many players in this game.

"Come on in, Aby."

The greasy young man opened the door wider and gestured with his arm for me to come in. I debated ignoring him. Spiting him by standing right there on the porch in response to his mockery. But he knew me. I hadn't introduced myself, and still he knew me. Standing at the threshold, I realized I'd only be spiting exactly one person if I didn't follow through. And it wasn't him.

I stepped through the door. There was a narrow hallway that opened into the front room of the home. I followed him into it. I couldn't see into the house beyond this front room. It was a makeshift office of sorts. Vintage metal furniture—two desks, a few file cabinets. And computers. Rows and rows of laptop computers open and on but facing at an angle away from me so I couldn't tell exactly what they were searching. It was disconcerting. I wondered where all the other users of the laptops were. I hoped they were nearby. I hoped that I wasn't alone in the house with Gary.

"So. What now, Aby?"

"Well, I was sort of hoping you'd tell me."

"You really have no plan, do you? Monica warned me about that. She said she's been helping you every step of the way but still it's like pulling teeth."

"Monica said that?"

"Something like that." The greasy young man turned around to an olive green metal filing cabinet closest to him, pulled out a thick blue folder and slapped it on the desk between us. I opened it up and thumbed through it. Spreadsheets and excel charts of numbers and figures that meant very little at first glance, but I hoped it was what I had come for.

So I could leave.

"What is this?"

"Information that I would think you and your boyfriend would be very happy to have. This here's the subscriber information for every new IM account in the last three days."

I flipped through the pages. No identifying information was listed as far as I could see. No names. No addresses. Just file numbers. This was starting to feel like a giant setup. I started to get nervous, wishing that I had told someone—had told Jude—where I'd gone. But of course, I hadn't told a soul.

Gary reached back into the file cabinet and slapped a thumb drive down on the desk next to the blue folder. "And this is the subscriber information for every new IM account in the last 360 days."

I decided to swallow my pride and my insecurity and ask the question that was plaguing me. "Assuming this is indeed useful and incriminating information against Innovative Media, how exactly did you get your hands on this?"

"Are you not impressed?"

"Honestly, I don't even know what I'm looking at here."

Gary slapped the folder shut, and snatched the thumb drive away before I could pick it up, and locked both of them away in a nearby metal cabinet, before standing. I had insulted him apparently and the meeting was adjourned unilaterally. I started to wonder if maybe this whole thing had been one wild goose chase. This guy might have promised Monica something he didn't even have. Who knew what those numbers on the printout even meant? And the thumb drive could have contained nothing more than this guy's last American History paper. I looked around at the rows of computers and the dinged, dented metal furniture. The whole setup might be nothing more than a hoax.

"Goodbye, Gary." I got up and hurried out the door, feeling a little surprised that he let me leave, as I'd started to deduce that he was a fraud, and maybe even a serial-killing sociopath.

As I hurried back down the blocks to my car, I tried to blend in with the bustle of the city street. In a short time, many of the faces and cast of characters out on the street seemed to have changed. New lovers appeared. New children, new grandmas, and new teenagers. Or maybe I hadn't been looking as carefully as I thought I had been.

As I raced down the street away from 2319, with my keys and mace attachment firmly gripped in my hand, I practiced telling the story of the day to Monica. She'd need to know how scared I was when I left. I'd need to convey to her that this had to be all one big hoax. And when Monica found that out, she'd have to drop this angle of the story. Wouldn't she?

I got to my car finally, relaxed my hold on the mace, and beeped the car door twice in a fluid motion as I got in.

I clicked the door to lock it and exhaled, with my head back on the head rest, my eyes pressed firmly shut.

No more wild goose chases for me. No more taking calls from Monica. I thought about what it might mean if Monica refused to drop her insistence on using me to help her get her story, but I dismissed it quickly. There was nothing to be afraid of. I'd talk to Jude. It was long overdue. I wouldn't let Monica get the best of me.

But God, why did it all have to be unraveling now?

With less than a month until the election?

I opened my eyes and started the car.

And then I screamed.

Because young, greasy Gary had appeared at my car window, and he was rapping on it angrily.

⌐

I sat for a few scared moments wide-eyed and staring at Gary. He was sweating and red-faced and as his knuckles knocked incessantly on my window, I felt like karma was finally catching up with me.

He stopped long enough to motion me to put the

window down. I shook my head, and tested the door lock, locking it a few extra times.

Gary looked down at the door, taking in the clicking of the lock and seemed to understand finally how this all looked to me. He yelled through the window. "Ok, ok. I get it. I'm not a psycho or anything. Calm down. It's just that you really don't have all the information you need. You're getting played, Ms. Boyle."

My worst fears were being confirmed. What did this guy know that I didn't?

Was Monica playing me just as I suspected?

I pressed the window button a millisecond to release it a fraction of an inch. Enough space for sound to pass through, but not an axe.

"Who do you think is playing me? Is this about Monica? Was I wrong to trust her?"

"No." He looked disgusted with how little I knew or understood.

He looked left and right as if looking for someone. "It's someone much, much closer to you. Someone who has reasons to take down Kylie Rutter that have nothing to do with the LessThan app or cyber-bullying. Some pretty powerful people are at the helms here. And you're being used in a game that started many years ago. We've all got our reasons, right? But make sure your reasons are clear."

He slipped the thumb drive through the crack in the window and turned and headed away from me, back in the direction of 2319, leaving me with the IM subscriber list and a host of new questions.

Chapter 19

Monica called again at my Appletreese office the day after the trip to 2319.

I picked up the phone, preparing for the worst, and in the end, became confused about what the worst would actually be.

"I have the lists, but I'm not exactly sure what to do with them."

"So why didn't you call me?" Monica sounded tired. I wondered if she was tired of having to explain things to me. "Aby, time is of the essence. I thought you understood what we were trying to do here."

"Are you going to threaten me again? Because I don't care what you tell, Jude. I really don't. You can tell him anything you want. I made my choices, and I'm living with them. I have my reasons for all of it, including ChelseaCat. I always meant to tell him everything one day. If one day is now, so be it. Your threat has no power anymore."

I was bluffing.

It worked.

"Aby, I have no interest in having a conversation with Jude about your past or about ChelseaCat. That's a conversation the two of you need to have."

My relief was short-lived, as she immediately followed with, "But Aby, I have some bad news that will be in the later online version of the paper."

A moment later, I was embarrassed that I had actually thought "some bad news" would be something about the election. "Corelle. She's taken her own life."

I felt all the air leave my body. I hadn't seen Corelle lately. I figured she was busy with high school. I thought about her sad thin recorded voice I'd heard only a few days ago, courtesy of Monica.

My voice cracked and then broke. "How do you know this?"

"We've been in constant contact with her over the last two weeks. I never thought—"

I heard Monica's tone match mine.

"We've spoken with her mother. She's asked us to go forward with our exposé. She wants to punish the assholes she believes are responsible for this tragedy. And by assholes, I mean Innovative Media."

I laid my face down on my desk and felt the cold wood against my burning face. Corelle had been full of promise and light and someone had stolen it from her. I had known the bully only as "Donny"—someone who had plugged Corelle into the LessThan app. Someone who was apparently a fellow classmate at her school with a powerful or notable mother. Someone who had told Corelle repeatedly that she was too ugly to exist.

"So what now? We have the Innovative Media subscriber lists. What do we do with them?"

I reached into my bag that was splayed open on the floor and pulled out the thumb drive Gary had slipped to me the day before. I thought briefly about a porn virus taking over my work computer, but I jammed it into the side of the computer anyway.

While Monica talked, I waited for the files to open. I wondered if they'd be searchable.

"Well, things are evolving even as we speak. Innovative Media has moved into a space far, far bigger than LessThan. And there is still time to stop them. This will be the new focus of my piece. We are rapidly tweaking the angle and we want to use real bullies in the piece. We want to expose Innovative Media before they become even bigger than they already have become. There is a movement within Innovative Media for some other strategic app takeovers."

"Something worse than LessThan?" Tears for Corelle

stained my cheeks.

Why?

How?

An hourglass twirled on my screen while the drive fought to be readable by my computer.

"Innovative Media needs more than LessThan. Its appeal has already waned somewhat and they are focused on the next big thing."

"What?"

"It's more of a question of how, rather than what."

"I'm not following." I cleared my throat and tried to set aside my grief for Corelle while I waited for the file on my computer to open.

"They've started a pyramid scheme of sorts. They've already beta tested it and it seems to be out in the world already. They have an app used to issue trophies, buttons, words of the day, memes of the day, exclusive GIFS. And then, because it's linked to LessThan and Innovative Media, it has enough PR juice to get kids to sign up. To the tune of millions. To the tune of *tens* of millions, actually.

"After IM connects enough teens to their app, they create a new app that pulls those millions to a new product. They keep making the former product obsolete. Each app is like a gateway to more sophisticated apps. The earlier versions reward their followers with freebies and virtual goodies that can eventually only be used in the new versions of the app. Four and five levels in, the apps range anywhere from $10 to $100.

"Why would anyone pay that kind of money for virtual trophies?"

"Membership is considered a privilege—a status symbol, and those who can't afford it are shamed mercilessly online."

I was gobsmacked. "Why are people doing it? Spending that kind of money on a digital app?"

"Why did we spend money on cigarettes? On the latest trend of the day? Why do today's parents spend money on college admissions experts? On Porsches?"

I shook my head. Was this all part of the same spectrum as a useless app?

Monica certainly seemed to think so. "They are buying belonging. Buying membership into an elite, exclusive community."

"How exclusive can it be if everyone belongs to it?"

"Right. Exclusivity is the great lie that draws them in like moths to a flame. Once everyone belongs, the community no longer becomes exclusive; all the current users are mocked as irrelevant, and a new app pops on the market under the IM umbrella. Everyone wants it. The stakes get higher. The cost gets higher."

"When the cost gets higher, does the club become smaller?"

"Only temporarily. The peer pressure seems to feed the thing. Eventually it becomes wider and wider until its community resembles something like 50 million as well. And then the cycle begins anew. Like I said, it's still in beta—but this is the model and it's working with beta testers. And we have learned that some of the kids are being rewarded with $100 'refund' checks to their accounts sporadically throughout the year—to select VIP members."

"This is insane. There's no way this could be a viable unchecked thing in this day and age."

"Oh, I assure you, an ever growing billion-dollar a year industry would disagree with you."

"Even with the era of helicopter parents watching over their little precocious tots like hawks? How are they not stopping this?"

"Stopping it? They're feeding it. Where are the teenagers getting their money? From mom and dad—mostly with permission. There is nothing that tugs at a parent's heartstrings more than a teenager who isn't fitting in with the crowd. The parents are buying them apps for Christmas, birthday, Hanukkah, and bar mitzvah presents. This is as harmless as candy crush in their eyes until Johnny is asking for membership to a $100-a-month digital app that he believes—and now mom and dad are starting to believe as well—defines his very worth.

"There are reports of taxable withdrawals being taken from 529 funds and parents incurring whopping tax penalties just to fund the app pyramid. And it's only in *beta* right now."

"Come on. This is a lie. You're a liar."

"Really, Aby? Think about it. These are moms and dads whose glory days are long over. Who remember all too well what it was like to be the least popular kid in high school—or worse—to be the most popular one day, only to have it taken all away the very next day. This app scheme is fed by an insecure generation raising the next insecure generation. And frankly, Aby, there are some powerful people who don't mind a new source of federal tax revenue that seems to be happening with very little whistleblower attention."

"Holy hell. This is starting to sound bigger than me. Bigger than all of us. I'm going to have to talk to Jude about this. I don't want to keep this from him."

"Well there's a brand new twist that's developed since we first spoke, Aby. Here's the problem now. IM—they are courting *Out The Bullies*. *Out The Bullies* is working on some new app development outside the *Out The Bullies* forum, and IM wants to buy it from them. A merger of sorts."

"Well that's crazy. How could *Out The Bullies* be thinking of selling out like that?" I didn't trust the defensiveness creeping into my voice.

"It's business, Aby. *Out The Bullies* is a business and they want to stay *in* business."

"Well, I am going to—*we* are going to have nothing to do with them from here on out. I knew it was all too confusing. Don't call me again. I'm done playing games with you, Monica."

I took a second too long to hit the disconnect button.

Or maybe I knew exactly what was coming next.

"Aby, *Out the Bullies* has been openly supporting Jude Birch. *Out The Bullies* is thinking about selling out to a company that is going down spectacularly in my exposé. So you could see how this could make Jude look."

I saw the room spin. I thought about my seemingly innocent coffee meeting with Laila. The one I did on his behalf. And now I'd unwittingly gotten him mixed in with this mess.

The file on my computer screen finally opened. Sheet after sheet appeared at the bottom of my screen, dated with month ranges going back a year. I went back to the first one—to the earliest subscribers available and typed in one word, Donny.

The result popped up quickly. Field A: IAmDonny; Field B: Kylie Rutter

I gasped so loudly, Monica asked, "You ok? What's going on, Aby?"

I toggled out of the subscriber list and googled Kylie Rutter. She had a daughter, Deirdre Rutter, who was a senior at Corelle's school.

The one Corelle *had* attended.

Kylie Rutter was more than owned by Innovative Media. She was a paying customer. Likely buying status for her daughter, who had probably killed Corelle with meanness.

Did Laila know about Kylie Rutter's daughter? Did she know any of this? Did she trick me into getting mired in this mess? I gripped my hands. Was Laila working for *Out The Bullies*? Maybe lining up a little gig for herself after the election was over? A very lucrative one for a company that Jude would now be beholden to if he actually won this thing?

I opened and closed my grip on the hand that wasn't holding the phone. I wanted to wring Laila's neck. And then I wanted to wring my own.

And who were these people who would do anything to survive high school?

I knew exactly who they were.

And I wanted Jude to defeat them.

"Where should we meet? I want to bring you this thumb drive as soon as possible," I managed to whisper through tears.

The Washington Truth, dated July 15, 2018
Excerpt from the Op Ed piece, by Nate Essuzare

...For the last several years, we've seen a growing back-lash against an entire generation of parents known as "helicopter parents."

This generation of parents who "hover" protectively over their offspring, lining up college admissions coun-selors in elementary school, handing out little league participation trophies to the entire team, while simulta-neously investing in sports camps for junior and little miss, with costs rivaling the family car, have been under fire from far too many of us in the media for too long.

I'd argue it's time to celebrate—and not dismiss—the helicopter parent.

After all, these are the parents *we wanted* as children. While our parents were climbing corporate ladders, rebelling from their post-War, middle class ancestors, we were inhaling second-hand smoke, eating lead paint, and getting sunburns. We were clamoring for attention, and coming up short.

Who are we to judge the new generation of parents giving their kids exactly what we always wanted?

Chapter 20

Monica mentioned a coffee shop in Adams Morgan and I agreed it sounded inconspicuous enough.

"How will I know you?" I asked.

"The old fashioned way. I'll introduce myself to you."

I arrived early and ordered a matcha green tea. An attractive woman about my age was standing in line behind me and I wondered if that was Monica. She looked at me blankly as I stared back at her perhaps a little too often.

Monica in fact turned out to be a plain-looking woman considerably older than me. She walked in and approached me as I was sipping matcha.

"Aby. It's a pleasure, finally. Monica."

She was efficient with her words, and sat down across from me without ordering anything. I reached into my bag for the thumb drive, and handed it to her.

"I still don't understand how this whole thing is going to work."

Monica leaned in and whispered.

"Ok. Here's the thing. This thumb drive is even more valuable than we once thought. It contains subscriber lists to both IM and *Out The Bullies*."

I felt had. My mouth went dry, and large drops of sweat slid down my armpits. I thought about grabbing back the drive, but Monica had already dropped it into her oversized bag.

I hadn't really known what I was looking at. I hadn't looked for anything but Donny.

"Innovative Media is now courting *Out The Bullies*. IM is hoping for a giant merger that will drive business away from all other social media. But these two companies have already taken a large portion of the market share of new social media apps, as these subscriber lists prove." Monica tapped her bag containing the evidence.

"If Innovative Media succeeds, it could create a monopoly and accomplish more in the next year than Mark Zuckerberg accomplished in the last decade. In creating their monopoly, they will drive up prices astronomically. They will have made money on the insecurities of teens, to the tune of billions."

"Wait. Aren't monopolies illegal? I feel like I learned this in a high school economics class once."

"Yes and no. You have to prove it first. Remember when everyone said no one would let two giant satellite radio companies merge?"

"XM and Sirius?"

"Yep, they used to be the only two satellite companies on the block, and they got the Department of Justice to agree they could still merge because of other competition in the market from free radio and other radio apps. Innovative Media and *Out The Bullies* are going to make the same argument, but the truth is they *do* have a monopoly in this space, and they are hoping the Department of Justice turns a blind eye to this."

"Department of Justice?"

I felt a sinking feeling, and wished I still had that thumb drive in my possession.

"Yes, that's who makes these decisions."

"I guess a litigator from the DOJ's D.C. U.S. Attorney's Office would be quite a valuable point of contact for IM and *Out The Bullies*, yes?" I felt pure dread.

Monica nodded slowly.

"And clearly, Innovative Media is looking for some support from the man who's made himself a name on the biggest internet litigation of this decade?"

"I think that's fair to say."

"Jude will never go for it. He'll press for litigation. He'll never support IM."

"Well, I think that's why they are so hot to acquire *Out The Bullies* as opposed to another competitor. Previously, IM never really gave *Out The Bullies* the credit they deserved. That's how *Out The Bullies* was able to function under the radar for so long and grow their company."

"So, what made IM interested in them?"

"Well, frankly, Aby, the fact that they supported Jude in this election. And that he didn't shun their support. I think that has established them as a real player in this game. At least as far as IM is concerned."

I looked up at the ceiling. I'd done this. I'd been played, and I had to accept it. The question was: by whom exactly? Laila? *Out The Bullies*? Monica? All of the above?

"And there's more."

Of course there was.

"IM's new model is to recruit new members to the app. You get credits paid in badges; but now, for certain members, money is showing up in their accounts, and because their accounts have to be linked to an automatic debit app called PayUp, they are able to access the money instantaneously. It's literally becoming a windfall for those members who recruit new members."

"You mean, it's become an actual pyramid scheme? App users are getting lured with real money, now?"

"Yes. That's exactly what I'm saying."

"Why is no one reporting it?"

"No one can prove it. It's only happening to a select number of teenagers and they are recruiting like mad. New members buy the app for $2.99, but they are secretly promised a windfall later on if they sign on and recruit new members. No one will talk about it online in social media. Only in the newest IM beta app."

"Well, how did you find out about it?"

"The Watchdog Group—you met one of them at 2319—is helping us."

Monica read my expression. "Aby you're on the right

side here. They are the good guys. So you've done a good thing."

"Dear God. What is *really* going on here? Monica, it's time you come clean." I could hear the panic in my own voice. I thought about Gary who seemed a little erratic in the house, insulted that I wasn't more impressed with his espionage skills, and then following me and rapping on the window crazily before giving me the thumb drive. I remembered his warning about all the competing agendas at issue here.

"Oh, I assure you this is legit and completely on the up and up. The Watchdog Group uncovered the largest pyramid scheme in the country last year. A so-called health food company selling caffeine pills masked as herbs to teenagers too broken to resist. They had become the biggest drug dealer in the United States in just a couple of years. Watchdog outed them and now they've moved on to IM and *Out The Bullies*."

"Couldn't Watchdog be a brand new tech company trying to get rid of their biggest competition? I think we have to be a little skeptical about this. We can't take their word for it. In the meantime, if teenagers are being taken advantage of, there are actual channels we can go through. We don't have to wait around for some competing tech company posing as a watchdog group to gather up so-called evidence."

"I don't think you understand. IM is working with very influential people. How do you think they even got funding or access to this type of information—this type of technology? They couldn't have done it without help at the top. They have friends as far up as the White House."

"The President? Come on. This sounds crazy. Like some kind of conspiracy theory. Two shooters. The government planned 9/11. You're not one of *those* reporters are you?"

"I'm simply interested in the truth, Aby. And I know you are, too."

Every time I thought Monica knew me, understood me, she went and said something that contradicted that.

"Monica, if that's even your name," I took a defensive dig unnecessarily, "that's what police stations are for. I'm done being the voice of righteousness for the world."

"Let's just say, Aby, that IM has very powerful friends. And if you think you can waltz into a D.C. police station and ask them to stop investigating their current homicide investigation for this so-called emergency, you're being pretty naïve."

"Well can't we report them? Like, I don't know, to the Better Business Bureau? Or the FTC? Or whoever is in charge of this sort of thing?"

"Absolutely—and we have. We've filed all the paperwork we could. All the right agencies say they will look into it. But in the meantime, real damage is being done. Right now, IM looks to be as harmless as Snapchat—rewarding users with trophies and hearts and virtual badges. But we know an increasing number of those users are getting monetary deposits marked only as "refund" directly to their PayUp accounts. We are even trying to ascertain whether PayUp is complicit in all this. We have documentation from four parents who, as part of a local activist group, set up accounts pretending to be teenagers, and received PayUp payments."

"Four? Out of millions? This doesn't sound very convincing. If this conspiracy is so far reaching, why aren't more people coming forward?"

"Why aren't more teenagers coming forward to say they've gotten windfalls of payments made to their PayUp accounts so we can stop it from happening? Is that really what you're asking, Aby?"

"Well, ok. That sounded dumber when you said it like that. But seriously—why aren't more activist groups getting wind of this and doing what that whistleblower group did?"

"Because IM is on to the fact that they are the subject of investigations now. They are no small-time operation. They have an entire team dedicated to vetting new-account openings now. I've tried to open a phony account under various teen aliases for four months now. Nada."

"I bet I could do it."

"Ok, vigilante. You go for it." I heard the mocking in her voice.

"So what are we left with?"

"Well, if we could get some true influencers from the *Out The Bullies* fanbase to help us, we might be able to get some momentum on our side."

"Influencers?"

"People with enough followers to make a difference."

"You have some in mind?" I felt warm air blowing on the back of my neck without any identifiable source.

"Well, Aby, I'm going to scour these lists."

I felt the sweat dripping down the middle of my back.

"But we already have *one* in mind."

"But Corelle, she's gone." I looked up at the fan with tears biting at my eyes. It was turning, but all I felt was a warm hot wind blowing eerily on my neck.

"No. We want you, Aby. We know you've been posting as SassyCorelle. And as ChelseaCat. I mean, this drive will prove it now, but we know you've been active on *Out The Bullies* for quite some time. And we want you to help us bring IM down for real now."

Chapter 21

I left the meeting with Monica feeling like I'd been run over by a truck; I headed right for the campaign office.

I didn't like that when I got to the office, only Laila was there. It didn't happen often, but when it did, I tried to make small talk and avoid substantive talk until Jude got there.

"Working later than usual, Aby?"

"Yeah, in the middle of a big fundraiser. I feel a little scattered between that and the campaign right now."

"Oh Aby, I really feel sorry for you."

I ignored the fake sympathy dripping in her voice. "Me? No thanks. How about if you direct all that newly found sympathy in someone else's direction. Like some of the kids at my Foundation who don't have running water or heat this week? I'm good. I don't need your sympathy. I don't feel sorry for myself. Plus, Jude deserves this. I don't mind spreading myself thin for him."

"Ah, there she is. The consummate do-gooder I've come to admire so much." Laila added her trademark wink, and much as I always coveted one, I didn't enjoy her words on this occasion. Especially when she added, "Plus. Plot twist. Staunch stand-by-her-man stance. You're like a country song now."

"What's that supposed to mean? What shouldn't I stand by Jude? Aren't you standing by him as well? Isn't that what you're being paid to do?"

Laila shrugged and started to back out of the room. I tasted her almond cologne on my tongue and started to cough.

"Ack. Cool down, Aby. Just kidding around. Killing time until Jude gets here. Isn't that what we were doing?"

Another misplaced wink.

I wondered if Laila knew or would care that Kylie Rutter's daughter was a mean girl on LessThan. Would it be helpful information to pass along? But then I'd have to tell her how I knew. That could get complicated. I was still working through this stream of thought when I noticed Laila looking down at some files I'd placed on the table. I'd brought some work along with me.

"Foundation work?"

I nodded, and then I dove into one of them, trying to ignore Laila. It was Isaiah Morris's file. I wanted to use some of it for a fundraising brochure I was putting together. But there were problems with that. Hypocrisies.

Isaiah was an 11-year-old student who spent every weekday at Appletreese's D.C. playground program. I tried hard not to think about how he spent Friday night through Sunday night. I wanted to believe his days at Appletreese were formative, were imprinting him—in a way the other days in the other places were not.

He wanted—no needed—to stay with his friends at Third Street Elementary. He had a close-knit group of friends who played basketball after school and came together on a neighborhood program-funded bus to Appletreese. Third Street Elementary had a vibrant after-school program in which the students studied contemporary and local artists. They made murals together on walls around the playground. Walls for which the neighborhood program bartered for additional funding for the bus and the program. He'd been through so much transition in the last two years. His older sister had succumbed to drugs the year before at age 16. His mom had succumbed to depression around the same time. Dad had left two years earlier and was nowhere to be found. He could have been alive. He could have been dead. It wasn't exactly clear which or if it mattered.

When mom was hospitalized with depression and Isaiah went to live with a foster family in a neighboring floundering school district, he was going to lose his spot at Third Street

Elementary and with it, access to the neighborhood bus, his basketball squad, and his mural projects. I could not let that happen.

I filled out forms and forged absent mom's signature to say that Isaiah was going to be staying under the legal guardianship of his paternal grandfather. I worked out a deal with the foster mom, that she would drive Isaiah to Third Street Elementary in the mornings and the Appletreese bus would get him to the playground every day and back home again by dinnertime. Foster mom received an extra subsidy each month. She never questioned why it was in the form of a money order signed directly by a Chelsea Boyle. And I never volunteered that the additional subsidy was neither sanctioned by nor financed by Appletreese officially.

Isaiah was safe for now. The gymnastics required to keep him so seemed worth it. Or at the very least, warranted.

Still, with Laila clucking nearby about me being a consummate do-gooder, I felt a little shamed.

She started reading the file over my shoulder, and I shut it quickly, too quickly.

Jude walked in then and saved us both from ourselves.

⌒

On the way home later that night after a late night campaign meeting, I looked at Jude's profile while Washington D.C. continued speeding by behind him, and wondered why Laila seemed so disappointed that I was still standing by Jude.

Even though we had agreed the night would be a late one, and everyone was tired, Jude had insisted on driving instead of Uber'ing home. My car was in the shop, finally getting an overdue new windshield, and I had been taking the Metro and Uber'ing everywhere. But Jude declined my suggestion. I knew that Jude felt in control in his own car. More than the ability to choose his own music, his own route, and his own seat reclining options, Jude liked to be in the driver's seat, both figuratively and literally. Was that what Laila hated so much?

Or worse—was that what she loved?

After a late evening of pouring over demographics and reports and website changes and additions, I decided to hold onto the silence for the ride home. Jude hadn't mentioned money. He didn't even ask why Laila hadn't mentioned money. A new round of just-released *Out The Bullies* ads endorsing Jude hung between all of us like a dangerous secret.

I wanted to talk to Jude about *Out The Bullies*. About how I had discovered them when I was doing some research before meeting him years ago. I wanted to tell him about how I used *Out The Bullies* to stick up for Corelle when I suspected she was being bullied by a high school classmate.

I wanted to tell him why that had struck such a powerful nerve for me.

I wanted to tell him that lying on my resume and lying to Mena and lying about breaking down outside Little Miss Whiskey's, and lying to Sol about my school status, and lying to my mom when her cancer diagnosis got too real—that none of those lies were the ones I was ashamed of.

I wanted to tell him about the one lie I'd told, when I'd reached my breaking point, that ruined everything.

But instead I sat in silence and Jude hummed along to Ed Sheeran, and I leaned my head back and closed my eyes to the sound of Jude's growling hum, and pushed out all my guilt and other thoughts. I needed the music louder. I reached over and pressed the volume higher and higher, until Jude finally called out, "Aby!" He must have had to yell it several times, because when I opened my eyes, we were stopped at a stoplight and my hand was poised on the volume control of Jude's car, and Jude was closing his hand around me trying to pry my hand off the knob. "Aby." He said it this time more gently. "Stop, it's too loud. What are you trying to drown out?"

Chapter 22

The first time it happened, it was a pen cap.

Just a small little pen cap in my back. Jabbed so hard, it broke the skin below my favorite white Abercrombie and Fitch shirt and made a tear drop-shaped blood stain that I couldn't get out after pre-washing and soaking the shirt for hours, until I had to give up and throw it out.

But it was just a pen cap, so that didn't seem like big enough news to share with anyone.

"Chelsea, stop being a freaking bitch. You have to finish my math homework before you leave. You're not even late yet." I was sitting on the edge of the bed, putting away my homework, telling Rafe that I had to get home because my mom would be home from chemo soon and I wanted to be home before she and Kane got there. He was so angry that he jabbed his pen into my back.

I massaged my back while I finished his homework, and he told me to stop being such a baby, and I thought about my now completely bald mom who would be hovering over the toilet shortly, heaving up her guts and I agreed that I was being kind of a baby over a little bruise on my back that I'd asked for anyway, because I knew packing up my homework early was going to piss him off, and I'd done it anyway.

And then things escalated. It wasn't pen caps anymore, it was hits to the back of the head. It was shoes thrown across the room. It was grabbing my hair by the fistful and hissing at me that I was an "ungrateful bitch, and probably a little crazy, too. Isn't that why you have to go to a shrink?"

I had told Rafe about Dr. York, hoping to receive a little empathy, a little compassion from someone who was supposed to care about me. He used that information and more against me.

I wondered in dark moments why I had confided in Rafe. I didn't tell Dr. York about Rafe. I lied and told Dr. York I wasn't seeing anyone. I wished I had lied to Rafe. I wondered when I'd stop lying *about* Rafe.

My mom rolled out red carpets for Rafe when he came over.

He'd charm her with stories of his plans for the future. The lacrosse scholarship. College degree. Law school eventually.

"He seems so good for you, Chelsea."

She didn't appear to notice that his future plans never seemed to include me.

"You seem happy. I'm so glad you have Rafe."

"Me, too." I nodded and wondered why my Mom knew when I was lying about eating brown rice cereal, but couldn't tell I was lying about Rafe Wilson.

Rafe Wilson, who was in jail now. Finally. But not before I told the lie I was most ashamed of.

﹌

The abuse went on throughout high school. And still I told no one. Until one day—with graduation looming on the horizon, I finally found a pained voice deep inside myself. We were in a small sound-proof study room cordoned off from the school library where Rafe was standing too close to me waving history notes at me. My own history notes. I had just finished tutoring a younger student in geometry and was packing up my things to go home and study for my own finals. But Rafe had other plans.

"This is no joke. I swear to you, Chelsea. You better freaking fix this. I'm failing history. Do you understand me? I'm *failing* history. You said you'd do this paper for me, and it's due tomorrow and I need some words on a paper and fast. And I need them to be words that get me an A."

I leveled my gaze at Rafe. I didn't dare turn my back on

him. He'd punched two holes in my bedroom wall in the last week. My mom had been too weak to notice them. I'd told Kane that I'd done it in anger. He'd nodded at me slowly and sadly, like he understood. Even though he didn't understand at all.

After he'd put the holes in the wall, Rafe had hissed, "Do you know how lucky you are that I have the self-control not to put your freaking head through that wall? You are so damn lucky, you whore." I had assumed this was an apology, and had accepted it as such.

"Rafe, I have a calculus final tomorrow. I can't finish your paper for you. I gave you the notes; you have to work on it yourself."

I held a protractor in my hand from the geometry tutoring session as Rafe balled and unballed up his fist. He continued with his tirade. "You are an ungrateful pig, you know that. You might not have a future outside that little peep show gig of yours. But I do."

Then he shifted gears. The mention of my night job aroused him as it usually did. "I'm sorry. I shouldn't have said that. You know I think it's hot that you work there. When are you going to get me in there?"

I'd wanted to spend fewer and fewer nights with Rafe, so I'd been avoiding him, but when he asked me one night whether I had a night job or something, I snapped. I made up a lie about a gig at Divas, the exotic nightclub on Route 25B. I actually hoped it would disgust him. That he'd become less interested in me. I'd hoped it would get rid of him but it seemed to have the opposite effect. He couldn't pass as 21, and he didn't have access to a fake ID yet, and so he couldn't even go there, but still he was overly excited about the news. He kept making me promise I'd get him in there one day. And I kept the lie alive by saying "yes."

The truth was, with my mother dying, and no plans for college or a job after high school, Rafe was the only thing I had in my life at that point, and he had cast some sort of spell over me that I was anxious to rid myself of. And yet, every time I tried to break up with him, I couldn't. I was captured by him. I'd thought the Divas gig would be his undoing. But no such luck. Sure he called me a "whore" more often than usual after that one, but he also kept trying to make surprise visits to the club. I realized I was going to have to think of another way to get rid of Rafe. To get out from under him.

"I'm in the middle of finals, Rafe. They know I can't work this week. They let me have the week off."

"Classy," Rafe smirked. Then he resumed his tirade. "Chelsea, listen. This history thing. This is it. Last chance. Or you will be sorry." He kept waving the notes at me. He was too close. I felt dizzy.

I felt the protractor point against my thigh. I slid it up and down while Rafe screamed and yelled about a history paper and how his parents would kill him if anything happened to his lacrosse scholarship and I wondered why no one would kill Rafe for torturing me day after day for the last three years. I'd called him Prince Charming when I first met him. He shared orange Gatorade with me from the secret employee frig, and he remembered me from a year earlier. At a time when I needed attention, he showered it on me. He was my first love. But first love had turned gruesome in no time at all. I was too embarrassed to tell my mom and Kane that I'd been utterly wrong about him. And what could I tell them anyway? That he called me a whore because I lied and told him I danced part-time at Divas? That he yelled at me when I backed out of promises to do his history papers for him? These seemed like sins of mine, really. And things I couldn't exactly reveal to my parents without severe consequences to *me*. It felt selfish to even think about burdening them given all my mom was going through at the time.

I was trapped in the relationship, and it was all my fault.

These were my thoughts as the protractor stung my

thigh. I imagined myself driving its pointed end through Rafe's heart. But no. I loved him. I wouldn't kill him.

Only his parents would kill him if I didn't help him with his history paper.

But dear God, I didn't want to write his history paper. I wanted to finish my calculus studying and I wanted to go home and be with my mom, and I wanted Rafe gone before high school graduation.

I heard myself yell out before I felt the pain of the slice.

Rafe was looking at me funny. His face was twisted in on itself, and he was pointing, and it took me a moment to look down in the direction his finger was pointing. My outer thigh below my shorts was pierced and the protractor was digging its way in deeper and deeper. There were long white fleshy rows surrounding the protractor. I stared at them in disbelief. How could I have sliced my leg open by accident? When I was really thinking about slicing Rafe open?

And how was the gash in my leg not bleeding?

With that, the white flesh started to bubble pink and then red as the blood rushed forward and leaked out of the gash and down my leg.

I thought I was screaming, but after a fuzzy moment, I realized it was Rafe. Rafe was screaming. "You crazy bitch. What are you doing? What the hell are you doing? You're bleeding all over the rug."

I felt myself on auto-pilot as I walked out of the room, with blood streaming down my leg. "He did this. Rafe did this to me," I pointed at Rafe as I walked toward the school librarian, blood running down my legs and a loud static in my ears.

Rafe raced up behind me. I heard him behind me. "Chelsea! How could you lie like that?"

I wheeled around on him, emboldened by the eyes of dozens of other students who had turned to watch what was unfolding.

"How could *you*? How could *you* lie like that? You said if

I didn't do your history paper for you, I'd be sorry."

"Dear God, Chelsea, I didn't mean it!"

Victory.

It made my fingertips tingle. The cut on my leg started to throb and I reached for a chair. The librarian helped me into it.

"Rafe Wilson, did you threaten this girl?"

"Well, I—she's lying."

"Did you or did you not?"

"I was mad. I didn't mean it."

The librarian's eyes bulged. "You did this. You did this to this girl."

I nodded violently as I pointed to my leg. "Yes. He did. He did this to me."

As the librarian rubbed my back, and phoned for both security and the Vice Principal of Discipline, Rafe stood dumbfounded. I felt relief. The kind of relief one feels when one is finally heard and believed. For me, it was the kind of relief I'd been waiting on for way too long. And the confusing realization that it took one more lie to be believed was heady.

As the Vice Principal escorted Rafe out of the library and *away* from me—*finally*—with his mouth still wide open, I thought:

My mother and all my therapists were wrong.

Lying isn't wrong.

Lying can save me.

But telling everyone that Rafe hurt me with the protractor that day? When he really didn't?

That isn't the lie I'm *most* ashamed of.

The Washington Truth, dated October 8, 2018
Excerpt from the Op Ed piece, by Nate Essuzare

...Is it possible, just possible, that we all want too much for our children?

We seem to be disproportionately excited and anxious about our children's success in this country. This is a country of parents who claim to want only the best for their children, and yet, too many are clogging their children with ambitions that can only lead to failure.

Or worse, success.

I say this is because we have come to define success as more.

More things. More work. More money. More responsibilities. More cares. More. This is a unique problem in this country—an epidemic of more. In so many countries around the world, parents and families struggle to give their children enough.

We look at those countries and pity and patronize.

Maybe we should be learning instead.

Maybe we should stop giving our children more. And give them enough instead.

And maybe we could admit then that this success we have sold them on all their lives, was really, just one. Big. Lie.

Chapter 23

"Look at them." My mom was pointing to the television screen during her treatment. A circus was playing out on the screen in the form of the evening news. "Look at all those politicians. Everyone promising to help the kids and no one really doing so. Washington D.C. is the land of liars, you know?"

I'd nodded.

I knew a thing or two about liars. Maybe they had their reasons. I felt myself warming to politicians as I sat there with my mother. But still I sat silently.

I sat with my mother in silence a *lot* while the chemo was strapped to her arm for the long hours it took for the doctors to poison her.

"It's for her own good," they'd say.

The ultimate lie.

They had saved her the first time, but within five years after high school graduation, the cancer came back. My mom and I had been working side by side at the local diner, me serving up coffee, her serving up dreams and aspirations to the local kids.

And so in many ways, the years had gone by very, very slowly. From what I'd heard, Rafe had gone off to school on the lacrosse scholarship as planned, but lost it sophomore year as his GPA tanked and his drink of choice changed from orange Gatorade to grain alcohol. His parents tried to intervene, but apparently helicoptering is frowned upon for young adults in college.

The library incident had not resulted in any negative ramifications for Rafe. He'd told everyone I was a liar. And it was pretty easy to figure out that the blood was all over me and not anywhere near Rafe. I hurt my own leg, and blamed it on Rafe. I was a liar. Rafe wasn't. Case closed.

In the meeting with the Vice Principal and my mother, I tried to say, "But he's been hurting me. I snapped. He *did* do this to me in a way." The Vice Principal clucked his tongue and said, "These are serious accusations, young lady. I think it's time you tell the truth." Then he told my mother to keep a better eye on me and find out exactly how I'd been spending my nights. Rafe sat in the corner with his own doting parents, like a kid in a candy shop. I knew he'd told them my made up story of working at Divas. Not even he could believe that story at that point. But it was yet another strike against me.

I asked my mother if she at least believed me that Rafe hadn't been the Prince Charming she'd always thought? She sent me back to Dr. York. So I figured that was her answer.

And I couldn't blame her. Because I was—at my core—a liar.

I'd cut my own leg and tried to blame it on Rafe at my breaking point, and that meant that no one believed me about anything else either.

Sometimes, while Rafe was away at college, I started to get confused and believe that I was wrong about him. That I'd been the problem, and he'd been a perfect gentleman. But then he came home from college, and started helping out around the motorcycle shop again. I'd see him at the diner occasionally, and the way my heart would race uncomfortably when he'd come in and smirk or wink at me helped me remember that I didn't trust him. That I was right about him.

The diner was a breeding ground for gossip, and before I discovered *The Washington Truth*, it was the diner where I got all my news. I heard Rafe wasn't headed to law school or anywhere else, actually. His grades hadn't landed him too many opportunities beyond one year of collegiate lacrosse. I guess he couldn't find a girl as dumb as me to do his history papers any more. I also heard he was dating Demi Poole from high school, and I'd seen them around town together occasionally.

I had a lot of first dates, and not too many second dates. It was a small town, and after people connected the dots that I was the one who lied about Rafe Wilson hurting her, I was usually pretty untouchable. I knew I'd have to leave town eventually. But I tried not to think about the catalyst that would have to happen before I'd be free to leave. I knew I'd never leave town while my mom was still alive

During the final round of my mom's chemo, with her hair, eyebrows and most muscle mass gone, I'd take turns with Kane, sitting in the bathroom with my mom while she vomited violently for hours on end until it seemed there was little left of her body but fight and spit.

I'd distract her with tall tales of a different life. Tales of a girl who moved away and started adopting thousands of children in the inner city and who was a celebrated hero.

Be that girl. When I'm gone, don't stay here. Don't stay here. My mom would elicit promises from me from her bed, and I'd whisper through my tears, "Of course not. What could be left for me here when you're gone?"

Saying the words out loud made me feel as though my very ribs were breaking open and my insides were flowing out onto the bed beside my mom.

Sometimes I'd read to her and sometimes we'd talk and sometimes we'd sit quietly. The quiet hurt me. I'd find my mind traveling to Rafe.

I was so jealous thinking of him with Demi, and yet so torn because I knew it would only be a matter of time before he turned on her, too. I thought about warning her—about knocking on her door and telling her to get in her car and run away. Run as far as she could.

But I didn't. I sat with my mom, day after day and pined for him a little.

Demi wouldn't believe me anyway, I told myself. *No one does.*

"Rafe Wilson is a lying, cheating asshole." I said it aloud, but not to anyone, as my mom was in and out of consciousness those days. I rambled on and on about him. About all the times he hit me. All the times he called me a pig when I'd order food out in public. All the times he called me stupid and a loser when I couldn't find time to finish his homework for him. I fingered the gash on my thigh that was now a scar. "I should have had him arrested a thousand times over. I should never have let it get so out of hand," I said.

I thought I was talking to the empty air around me while my mom slept. But my words made her perk up. She seemed really agitated, and I was afraid that somehow she actually heard and understood my words. Years of hiding the abuse from her was unraveling on her deathbed. I felt guilty. But it only lasted a moment, as she leaned up on her elbow, reached over and touched my thigh, and said "Chelsea. You have to move on. You hurt yourself, honey. Rafe didn't do this to you. You picked Rafe. I know, I know. The heart wants what the heart wants. But now you have to move on. Just move on."

She laid back deep in the covers and brought the duvet up to her chest with thin pale fingers. I always imagined that if I ever got the nerve to tell my mother exactly what Rafe had done to me, she'd become enraged and make all sorts of violent threats, only some of which would she actually carry through on. I was certain she'd be appropriately indignant on my behalf.

As she laid back in a morphine haze, I was furious at her actual reaction.

I was even more furious when she died the next day and those became her final words to me.

⁓

Madelyn Boyle died in her sleep.

At first I thought Kane was saying that to make me feel better. After my mother was admitted to hospice care, and after around-the-clock vigils, I had taken an hour to go home and get a shower. I'd fallen asleep by accident. Kane called from the hospital to deliver the news. I thought he'd been trying to spare me some gory details about how my mother choked on her own tongue in a seizure, or bled out in the hospital bed, or some such other gruesome fate.

But when I arrived at the hospital 15 minutes after that call and saw my mother laid out looking like she'd stilled for an afternoon nap, I knew Kane was telling the truth.

My mother had simply stopped breathing. A heart could stop beating. Lungs could stop breathing. A person could stop living. The morphine was being delivered in slow steady doses to eliminate pain from the whole sordid mess. Madelyn Boyle had fought the cancer for years, and yet, if her body was done, then there was probably no talking her out of going ahead and dying.

The funeral arrangements were perfunctory and planned and I was not at all surprised by how carefully everything had been pre-arranged. The town turned out in droves to honor her.

I saw a few familiar faces from high school at the church. But not Rafe. I looked for him, though. I hated myself for that, but I did.

I didn't thank those high school faces who did come. I didn't say anything to them all. It had been years since graduation. And other than the occasional drop ins at the diner, I hadn't seen any of them since then. I'd been preoccupied with my mom's living. And dying.

The diner was shut down to the public for a private post-funeral reception. The owners loved my mom. I knew they tolerated me in her honor and I was grateful for that. A shrill-sounding girl named Sandy Richards came to the diner after the funeral and hugged me before I could stop her. She had been part of Demi's Posse, but I had only the vaguest of memories of her. I wasn't sure at all why Sandy had come, other than to gawk at the floral arrangements and report back to the others whether I was still a lying, crazy loser.

During the awkward silence that followed Sandy giving empty condolences and me giving even more empty thanks, I was scrolling through my memories of Sandy. Most of them were benign. Just episodes of Sandy ignoring me in the halls, or in class.

There was something, however, at the corner of my memory, trying to resurface. I looked at Sandy, measuring her.

"Hey Chelsea, did you know? It's actually our reunion weekend—five whole years. I'm heading over to Carmine's Pizza shop to meet up with the others. Want to meet us there?"

I shook my head perhaps a bit too quickly. "Thanks, but I don't think so."

"You should come. Demi and Rafe and a bunch of people from the old crowd will be there."

I paused for a moment. Maybe I would go. Maybe I'd warn Demi about Rafe. Maybe I'd tell the truth and maybe someone would finally believe me. Maybe I'd be a hero. "I don't think so."

"You sure?"

I nodded slowly, thinking.

"Ok. I'm really sorry about your mom. You want anything? A cigarette or anything?"

And then I remembered.

I was in the girls' bathroom—in the last stall—in the final weeks of our senior year when Sandy and Demi came in. It was the day before the library incident. I recognized their squealing giggles. Sandy didn't seem to have outgrown the squeal yet if her greeting of me at the funeral was any indication.

"You want a cigarette?" I'd heard Sandy ask Demi, her voice thin and high.

"No. You know I don't touch those things." Demi's voice was thicker and lower and definitely recognizable.

I stayed still. I didn't want to show myself. I wasn't sure if they were putting on a show because they already knew someone was in there. Maybe they knew *I* was in there. But I decided not to take the risk anyway.

"Hoping to have fresh breath for Rafe after school? Don't worry, I have gum." Sandy's giggle reverberated off the cinderblock walls and hurt my ears physically.

"Shut up," Demi said.

"Demi, come on. It's time you guys come out in the open and stop creeping around behind that girl's back. I mean, God, her mom is like dying or something. Can't *you* do Rafe's homework for him, and let him leave that poor girl alone, already?"

At my mom's funeral, I glared at Sandy with the memory now as fresh in my brain as if it had happened yesterday. I fingered the scar in my thigh through my pants, and Sandy looked down at my hand as it caressed my thigh.

"Hey, Chelsea." The squeal was gone and her voice was softer now. "I've been wondering something. You know, now that I see how Rafe is with Demi. They've moved in together."

"Give them my congratulations," I said wryly.

"Chelsea. Rafe wasn't that, you know, nice to you back then, was he?"

I decided to let the chips fall where they may.

If Demi wanted to lie to herself about Rafe, who was I to judge?

"Rafe? Nah. He was fine. We were just kids, you know? It was no big deal. I wouldn't worry about him and Demi."

That was it.

It was no big deal.

That's the one.

That's the lie I'm most ashamed of.

⌒

A few days after my mother's funeral, I was sitting up all night crying, so the wailing police sirens didn't wake me up. I wondered briefly where they were headed, and why there were so many. It was a small town, with not a lot of crime, so the sheer number of police cars all headed in the same direction was newsworthy on its own.

The next day I got the news at the diner.

Rafe had beat up Demi after a fight. The details of the fight varied depending on the gender and the age of the source, but suffice to say, I figured out that he'd left her for dead in their bedroom, bleeding and naked. He had made it look like someone had broken in, breaking all the windows to the house from the outside. Then he'd left, and had some beers at the bar in town, trying to make an alibi for himself.

Demi had pulled herself across the floor of her bedroom, and dragged herself down the stairs and out the front door where she'd mustered the strength to scream for help.

The neighbors had been annoyed at first at the racket, but then they'd saved her life.

Demi ultimately pressed charges and Rafe had pled guilty without a trial. It all happened pretty quickly and he got five years as a result of the quick and speedy plea bargain.

Only five years for all her bravery.

I was tempted to gloat every time I saw Demi after that.

See. It doesn't even pay to tell the truth. The bad guy always wins anyway.

But I couldn't gloat, because I knew what had happened to Demi was my fault. I hadn't warned Demi about Rafe. And worse than that, I had lied about him, and so no one believed he was capable of doing such a thing.

Months after the attack, I couldn't bear to see Demi in town. One of her eyes still looked off to the side as she'd been nearly blinded by the beating. I avoided her every time I saw her, and I knew it was only a matter of time before something convinced me to finally leave.

I didn't know it would be moldy food, but that turned out to be as good a reason as any.

I was over at Kane's for a weekly check-in dinner. He'd started these immediately after my mom died. He planned the first one at her funeral. "Don't disappear. Come Tuesday for dinner. And every Tuesday after that."

I'd moved out shortly after high school graduation. The tension between my mom and I after I'd hurt myself in the library had grown uncomfortable and I needed my own space. The space and the tension had dissipated as my mom relapsed.

I didn't like coming home—but I'd done it often after my mom's relapse, and I complied with Kane's dinner-date command after the funeral. As expected, the dinners were usually filled with awkward silences, punctuated with the occasional:

"Are you going to the new therapist?"

Yes. Every Monday now.

"Are you taking your meds?"

Sometimes.

"Do you need any money?"

No.

We both became increasingly and painfully aware how much a part of our lives my mother was. We could barely carry on a conversation without her help.

One night, I arrived to find Kane making something that looked a little more complicated than his usual toaster muffin pizzas. I was touched by his effort. "Can I help, Kane?"

"Sure, how about you cut up an onion or two?" Kane gestured carelessly toward the refrigerator with a paring knife.

I was embarrassed by my instinctual but exaggerated wince at the waving knife in Kane's shaky hands. I ducked my head into the refrigerator where I spotted a few onions settled behind the milk. Reaching deep into the back of the refrigerator, I accidentally backhanded a small carton which rolled forward through a narrow empty alley of the shelf, careening off the edge. It landed on the floor, spilling its contents all over the kitchen floor and onto one of my bare feet.

"Oh my God! Kane, what is this? It's disgusting!" I tried not to gag as I hopped over to the sink with a thick pile of curdled moldy goo winding its way around my right foot and between each and every toe.

Contorted and messy, I stood on my one clean foot at the sink, as I tried to reach the roll of paper towels situated just out of my unbalanced reach. I gasped with frustration at Kane standing paralyzed in his spot by the table, not moving, not helping.

"Kane!"

He continued not to move. Not to help. A tear rolled down his cheek, and for a minute I thought it was the onions until I realized *I* was the one who was supposed to be cutting up onions.

"Kane?" I was gentler the second time. With effort.

"Please, Chelsea. Don't."

"Don't what? Hop? Make a mess on your floor? I'm trying. I really am. Please, Kane, hand me a paper towel." I balanced my hands on the sink's edge with one coated foot still in mid-air.

"Don't clean it up, " Kane said as he walked past me at the sink and bent down to the floor where the carton was still dumped on its side. He picked it up gingerly like it was fragile, and only then could I see what it was. It was yogurt. Strawberry. Nonfat.

It was hers.

I tried to push away the discovery that my foot was actually coated in what had to be at least six-month-old yogurt remnants as I finally reached the paper towel roll and began cleaning my foot, the sour smell filling the space between Kane and me.

"Look. Kane, I'm not saying you need to clear the house

of every last memory. But you need to throw away things like... *this*." I pointed at the carton he was still handling oddly. I threw the paper towels, now sopping with my mother's leftovers, into the sink. I held onto the edge of the sink and shook my head angrily at the stainless steel basin, and thought *I'm tired of being alone.*

I'd stayed in the town my mother had died in, the one my former abusive boyfriend had lived in with his new girl-friend and baby on the way, before he'd beaten her senseless and ended up in jail. I'd stayed in the same waitressing job waiting on the same tables my mother had waited on all those nights before me. I'd stayed because everything was familiar and that's what I thought I needed. After everything I'd been through, I thought I didn't want to be surprised anymore.

I stared at the sink a few feet from Kane, who was still crying over the near-empty yogurt carton, my purse thrown atop my mother's usual chair at the kitchen table, with a journal poking out the top filled with stories and lies, and a buried pill bottle half full of useless medication, and I thought: *It's time to go. There's nothing familiar about this any-more.*

I got into the car and headed south and I stopped when I ran out of gas.

In Washington D.C.

The land of liars, my mother had called it.

It was where, ironically, I thought I could make a fresh start.

And the funny thing is, other than the complete fiction I'd created to get the job at the Foundation, and up until Monica Landsberry crashed into my life, I felt like my lying was otherwise under control.

I loved Jude, and that was the truth.

I supported Jude's political career and that was the truth.

I was committed to my work at the Foundation and that was the truth.

When I'd learned about *Out The Bullies* while researching them for my planned first date with Jude, I couldn't help but become interested in a company trying to change things for so many. I applied to be a beta user that same day I had lunch with Jude at the Ethiopian restaurant, and I was approved.

I wrote as SassyCorelle and ChelseaCat and a variety of other monikers. I wrote about bullies and I wrote about the truth.

Words have power. I grew to understand that.

I thought maybe, just maybe, I'd become the thing my mother had always wanted me to be.

Cured.

Chapter 24

The final weeks before the election were filled with an onslaught of *Out The Bullies* ads in support of Jude Birch. I spent my downtime working up the nerve to tell Jude about Monica Landsberry.

The thing was, Jude's poll numbers were still abysmally low. Eleanor Norton abstained from an endorsement, stating only that she'd be honored to work with the new representative for the great District of Columbia. Jude was distracted and there never seemed a good time to fill him in on what had been going on behind the scenes.

I wanted to tell him. But time was simply moving too fast.

And it didn't seem like any of it was going to matter anyway.

We were losing.

And then it was the day before the Special Election, and *The Washington Truth* told him everything.

"What the hell is this, Aby?"

Jude had arrived at the campaign office earlier than me to tape a new set of robo calls that was scheduled to go out to super voters at noon and 6 pm that day. When I got there, I was already one-and-a-half coffees in and I was still exhausted. I'd been up tossing and turning all night in the guest room trying to figure out how to tell Jude about my secret conversations with Monica, and trying to reconcile my feelings about being on the same side of the table as Laila in this whole duplicitous endeavor.

I was also wondering what had happened to Monica, as she had disappeared in the last week. No phone calls, and when I tried the number I had for her, it went to a disconnected recording. I wasn't sure, frankly, if the number had ever been in service as I'd never tried it before. Monica had given it to me one of the first times she called, but I never had to call it before. Monica's phone calls had been regular and predictable over the last few weeks.

Until they weren't.

With no contact with Monica and no whiff of the story in print, online, or even a blog post, I had started to lose faith that Monica was going to print anything at all. And I wasn't sure how I felt about that. It seemed a long shot that Jude could even turn around his numbers at that point, but there was still a part of me that believed Monica had been telling me the truth about who were the good guys and who were the bad guys.

But with the media silence, I had no one to rely on to turn things around for Jude—other than Laila. I hated that fact.

Meanwhile work at the Foundation had been plodding along. Mena had been tremendously kind to me, letting me leave early and understanding that I was torn in my attention between my work that I loved and the man that I loved. I wondered on more than one occasion whether it bothered her that her Executive Director's fiancé was running against a candidate backed by her father. But from my point of view, Mena had left her political and financial allegiance to her father behind with disavowing his money. I was sure she loved her father as any good daughter does (how would I know, really?) but she didn't seem to share or support his politics. She never went to campaign events for either candidate, and she never spoke publicly about either one, although I felt like she was probably going to vote for Jude. After all, she had offered her own money to the campaign.

I'd been too embarrassed to return her check to her directly. I'd taken it to the bookkeeper who also handled Mena's personal finances and told her to discreetly void the check, as I didn't want to mix business with politics. She'd looked at me like I had three heads and said, "But this is D.C.

Politics is everyone's business."

I had nodded, and said, "Well, we want to do this on our own. Without Mena's generous help. You know, the way Mena has inspired me with her own path."

And the bookkeeper had looked at me with the same three-headed look, but she'd shredded the check and then clicked a few buttons in her accounting software. And Mena never mentioned it.

No, if Mena felt any conflict about her and my respective relationships to the adversarial candidates, she never let on.

⮌

On the eve of the election, I was heading into the campaign office and I was in the middle of leaving a voicemail for my admin about a few letters I wanted her to print out and leave for my signature later in the day since I'd only have a few moments pre-election to pop by the office. So when Jude screamed out, "What the hell is this, Aby?" as a greeting, I shushed him, and kept on leaving the balance of my message.

"What the hell was *that*?" I replied as Jude stood staring at me. I was aware tensions were going to be high on this day, but that didn't mean I liked it. I noticed then the copies of *The Washington Truth* sitting on the table in front of him, and Laila looking like a barn cat who'd gotten her quota of barn mice already that morning.

"What?" I grabbed a copy to read for myself.

The Washington Truth, **November 5, 2018**
Which Side of History Will You Be On?
By Monica Landsberry

By some reports, tomorrow's Special Election, in which two District of Columbia insiders vie for a newly created non-voting representative position is a typical D.C. political struggle—one that no one outside the Beltway cares about, and less than half of those inside the Beltway intend to show up for.

But our sources reveal a much different picture. One of corporate greed, power grabs, and grown up bullying playing out on a national stage.

Jude Birch, an attorney who has focused his career on making sure companies cannot make money on the backs of innocent children and other underrepresented populations, has been outspent in every mile of this campaign by Kylie Rutter, the candidate notoriously backed by Innovative Media, the creator of the loathsome app, LessThan, as well as investor and construction mogul, Dominic Treese. The unmitigated support of Dominic Treese and Innovative Media has raised eyebrows about exactly what type of quid pro quo these mega-companies hope to gain with bought support in the Capitol.

On the other side of the aisle, Jude Birch is supported by a small but mighty up and coming company, *Out The Bullies*, formed by a band of a techie whistleblowers who have stood up to Innovative Media, refusing several offers to be bought by the mega company.

Jude Birch, previously employed by—and indeed mentored by Dominic Treese—has not let those early years influence his decisions to prosecute Innovative Media for COPPA violations. Sources say that Treese met with Birch personally at the outset of the U.S. Attorney's case against the company he is heavily invested in, but like *Out The Bullies*, Jude Birch refused to be bought.

So, D.C. Special Election voters, will YOU be bought this election?

Which side of history will you be on?

For more about the path of money from Treese to Innovative Media, turn to pages 4-5. For a profile of at least one suicide linked back to misguided use of IM's popular app, LessThan, and the unfortunate connection between the victim and Kylie Rutter's teenage daughter, turn to page 3.

I knew without turning the page that Corelle's smiling face would be beaming up on page 3, and I folded up the paper and turned it face down on the table.

"Jude, this is a fabulous piece and the timing is impeccable," Laila piped up from behind Jude.

He turned to me instead of her. "Just who are their sources? Have you talked to them? Did you and Laila organize this?" His voice was softer but his eyes were still hard. He was angry at the deception, and he still believed I was the link to *Out The Bullies*.

I sighed with the realization. Laila had sought out and seemingly locked in the *Out The Bullies* money. But because I'd started my whole relationship with Jude with a made-up story—based strictly on Google research—about a boyfriend who'd dismissed me and the whistleblowers who started *Out The Bullies* and Sarbanes Oxley, he still believed I was the missing link. My misguided lies were always messing up people's ability to believe a word I said.

The truth was, even though I'd been a beta user for years, using the *Out The Bullies* app strictly as therapy, I didn't know any more about *Out The Bullies* than *The Washington Truth* had told me. But they'd made good on their promise to publish the exposé on the eve of the election. I couldn't help but be proud of my part in all this. Jude might be mad now, but if he could do it, if he could actually pull this off, then he'd have no reason to be mad starting tomorrow.

I inhaled deeply and said as much. "If I had it to do over, Jude, I wouldn't change a thing. Now let's get to work."

Probably given the timing and amount of work there was to do, he agreed. He turned back to Laila and with that my phone lit up with a strange 202 number. I headed out of the office to take the call, while Jude and Laila huddled heads down over a stack of paper. Laila glanced up at me as I was about to take my call, and gave me one of her trademark winks.

◡

"Did you see the piece, yet?"

It was Monica calling from a brand new number.

"I did. Thanks. It's not exactly the full-fledged factual exposé you promised. More like a fluffy op ed piece. But it might do the trick. Thank you."

"Thank YOU. Ok, I know you have a ton to do. But listen. Assuming Jude can actually win—and I think he can, then you and I need to chat again tomorrow. I need something from you, and I think you'll agree I'm due a returned favor if Jude wins this election."

"What are you talking about?" My heart sunk. When would I stop being beholden to Monica?

"Well, it's just that—you're right. The piece today is not quite the full-on exposé about Innovative Media that I intended to publish. But the fuller piece isn't ready yet. We need a better—more authoritative—source about a major piece of the story that we want to publish. But don't worry about all that today. Just worry about winning. Talk soon."

Click.

I went back to work, hoping Jude's numbers would reverse and that he could actually win the election with this new *Washington Truth* piece, but worrying, based on Monica's vague words, about just what a victory might cost.

Chapter 25

Spoiler alert: Jude won the election.

Kylie Rutter gave her concession speech within minutes of the last poll closing. In one of those weird plot twists, the good guy won.

The day after the results came in, Jude woke me early in the morning; he raised up on one elbow and asked me the question I'd been half hoping he would never ask.

"Aby. How about we get married?"

I looked at him long and hard, waiting for the fog to erase from my brain long enough to weigh all the decisions I would have to make before I could say yes or no. I wouldn't be able to marry Jude unless I came clean about what I'd left behind. About who I was and what I'd done to get here. I knew that for sure.

"Aby," Jude said, and that sound alone reminded me of all the lies still between us.

The silence stretched like an empty hammock between us.

⌒

"Mrs. Birch, I have a delivery. Can you sign for it?"

I turned to face the delivery man standing in Jude's new Capitol Hill office. It was a few weeks after the election, and we were still moving in. An engraved clock that I'd ordered as a surprise had now arrived. And I was being asked to sign for it.

"Sure."

I hadn't planned on marrying Jude with the biggest lies still standing between us. But I hadn't planned a lot of the landmarks along this journey, either.

We got married the week before the clock arrived. A female minister came in to check on Jude on one of her rotations through the building for a non-denominational prayer service, and Jude asked her to marry us.

"We're already engaged," he said.

I looked quizzically at Jude. I had never even said yes. How could he call us engaged?

But I wanted to marry him. He knew that.

"Can't you do the honors?" He was persistent.

"Jude, she can't marry us. There's paperwork, and witnesses and things to actually take care of."

The filling out of a marriage license was a big holdup for me. I assumed I'd have time to come clean before Jude and I actually had to sign both our names on a legal document, but the minister seemed a little militant about her authority.

"I most certainly can marry you."

She answered my confused expression with, "Marriage is a covenant between you and God. Not you and the state. So if you want to declare your love and have me sanction it— go for it. And let me be the witness and facilitator."

So we got married. Right there in Jude's new office. I have no idea if it was legal or not. Like most of what I was up to at that point. But—also like most of what I was up to at that point—it just felt right.

⤚

We announced our wedding as if it had been an official one before God and everyone. The press gave us a little— just a little—bit of time to ourselves, and we holed up on *Front Runner* for a long weekend. After a campaign that had pulled Jude in a million different directions, we weren't used to spending every waking moment together. I realized that simple fact, as I swallowed my pill the morning after the "wedding" with some left over tonic water on the nightstand,

and noticed Jude looking at me curiously.

"Oh no. Don't get any ideas about getting me barefoot and pregnant any time soon."

"You'd be a fabulous mother, Aby."

Jude tilted his head at me to show he was serious and not simply trying to get me back into bed.

"Well, that's a conversation for another day." I smiled at him lifted my water glass to him. "Cheers."

"To later." Jude toasted me with an air glass, and I smiled to hide my fears.

With my history, I don't really think I'm cut out to be anyone's mom.

Mothers show up late at night with power bars and false confidence in their daughters' ability to make deadlines. They tell their only children they can be anything they want. They tell their daughters they can be something good and beautiful and amazing. They tell their daughters they can move on.

In other words, in my experience, all mothers do is LIE.

And then the realization: *Well actually, maybe, I'd be a good one after all.*

∽

Having taken a backseat throughout the campaign, the marriage announcement pushed me into the spotlight as I always feared it might.

The press tried to dig up a little information on me, but came up only with my Foundation work, and luckily for me, bigger issues made them lazy, and they focused on my role at the Foundation.

There was one article by *The Washington Truth* published on the eve of the swearing in that got under my skin a little, asking whether Jude and I would go the way of other young and hungry political couples of late. I wondered if Monica had anything to do with that piece. She hadn't called immediately following Jude's victory as she'd threatened. I started to think maybe she and I really were done with each other. I breathed a sigh of relief. I told myself if the worst the press had was that Jude and I might become another cliché, then that wasn't so bad.

I guess if they had had much more time to dig, I'd have been in trouble.

But of course, they didn't have much more time. Because soon afterward, Jude was shot.

Chapter 26

The honeymoon ended a few days after the swearing in.

I showed up to the campaign office to help clear it out before we gave up our short-term lease.

I expected the office to be empty and locked, so I was surprised to find the door open and even ajar. I pushed it open gingerly and waited as my eyes adjusted to make out the figures who were standing in the office. It was Jude. And he was holding Laila in the dark.

I switched the lights on to reveal them completely. Jude's arms were pressed around her and Laila had tears running down her face. Mascara-streaked tears were running down a face I was so used to seeing locked down in ironclad expressionless icy strength. Its seeming evaporation was a sight almost more startling than catching my husband with his arms around her.

I gasped. At her tears, really.

Laila quickly excused herself, hissing as she left the room. "This isn't at all what you think it is. So be very careful."

Be very careful? This woman was almost more than I could bear.

The second she was out of the room, I screamed at him, "Jesus, Jude. Have you really become a cliché?"

He stood silent and sad.

"Are we what *The Washington Truth* has predicted? Just another political couple who can't be honest for one second. Who won't last much longer than the campaign itself?"

"Aby, stop. You know I love you and you're jumping to conclusions here. This is me. And Laila."

"Exactly. You're not helping your cause, Jude."

He sat down at the table, groaned loudly, and put his head in his hands. It occurred to me that something was bothering him and that it wasn't me walking in on him holding Laila. It occurred to me that a good wife might actually ask what was wrong.

It also occurred to me that I was not technically his wife. Or good.

"Be honest with me for one second, Jude. Is our entire life together one big lie?"

Yes. I answered silently, truthfully, for him, while waiting for his answer.

Because *his* answer would be everything. It could be the turning point.

"No!" Jude yelled, and then jumped up from his seat at the table and grabbed at my arms. His grip felt too tight, unfamiliar. Everything about him felt unfamiliar. He even smelled unfamiliar. He was coated with Laila's almond scent. I turned away from him to keep from gagging.

"*We* are not a lie, Aby. *We* are not a lie." I wrenched away from his grasp. His tight hold was making my heart race and panic spread up my back.

"How can I tell? How can I trust you?" I was sobbing now. The kind of loud choking sobs that made me feel out of control.

"You have to. You have to know that by now, Aby. Or this is all for nothing."

"Jude, I don't want her in our lives any more. I don't want to see her—with you or without you ever again. Promise me. *Promise* me."

Jude looked down at his shoes in response and I left him behind, swirling in the stink of almond and betrayal. I walked down the hall to a bathroom and splashed cold water on my face. I looked into the mirror at my pores as they opened to soak in the cold water, and I splashed again and again, while my pores opened wider and wider and my makeup ran down my face making longer and longer streaks at first and then smaller and smaller ones, until the streaks faded and nothing was left but my face—clean and clear.

I stared at myself in the mirror a moment. I took in all the doubt and emotion and clarity. It was the face I was not used to showing in public. And I smiled triumphantly at my reflection, certain in that moment that I was the only person in my entire life I could trust. I was the only person I could count on being honest and authentic.

"You can trust no one but yourself," I whispered to my reflection. "Stop believing otherwise."

"You are the one authentic and true person in your own life," I repeated, searching for more affirmations in my memory, flipping through recalled images like an old-fashioned projector until I gasped aloud.

Because of course, even that. Even what I was telling myself right that moment...about my authenticity and reliability.

It was all one. Big. Lie.

As I walked out of the bathroom and exited the campaign office, leaving Jude and Laila to clean things up, my cell phone lit up with a brand new 202 number.

Monica was back.

Chapter 27

"Aby, you have to help me talk to Jude."

"What are you talking about? We're done. I helped you get your story. I helped you get your information on Innovative Media, and I helped you give credibility to *Out The Bullies*. We're even."

"Even? Come on, Aby. Even you can't be that naïve."

The words stung. I knew I was a lot of things. But naïve? That didn't feel good. Especially with what I'd just walked in on in the conference room.

"Monica, Jude is the real deal. You printed it yourself. And while you might not believe it, I do. If he wants to talk to you, he will. Call his office. Make an appointment. Do this through the normal channels. If he decides not to talk to you, there's really nothing I can do."

"So you're fine with Jude knowing about your past."

I signed with exasperation. Is this all she had?

"Yes, Monica. I am fine with that. He and I are going to sit down and have a long talk, and what happens between Jude and me personally has nothing to do with you, and frankly, I couldn't care less about your threats anymore."

"Fair enough. But let me give you a bit of advice, Aby. This next installment of the Innovative Media exposé? Without Jude's side of the story, it might be a little one-sided. And if that's the case, I can't promise it's going to paint Jude in the most flattering light. Think about that before you lose my number entirely."

Click.

Thud.

⤺

The next few days were numbing. I banished Jude to the guest room, telling him we'd talk when I had the strength. The truth was I couldn't demand the truth from Jude until I was ready to come clean. And despite my blustering with Monica, I wasn't there yet. Night after night, I'd write in the *Out The Bullies* blog under various aliases, or in my bright orange journal which was running out of pages, and I started to wonder whether I'd ever find the courage to tell the whole truth to Jude, or whether our relationship—our new "marriage"—would simply be over before it began.

I was thinking these dark thoughts one night while driving home from a donor event for the Foundation, when red and blue lights pulled up closely behind me. I didn't remember speeding, but given that I didn't remember much about the drive, I realized I better pull over.

"Sir, I'm tired and I'm in a hurry to just get home."

These were the first words I spoke to the officer who pulled me over on Michigan Avenue on my way home that night. It was a total face-palm moment.

I should have paid more attention to my words. I should have chosen more carefully and stopped to reflect more. But I was too busy staring at him. And the more I stared, the more worried I got.

Not because I'd likely been going over the speed limit.

Not because of the two glasses of rosé I'd had at the event that evening.

Not even because I'd spilled a little stale leftover wine on my dress while helping clean up after the event, and could only imagine the scent that was emanating through the small crack I allowed in the driver-side window. I figured that through even that small crack, I was starting to smell like a homeless woman from outside the Metro.

No, I was worried because the police officer wasn't wearing a uniform. He was wearing regular old clothes. Well, not regular clothes. He was wearing a tailored black shirt that looked a little expensive for the highway patrol and some matching tailored chinos. He was tanned and clean shaven and looked way too comfortable to be meeting monthly traffic stop quotas. So, even though he held a badge up to my window, identifying himself as a member of the U.S. Capitol Police, I figured this was some sort of scam that I'd fallen for and soon I'd be stuffed into my own trunk and dumped in the River.

I kept the window opened only a crack. "I'm sorry, Officer. You don't look like a D.C. cop, and I've seen enough horror movies to know I'm damned if I drive away right now, and possibly dead if I stay put right now."

I was questioning whether I should phone Jude. But my phone was across the car sandwiched in the fold of the passenger side seat, and I was afraid if I reached for it, the man posing as a police officer might shoot me on sight.

"Can I reach over for my phone?" I asked him through the crack in the window as I nodded in the direction of the passenger seat.

He shook his head, and spoke loudly through the cracked window.

"Ma'am. You're right to be questioning who I am. But I'd suggest you don't call your husband right now." I wondered how he knew I was sort of married. And how he knew I was about to call him.

"Hold on." The plain clothes officer motioned to someone in the car, and I felt the hairs on the back of my neck stand up as I watched Mena walk from the passenger seat of the patrol car around to my side of the car.

"What the—"

"Shhh. Aby, it's ok," Mena greeted me. "Put the window down. Officer Bruce needs to talk to you, and frankly, we haven't been able to arrange a quiet time with you outside the office when you haven't been with Jude. Sorry, but this was the only way."

"What the hell? You've been waiting for me? What's going on here?"

"Come with us, Aby. Back to the Capitol Police office, and we'll explain everything." I noticed that Mena was doing all the talking now, and Officer Bruce was standing silently next to her. Waiting. That Mena was there was reassuring at first, but that hair-on-the-back-of-my-neck feeling was not nearly as reassuring, and I was undeniably happy about the idea of getting the hell out of there. To a real police station. But how would I know where we were headed?

"For obvious reasons, I'm not that interested in following you blindly. Where are we headed?"

"Aby, this is a Capitol Police matter. We're headed to the Capitol. No place safer than that, right?"

Mena leaned in, and I saw one of her long manicured fingers tapping at the crack in my window.

I could leave both of them here and drive home, and call the police, couldn't I?

But if he really was a police officer, then what might that get me? Arrested? For evading arrest?

But what was I doing that was illegal?

Oh, right. Speeding, and driving under the influence. I mean I was feeling pretty sober by that point, but what would a breathalyzer say? And how would it look to Jude if one of the first official duties was to consider a pardon request from his new wife?

I had no choice really. "Ok. I'll follow you two."

Mena walked around to the passenger side and tapped on the window. She was saying something I couldn't quite make out. There was no light on that side, and I couldn't see her lips in the darkness.

"I can't hear you," I yelled through the still closed window while Officer Bruce started walking back to his patrol car.

She must have yelled louder, because I finally heard Mena through the closed passenger window. "Let me in, Aby. I'm driving with you to the Capitol."

At the Capitol, we drove around to an annex of the parking lot I'd never been to in my weeks of moving Jude into his office. I stayed behind Officer Bruce, and Mena barked a few directions, but other than that, she remained silent.

"Mena, what's going on here? Am I in trouble? Is the Foundation in trouble?"

Mena kept barking directions, and pointed ahead for me to follow Officer Bruce around several dips and curves in the Capitol parking lot.

I kept peppering her with questions as I turned the car around the parking lot, but she ignored me other than to say, "Aby. Shush. Officer Bruce will explain when we get to the office. I don't want to give you half the story. You'll get the full story in a few moments."

"You don't want to give me half the story?" I laughed then. "You're working with the police, and stalking me to get me away from my newly elected husband to have me talk to Capitol Police. I'd say, all I've *been* getting is half the story up to this point."

⌒

After I parked next to Officer Bruce, the three of us headed to the nearest entrance—one I'd never been through in my weeks of near daily trips helping Jude moving into the Capitol building office since the election. We walked in through a nondescript door via an electronic pass that Officer Bruce pulled out of his pocket. He used the pass again to gain access to an elevator just inside the doorway. After the three of us stepped inside the elevator, Officer Bruce reached across me with his still unwrinkled black shirt and pressed 2. I laughed a little bit, breaking the eerie silence that had covered us since we all emerged from our cars parked side by side in the Capitol parking lot.

Mena responded to my inappropriate nervous laughter instead of Officer Bruce, who kept his game face on. "What's so funny?"

"I always thought these sorts of secret clandestine interviews happened in the basement. Not on the second floor."

Mena looked over at Officer Bruce, and I swore she stifled a laugh, but also she rolled her eyes, as she said, "Oh, Aby. Quit being so dramatic."

The room they led me to was much busier than I expected. As we made our way to the second floor, I was picturing a "Law and Order" room with a long wooden pock-marked table and cinderblock walls and a handsome good cop to go with Officer Bruce's bad cop routine. But instead I got a long hallway past some speckled glass with a fuzzy view of rows of screens on the other side, which were being monitored by a room full of men, and only one woman that I could make out as we walked by briskly.

"What's in there?" I pointed as we walked by, but Mena and Officer Bruce shrugged and kept walking. Eventually I was lagging and I sped up to keep up with them, not wanting to be alone here any more than I wanted to be alone on the side of the road not a half hour earlier.

We landed in a small but comfortably decorated office at the end of the hallway and past the speckled glass. I glanced around for a nameplate, but there wasn't one. I wondered how I'd get any reassurance that I was really talking to a man named Officer Bruce. Hypocritical of me, I know.

Officer Bruce took a seat in the institutional metal chair behind the desk in the office, and Mena took a seat in a bright yellow pleather seat on the opposite side of the desk and motioned for me to take the one next to her.

"So, Ms. Boyle."

"Mrs. Birch, please."

I thought I saw the faintest sign of his eyebrow going up. But just on one side. *What does he know?* I wondered, before he complied.

"Of course. Mrs. Birch. Can I call you Aby? Would you mind that?"

I nodded. "That's fine." Why bother getting hung up on legalities simply because I was speaking to a police officer?

He paused a beat, and I stifled my compulsion to fill the

silence with something. I looked over at Mena, who was looking directly at him, showing me only her regal profile, and I thought back to my initial interview with her. Was everything finally catching up to me? The interview, the false resumé? The conversations with Monica? How much did they all know? Only one thing was for sure—I'd need to be very careful here.

I waited out the beat with Officer Bruce.

"Aby, the important thing to understand is that we are all on the same side here."

I nodded, without any clue why.

"This will become abundantly clear as we are able to disclose more down the road, but for now, here's what we can tell you. As a newly elected Congressman, Mr. Birch's safety is our jurisdiction. It's paramount to us."

I nodded again, still without a clue why.

"Thank you, I—that's wonderful. But this was sort of a dramatic way to introduce your services to me, no? Thank you so much for your commitment to our safety."

Officer Bruce shook his head. "Here's the thing, Aby. I don't want to be crass, but your safety—it's not within our jurisdiction. Only Mr. Birch's."

"Ah. Ok. Got it. Well, then thanks for nothing." I smiled and winked, in Laila Rogers fashion, seeing if it worked to loosen up the good Officer. It didn't. He continued on, remaining expressionless.

"Aby, we receive hundreds of threats on elected representatives every year. We have to follow up on all of them. That makes our job quite difficult, as you can imagine."

I nodded. "I can."

Then an understanding started to creep into my consciousness. "Have you—" I put my hand up to my throat. "Have you received a threat against Jude?"

Officer Bruce nodded. "We have. A fairly significant and substantiated threat."

"Is it someone from *Out The Bullies?*" I blurted out. I

thought I saw a flint of surprise pass over Officer Bruce's face before it burned out and left the expressionless gaze again. "I can't give you the exact details, but suffice to say, there seems to be some connection between a failed campaign run by Mr. Dominic Treese some years ago, and the successful run of your husband last year, and that connection involves a substantial threat."

I looked at Mena. So this was why she was here? Her dad was involved, too? Was he being threatened too? But he wasn't a Congressional representative. From what I'd heard, his campaign was over before it started. How did Mena get him this level of security?

Wasn't it fascinating what money could buy, I thought for not the first time since I'd met Mena.

"I don't understand. I thought Mr. Treese ultimately decided not to run for office in Maryland. Are you telling me he was actually threatened?"

"He decided not to run in Maryland because he was courted for a much bigger office." Officer Bruce passed a plastic bag to me across the desk. I picked up the bag and crooked my head to see a crumbled note with cutout magazine letters spelling out, "If you run, you will be sorry." I shook off a chill. The letter was addressed in typed letters to a Mr. Dominic Treese, at the address I recognized as Mena's childhood home. She'd shared the location with me in connection with her Franklin Street shelter stories.

"Several years ago, the Republican party was going to put Mr. Treese forward as a Presidential candidate. Threats on Mr. Treese's life—such as this—caused him to back out of that campaign. Philomena brought her suspicions to us about who was at the helm of those threats—very well-founded suspicions—but because we didn't have any jurisdiction, we couldn't proceed."

I wondered why Mena didn't take her accusations to another police force—one that *did* have jurisdiction over death threats. In seeming answer to my thoughts, Mena chimed in silently, "And no one else in any local police force would give me the time of day. Too many other more significant actual crimes to deal with. No time for politics, said the Maryland police force. So, I had to wait for Jude to actually get elected and be under the jurisdiction of the one force that has actually paid attention to me."

Well, that's an odd reason to support a candidate, I thought. Could Mena really have been patiently waiting for Jude to be elected just so she could get the Capitol Police involved in her father's case? And how on earth could she know that Jude would be threatened? Suspicions I wasn't proud of rose up like stifling heat in the room. I felt warm and started to shed my cardigan to the seat back behind me.

"Now, we believe the same person who made the death threats against Mr. Treese is at work against your husband. And since his election, he is indeed under our jurisdiction, and we have commenced a full-scale investigation into the suspect."

"Wait. Does my husband know about this? Does he know about the threats?" I shuddered to think that Jude was receiving death threats and not telling me. Did he keep something from me, not wanting me to be afraid for him?

"We have several taped conversations supporting our case. Between your husband and the suspect."

"Taped? Is his phone tapped? Is mine?" I grew nervous, replaying my conversations with Monica. It had never occurred to me that my cell phone conversations might be recorded. Maybe Monica was right. Maybe I *was* naïve.

"All phone conversations at the Capitol are taped. The suspect has been brazen enough to call Representative Birch at his new office. And has made a credible death threat."

"Oh my God. Ok. Well, if you have this threat taped, isn't there enough to shut this down? Throw them in jail? Why did you have to pull me over under the cloak of darkness to try to get more information?"

I felt sick. To think Jude was fielding all this alone and

not sharing it with me was frightening. I knew he was probably just protecting me, but I felt sickened with guilt and fear and worry. And here I was acting like a jealous teenager over Laila Rogers while Jude was receiving death threats.

"Here's the thing, Aby." It was Mena now. She was the good cop to Officer Bruce, I finally realized. There'd be no others.

"Jude is protecting this person. He is not reporting it. The Capitol Police wouldn't even know about the death threats if they hadn't heard Jude talking to her himself."

"Her?" I was embarrassed that my feminist sensibilities would immediately imagine a male threat, and further embarrassed that the newly discovered gender of my husband's threat actually reassured me.

The reassurance—and the embarrassment—was short-lived.

"Aby, Jude's being threatened by the same person who threatened my father back in 2015—Laila Rogers."

Laila.

My mind flipped to a thousand unpleasant memories over the last years. All the times the hairs on the back of my neck went up. All those times I begged Jude to get rid of her, but he wouldn't. All the reasons I had not to trust her. So maybe she wasn't having an affair with my husband, but she was threatening him? I *could* trust my instincts after all. The realization was oddly reassuring.

So that's why Mena was patient with me working on the campaign? She knew Laila was up to no good. And she hoped I'd help her get Laila when Jude was an actual elected official.

She had bet correctly.

"What is it you want me to do?"

In that moment, sinking Laila Rogers became as appealing as sinking Rafe Wilson had once been. I had screwed that one up completely; I wouldn't screw this one up.

I refrained from saying what I was really thinking. *Whatever you need on her, I'll give you everything you need. I'll say whatever you want me to say, even if it's not true.*

"Would you consider taping a conversation with her? We know you and she worked together on the *Out The Bullies* angle of the campaign. And surprisingly, she trusts you. She trusts few people, but we have reason to believe she trusts you."

I wondered—not for the first time—whether anything I'd done during the campaign was illegal. Was this really a way of getting me, rather than Laila?

Officer Bruce seemed to read my apprehension. For the first time his expression softened somewhat. "Look, Aby, this is D.C. We know you're a bit conflicted about conversations you and Laila had about *Out The Bullies.* The truth is, there may very well have been campaign finance violations, but we're not focusing on those right now. And we know you're hiding things from your past with Jude. We're not here to play marriage counselors. We're just here to get the bad guys."

I laughed again—the way I had at the second floor button on the elevator. But still I paused to process all this new information, and the pivot that my knowledge base had taken. I thought Laila and I were on the same side of the table. I thought Laila and Jude were also on the same side of the table. It was Jude and me I hadn't been too sure about recently.

I might be in trouble, I realized. *I might be in real trouble*

Officer Bruce interrupted my considerations as he fiddled with the iPad on his desk and then said to me, "I want you to hear something."

He pressed a button, and Jude's voice came out of the iPad speaker. He sounded sad as he said, "Laila, why are you calling me?"

"Just wanted to wish you luck now that you're officially moved into your new office. You have everything now, don't you? You're the big winner." Laila sounded like she was slurring. She sounded drunk, and angry.

"Laila, I'm super appreciative of everything you did. Really. Aren't we even now? You got your last check for fees, yes? Can't we just move on? Go on with our respective lives? We won. We beat Kylie Rutter, and we beat Innovative Media. We even beat Dominic Treese. Isn't that what this was all about for you? Dear God, you even went behind my back with Aby and *Out The Bullies*, and I looked past it. Can't this just be over now?"

"Well, sure. You'd love that."

"I would, Laila, I really would." There was that unfamiliar sadness threaded through his voice again.

"Well, I'm sorry, Jude Birch, but it's not that easy for me. And it better not be that easy for you, either. I'm not done with you yet."

"Laila, I'm sorry. But I *am* done with you now."

"Jude Birch, how dare you." The hiss that came through the iPad speaker was barely recognizable as Laila's voice. I thought back to the time I overhead them arguing behind closed doors while hot lattes poured over my arms and tears spilled out of my eyes. I thought too about the day not too long ago that I'd walked in on Jude holding her in the empty campaign office and she'd told *me* to be careful. I still knew little about their history. But I knew how angry it made her. She was even more angry now. I heard her voice strangle out its final warning.

"If you hang up on me, Jude Birch, I swear to fucking God I will kill you."

And then I heard Jude whisper one last sad, "Goodbye, Laila," before a click and then an ear-splitting silence. I sat in stony fear across from Officer Birch.

The three of us sat for a few moments as I pondered the same question I'd been wondering for some time now—*what in the hell did Jude do to that woman?*

It was probably my desire to find out the answer to that question once and for all in addition to my fervent desire to get rid of Laila Rogers from my life, that prompted me to break the silence.

"Sure. I'll wear your wire. Whatever you need."

⌐

It turned out that I didn't need to "wear a wire." Once again, my Law & Order binge sessions had only served to confuse what was actually being asked of me. Officer Bruce gave me a tiny microphone that he said I merely needed to attach to my cell phone like a pop socket and it would tape any conversations within a three-foot radius. I had to sign it out with his front office like a library book.

"So, do you need a deposit?" I joked to the woman who handed me the piece of hardware. She didn't bat an eye. She merely said, "Nope. But you'll owe the federal taxpayers $2,500 if you lose it or drop it into the toilet. So don't." I hoped she was returning my joke with her own but she didn't seem to be.

I turned to Officer Bruce. "So what do you want me to tape her saying?" Officer Bruce suggested I get Laila talking about Jude. And the sooner the better. He seemed to think she was freshly angry enough to blurt out all sorts of things to me. The taped conversation had happened merely 24 hours earlier, and they'd recorded several hang-ups from her number in the hours since then.

"We merely want to stop her before she tries anything desperate in anger. She trusts you. Meet her for coffee. Ask her how she's feeling now that the campaign is over. See if you can get her talking about Jude at all. Things you think might not be important just might be. So whatever she ends up saying on mic, bring back to us. Don't assume any of it is irrelevant."

The next day, I put the microphone in my purse and headed into Georgetown. I went to a couple of coffee shops. I even took the subway to the Capitol area and ducked my head into Pete's. I realized that now that I wasn't seeing Laila every day at the campaign office, it was actually going to be difficult to run into her. I'd have to reach out to her. As much as I didn't relish the idea, I'd need to initiate contact with her—on safe grounds. I got an idea.

Hey, how about a celebratory drink tonight? I'd love to thank you for everything with a glass of pinot?

Three dots popped up almost immediately. I was nervous, and then: *Sure. I have a meeting near McPherson Square. How about Catch 15 at 6?*

It's a date.

I arrived a few minutes late. Maybe subconsciously, my earnestness was starting to evaporate. I was starting to fear that I'd screw this whole thing up, the way I'd screwed up with Rafe. It had taken another five years to put him away after I'd been caught lying about Rafe in the library. And he'd nearly killed someone in the meantime.

I didn't want to think about what might happen if I screwed things up with Laila.

I didn't have much time for second thoughts because as I arrived, there she was on the corner, with her back to me on her cell phone. She was wearing a bright red rain jacket cinched at the waist, even though there wasn't a cloud in the sky. I glanced upward ominously and wondered—not for the first time—what she knew that I didn't.

I was about to call out to her, but I saw her gesturing wildly, and I held back, not wanting to interrupt the conversation. I wondered briefly who she was talking to. Then I heard pieces of her conversation float over the still air to me. "I'm busy now. I have an appointment actually, but it'll give me an excuse to leave early. I'll meet you there in an hour. Sound good?"

She turned around then and greeted me with as false a smile as I'd ever seen plastered on her face. "Aby. What a nice invitation. Been looking forward to this all day."

I knew, just by looking at her, who she'd been talking to.

And I wondered where exactly she was meeting my husband in an hour.

⤸

The wine toast was strictly perfunctory and filled with tension. Laila was clearly anxious to leave, and not angry or ready to blurt anything out to me. I thought about that time I'd overheard that she'd love to tell me what Jude had once done and see how angry it would make me. I thought about asking her point blank, but I couldn't muster the courage.

I had the microphone on in my purse, I wasn't sure it was even picking up our conversation, and we certainly didn't seem to be saying anything that was going to help Officer Bruce, or even Mena.

Could you really make good on a death threat? I let my mind wander as we sipped our pinot. I wondered how many it would take to get Laila drunk and slurring the way she had been on the taped call with Jude. I wondered what drunk Laila would say to me if we had enough time to get there. But we didn't because she was in a hurry.

She finished off her wine in record time, and threw some cash down on the table. "Drinks are on me, Aby. It's been a fun year. Wishing you nothing but luck from here on out."

I pushed her bills back to her with one finger like they were dirty. "Oh no, I offered to take you out. I insist."

She shrugged and took her money back, and then gave me a quick awkward hug while I was still seated and said, "I have to run. Thanks again. For everything." She practically knocked her chair over in the hurry to get out of it, while I pulled some bills out of my own purse.

I gave her a 60-second head start. Then I followed her.

⤸

Laila glanced over her shoulder one time as she descended into the McPherson Square subway. I followed behind her at a safe distance, feeling a little like a deputized officer, and wondering if Officer Bruce would be impressed that I was taking my civilian duty so seriously and carrying it out so well. The D.C. Metro crowd made it easy to blend and still watch Laila ahead in that conspicuous red jacket. I watched her get into a subway car and I jumped into the car attached to it. I situated myself in the middle of the car where I could see the crowd in the car coupled to mine through the dirty window that separated the two cars. I could see that red jacket bobbing with the motion of the train and I kept my eye on it every time we stopped along the way.

After three stops, I was feeling impatient, and felt my eyes get a little drowsy from monotony as I stood on the train gripping the filthy silver bar that ran vertically down the backside of the train car. When I realized my eyes were closing, I blinked them open hard and tried to refocus on the red jacket.

It was gone.

The door chimes on my own car were blaring a warning at the L'Enfant Plaza Stop.

I stared at the closing doors for a nanosecond in a frozen trance before overcoming my own inertia and jumping toward the doors, leapfrogging a backpack and a woman with her small child. I barely made it out the doors, but my purse didn't. Out the corner of my eye, I saw Laila's red jacket disappear from view on the seemingly mile high Metro escalator heading for the Plaza exit. I wanted to run after her, but I was stuck on the platform attached to the train by my purse.

Certain I was now going to be dragged to my death, by the speeding train, I screamed wildly, banging on the train doors.

I needn't have screamed so wildly, I realized a second later, as the conductor leaned his head out of the car ahead of mine and yelled out, "Relax lady. The doors open automatically when someone gets stuck."

While I was banging, the doors opened under my rapping knuckles and I fell backward, my life and purse intact.

From my undignified position on the floor, I could barely make out the top of the high escalator and a red swatch of material darting away, oblivious of my plight. Which was a relief. I could still continue to follow Laila without being spotted.

If I didn't lose sight of her.

I jumped onto the escalator and ran up the moving stairs, taking them two at a time, playing a game of frogger with the commuters who were inconsistently following escalator etiquette of "walk left, stand right."

At the top, I ran full speed through the turn style and took the exit steps two at a time. There was no sign of the red cinched rain jacket, and I stopped and clutched my stinging side, trying to grab back the breath sucked out of me. All I could see were masses of people on their way to their lives. One of them somewhere was my husband and one of them was Laila, but that was all I knew. I couldn't see them. I could just feel them.

I was about to give up, head back down the subway escalator, when I smelled something familiar. Laila's almond scent wafting over the smell of stale coffee and urine—the permeating smell outside the Metro turn styles.

I walked toward the scent which took me outside the entrance onto the street and around the corner. I saw her then. Standing on a nearby corner, she was scrolling through her phone, stopped on the corner just long enough to let me catch up.

I was relieved and then instantly angry again, as she looked up from her phone at the changing "Walk" signal, and hopped across the road on her way to her clandestine meeting.

I followed behind her, both eyes on the ridiculous rain

jacket, under an unseasonably blue sky. I was still thinking about her odd fashion choices, when I saw her walk up the steps and through the open door of a small white brick-faced boutique on Maryland Avenue.

The mannequins in the window were in various stages of dress in the latest runway fashions, and I couldn't stop staring. *Why in God's name would Jude meet her here?*

I didn't have long to wonder, as I saw Laila hug a tall thin woman behind the mannequins. The windows must have been cleaned recently for the new display, as they were clear as air, and even though I'd only met her in person two times earlier, I knew her face and her sense of style well. There was no doubt who the woman was on the other side of both the window and Laila's hug.

Laila wasn't meeting my husband secretly. At least not on this occasion.

She was meeting Suzana Treese. And for some reason that scared me even more.

⤸

I was back at the Capitol Police entrance within the hour. I'd been able to get through the security of the lot with my new identification as Mrs. Jude Birch, but I hadn't yet received enough clearance to make it through the non-descript door without a lengthy conversation with a woman behind the Capitol Police intercom. She seemed surprised I even knew it was the Capitol Police office, which I thought should convince her even more easily that I belonged on the inside.

But it didn't.

"Please. It's Aby Boyle. Aby Birch. Jude Birch's wife. I have a meeting with Officer Bruce. I need to talk to him. It's urgent."

"Mrs. Birch. Calm down, please." I realized I was still out of breath from my trailing adventure. I made a mental note to get back to yoga this week with Mena.

Mena.

Did she know her mother was in on the threats to Jude? Did this mean her mother was involved in the threats to Dominic Treese as well? Had she threatened her own husband?

My mind was racing, and even though I knew I should be doing the very thing this faceless woman at the Capitol Police advised, to "calm down," I couldn't.

"Please. I'm begging you. Please just get Officer Bruce, ask him if he didn't tell me I could come here anytime with new information. Go ahead. I'll wait."

I pictured the woman on the other side of the intercom giving the finger to me grandly. I imagined she must be rolling her eyes and pointing at me in the video screen monitor doing a nervous dance leaning in and bending back out trying to get my message through the intercom onto sympathetic ears. I imagined Officer Bruce running in and bellowing, "Of course, I want to see her. Let her right in."

I stood outside in the cold for a few more minutes, my arms circling my own waist in a hug. Finally, the intercom buzzed with some loud static and a curt, "Hold on, Mrs. Birch. Officer Bruce will be right with you."

The door came open and standing there was Officer Bruce.

I practically fell into him as I'd been leaning against the door talking animatedly with the intercom. I was so relieved to see a human person, I almost hugged him.

"Aby, calm down. Calm down. You've got yourself all worked up. And my staff along with you."

"We need to talk. As in right now." I pointed my way to the elevator, and pushed past Officer Bruce, giving him no option but to follow along after me.

"Aby, don't you think you're being a little melodramatic here?" Officer Bruce asked as we exited the elevator and walked down the hall.

"You wanted me to spy on a woman you claim is

threatening to kill my husband and you're calling me melo-dramatic?" I hissed over my shoulder.

When we got back to Bruce's office, I slammed the door behind me.

"Why is Laila meeting with Suzana Treese?"

His look told me what I needed to know. He knew some-thing. He knew a lot more than he had told me.

"Bruce, you suck at poker. I need more information before I go running around town following and taping a woman who apparently has much bigger connections in this town than I do. Tell me, Bruce. What do you know about Suzana Treese and Laila that you're not telling me?"

"Aby, listen. We don't have a lot of information about Suzana Treese. She's an immigrant, who's kept herself fairly under the radar in recent years."

"But you're working with her daughter. Why don't you ask Mena some questions about Suzana?"

Bruce whistled through his teeth. "I didn't expect this right out of the starting gate with you. I really didn't. Listen, Aby. Here's what I can tell you. We have some reason to believe that Laila is working for a corporate client that's become incredibly powerful recently. That client has some very powerful enemies and if what you're telling me is cor-rect, then Suzana and Laila might be working together on the same side. This changes this case. Elevates its profile. And—well—elevates the level of protection you're going to need, Aby."

"What are you talking about? I don't need protection from Laila." I said it with more confidence than I felt.

"Aby, listen. Laila? She works for *Out The Bullies*."

I knew it.

"Are you saying that *Out The Bullies* is now threatening my husband?"

"Possibly. And that means that if Laila and Suzana are working together, Suzana may be working for *Out The Bullies*, too."

"But her husband is a huge investor in IM. Aren't there conflicts of interest there?"

"Or a huge double-cross."

Things once blurry started to come into focus. "Are you saying that both Laila and Suzana are trying to double-cross Dominic Treese?"

"I think it's safe to say they have both been working together to derail his political aspirations."

"Oh my God. Do you think Mena knows?"

"I don't. But if I were you, right now, Aby, I'd be cautious with everyone."

I rubbed my temples, thinking about Monica and Gary and the cat and mouse games I'd been playing the last few weeks of the campaign. How far into this thing had I gotten without even knowing? How much should I share with Officer Bruce? His own words rang in my head:

I'd be cautious with everyone.

"Well, as you already know, Jude's campaign was supported grandly by *Out The Bullies*. But it was at Laila's insistence. I think Jude and I have been pulled into something much bigger than a disgruntled ex-girlfriend threatening my husband. I'm not helping you any further unless you promise to protect me."

"It's fine, Aby. You can give back the microphone. We're going to need to amp up security here, and I'm going to have an officer follow Suzana Treese and Laila for a few days."

I thought about the money trail from *Out The Bullies* to me through Laila. I thought about all the times Laila had made the hairs on the back of my neck stand up. About the warnings from Gary that she had her own agenda here. She was dangerous. I knew that. And I'd already gotten in too deep with her.

"You know what? I'm not leaving here, until I get some protection. I understand I'm not within your jurisdiction, but I'm not going to just waltz out of here unprotected."

"Aby, the best way to protect yourself is to help us get to

the bottom of the connections between *Out The Bullies*, Laila, and Suzana. We know you've been an ardent user of the *Out The Bullies* beta app for years now. In fact, we think *Out The Bullies* may very well have been tracking you through its geofilter on the beta app.

"What?" I felt so foolish. Had I been helping *Out The Bullies* spy on Jude's whereabouts through me? What else had I been inadvertently helping them with?

And what about Laila?

"When we get to the bottom of all of this, we'll be able to trace everything much more clearly and iron out the vendetta Laila Rogers has against your husband. And Dominic Treese. Did you know there was talk of Dominic Treese being nominated by the Republican party instead of Donald Trump? We think there were some enemies of Treese even then who worked to make sure that didn't happen."

A long ago memory came to me: in Little Miss Whiskey's, the first time I met her. Laila high fiving with Jude when Donald Trump announced his plan to run for office. Jude admitted in the car on the way home that there was someone else the party was supposed to put forward. Someone worse. Laila and Jude were never fans of Dominic Treese.

What had he done?

I thought again about the familiar hug shared by Suzana and Laila no more than an hour earlier.

More of Laila's overheard words came back to me from behind that conference room door months ago—if I knew what she had to tell me, I'd need an apology from Jude, she had promised. Moreover, Monica had insinuated that Jude might not come out squeaky clean in the expanded version of the exposé that she was working on.

Laila had mouthed "Thank you" that night of the Donald Trump announcement to Jude.

What was he hiding?

Maybe Laila's hands weren't clean in all this, but neither were Jude's. I wanted to uncover the truth. And I wanted to out Laila. But more than any of that—I wanted to protect the man I loved.

"I think I can help you connect a lot more dots than you even realize. But I need protection."

"We've been all through this, Aby. We don't have jurisdiction to give you your own security."

"Not for me. For Jude. We can both help you, but, I'm not going to put him at risk without your promise. I won't go forward unless he can have protection. You have provisions for Witness Protection, right?"

Officer Bruce nodded slowly.

I nodded more quickly in response.

"Then that's what I want. For both of us."

"The thing is, Aby, if we were to even discuss this up the chain—up the ladder—you'd have to decide whether you were willing to leave everything behind. And everyone."

"I don't have any family. No family other than Jude. It's ok. I don't really do too much other than go to and from the office."

"Aby, you're not understanding me. You'd have to leave D.C. We don't have the manpower to protect you here—in this busy metropolis. So you'd have to leave. And you'd have to take on an assumed identity until the case was resolved. Or longer."

"I'd have to lie about who I am for the rest of my life?" The irony of Officer Bruce's suggestion was not lost on me.

"Right. Or until it was safe to come out again. We'd have to evaluate that on a year-by-year basis."

I saw the elephant in the room. The one Officer Bruce was dancing around.

"And Jude?"

"He'd have to be willing to go along with it."

"He'd have to be willing to lie along with me?"

"Yes, or—"

"Yes or what?"

I grabbed onto the "or" as if there really was an alternative.

Officer Bruce said, "He'd have to be willing to lie until we closed the case. Or we couldn't protect either one of you."

"I don't know about all this. I'll have to think about it."

"Ok, well, I'll write everything up. If you want protection from Laila Rogers, Suzana Treese, and *Out The Bullies*, you'll have to agree to some parameters. I'll send you the terms for your review."

I nodded, and as I drove home, I thought about how crazy it all sounded.

How could I convince Jude, the man who had never lived anywhere but D.C., to leave this city?

I thought about the sadness I'd heard in his voice during the taped conversation with Laila. Something was haunting him. *Laila was haunting him.*

I remembered all too well how Rafe had done that to me. How I'd wanted—no, needed—to escape him. Jude seemed to need that as well.

We could leave this crazy world behind for a while. Maybe we'd escape on *Front Runner* for a while? Maybe that was the way to convince Jude to go along with it? He could come clean about whatever role he'd had in threatening Dominic Treese. Laila could stop blackmailing him. And we could get on with our lives.

The thing is, I didn't have much time to try to convince Jude to run away with me. Within 72 hours of my last conversation with Officer Bruce, I was maintaining a vigil with Jude who'd been gravely wounded in a shooting ruled to be "gang related" by the D.C. police.

Of course, given all that I'd discovered in the weeks leading up to the shooting, I strongly suspected otherwise.

Chapter 28

"Jude, what's in the box?"

"Important documents. Like passports and such."

"And I put a letter in here. A few months ago. I think it was right before the shooting, now that I think about it. A letter to you. I hid it from you."

"You hid a letter to me?"

"It's a letter asking you to agree to lie. About everything."

Officer Bruce's letter detailed much that I'd wanted to tell Jude myself. The connection between Laila and *Out The Bullies*. The rise in stature that *Out The Bullies* had been able to achieve because Laila had green-lighted the ad expenditures. The possible campaign finance violations. It detailed the fact that Laila and Suzana were working together to threaten Jude and had probably been responsible for derailing Dominic Treese's campaign as well. It was conspicuously absent of any reference to Philomena Treese. It was conspicuously absent of any reference to Jude being complicit in any of their actions.

In the letter, which indicated that it had been served "Via Hand Delivery" on January 25, 2019, the date of the shooting, Officer Bruce stated that in consideration of evidence I would provide on the foregoing links, I'd get my own private security outside of the D.C. city limits, until the completion of any trial that came about as a result of the information, complete with new identification, new documentation, and new job assistance.

There was room for a notarized signature by me, and a conclusion that read, *We can discuss similar arrangements for Congressman Birch at his convenience. Contact me to discuss.*

Officer Bruce had been calling me constantly since the shooting, but I'd been putting him off.

We need to discuss the deal, he kept saying.

I'm not ready. I need more time.

I wondered if the fact that Jude had been shot kept him up at night, and whether he felt like a heel going along with the D.C. Police Department's ruling that it was a bunch of gang bangers, in light of everything he and I both knew. There hadn't been any follow-up to the original exposé by *The Washington Truth*. Monica hadn't called me in months, and I was starting to think that maybe our new normal had arrived.

Until Jude busted out the fire box.

I sat with Jude, next to the open fire box, trying to explain why I'd done all I'd done.

"I didn't want Laila to get away with threatening you, Jude. I don't know what you and she did to sabotage Dominic Treese's campaign, and I'm not sure I want to know. But I wanted to protect you. Do you understand?"

Jude nodded. "I do. I understand."

I proceeded more gently. "And the thing is, Jude, I don't think your shooting was accidental like they keep saying."

Jude looked down at the fire box sadly and silently.

"Would you want to go away, Jude? With me? Get away from Laila and the Treeses? Go where you might be safe?"

I waited for his answer, and I had no choice but to believe him when he said, "No, not like this."

I put my head in my hands. It didn't seem possible that our choices were so severely curtailed simply because Jude could no longer lie. Jude reached out and put his hand on my arm and I felt lighter, as if he'd absorbed some of the sadness I was feeling. And then he asked, "Do you think there's a way, Aby? Do you think there's a way to fix my brain so I can go away with you and pretend we're other people? At least for a while?"

I thought about Dr. Drake's prognosis.

Jude can't lie.

"I don't think so, Jude. But it's ok. I'm going to stay here and take care of you. I'm not going anywhere."

"I haven't talked to Laila since the shooting, have I? I'm having trouble remembering."

I shook my head sadly. I'd kept Jude here and away from the Capitol ever since he was discharged from the hospital. Officer Bruce told me they had been tailing Suzana and Laila the last few months, but that both were lying low. Possibly they were waiting until Jude reemerged back into the world.

Officer Bruce kept telling me we were running out of time. That he was getting a lot of pressure from Mena to wrap this case up. To link Laila to Jude's shooting, and to her father's case as well. Apparently, he hadn't shared Suzana's potential role. I had a feeling Mena wouldn't be pushing so hard if she knew about that.

In my last phone conversation with Officer Bruce, the day before Dr. Drake's latest diagnosis, Officer Bruce said his case had some missing pieces, and that he was going to have to subpoena both me and Jude. He said that we'd have to make a decision soon about whether we were going to tell all we knew and become cooperative witnesses in the case they were putting together, or whether we were going to have another role altogether. A less favorable role—one without police protection.

Mena and I didn't talk about the ongoing investigation. We did our work at the Foundation and ignored each other. We didn't go to yoga, and we didn't talk about her father.

Or her mother.

I wondered constantly whether Dominic Treese had showed up at the hospital that day in his black Mercedes to actually warn me about his *wife*.

Sitting with Jude and his fire box and my fears, I decided I'd call Officer Bruce and tell him that we'd cooperate. Even without police protection. We'd have to face down the threat of Suzana and Laila and *Out The Bullies* right here. Together.

Chapter 29

I left Jude in his room, and headed downstairs to my flamingo-flanked couch, and sat in it.

I was about to dial up Officer Bruce, but an odd number popped up, and I let it go to voicemail.

I wondered if Monica was returning yet again.

I gave it a minute, and then I listened to the voicemail.

"Mrs. Birch. It's Fiona, the Congressman's night nurse. Anyway, I'm calling from my cell number. Give me a call when you get a chance."

I realized I hadn't seen Fiona in a few days, and I wondered why. I called her right back.

"Hi Fiona. Sorry, I let the voicemail pick up because I didn't recognize this number."

"Yeah, sorry to bother you. I'm calling from my personal cell. I got fired and I didn't want to leave the Congressman without getting in touch with you."

"Fired? What happened, Fiona?"

"Well, my supervisor wrote me up for being a few minutes late a couple of times this month. But really, I think it was because I kept telling her she needed to call you. She thinks I'm getting too involved with some of my patients. Told me to stop trying to play God. Or doctor."

"Why did you want her to call me? What's wrong?"

"Well, according to the rehab doctor, nothing. But I know it's not nothing. The Congressman, whenever I've been working with him this month, he's forgetting things and acting weirdly. I know he was getting better a few weeks ago, but in the last weeks, he's been really erratic. I kept telling my supervisor she has to talk with you and even get the Congressman's surgeon involved, but she kept telling me that was not protocol, and I really needed to do my job."

"Oh, Fiona, you're doing the right thing. Thank you for contacting me directly."

"I needed this job, you know. I didn't want to go over her head, but now, you know, I really don't have much of a choice."

"Is there anything specific, Fiona?" I was starting to wonder how much of this conversation was disgruntled employee and how much was real.

There was a pause and then, "You know the little mouse figurine?"

"Yes, Fiona, I know it."

Fiona kept a mouse figurine in her pocket when she worked. Apparently it was a gift from her daughter—but when Jude had admired it, Fiona let him keep it on the table in the room where he did his rehab exercises. Jude had been so touched by the gesture. He swore to enjoy it daily and made a big fuss over it. He always made a point to tell Fiona when she came in for house calls, "I'm taking good care of that mouse, Fiona." He'd wink charmingly and Fiona would smile—a smooth, monotonous routine that I was afraid would grow old, but for Jude and Fiona, but it never did.

"Mrs. Birch, he's forgotten the mouse."

"What do you mean? Forgotten the mouse?"

"Last week, when I was there, he didn't mention it like he always does, and so when I was about to leave, I asked him, 'So Congressman, how's our mouse?' And he just looked at me. Blank. Mrs. Birch, it was downright eerie. I told my supervisor that and she told me he's probably as sick to death of me as she is."

Fiona sniffed a bit and I realized she had probably been crying this entire phone conversation and I hadn't noticed until then. There was something telling about Jude not remembering the mouse. I couldn't explain exactly why I knew Fiona was right, but I did. Jude was deteriorating, not improving. I'd been watching him get more and more confused in recent weeks. Maybe I was wrong that Dr. Drake's latest diagnosis simply meant Jude was "perfectly fine, except he couldn't lie."

I felt a tight grip of panic in my chest with the thought. I thanked Fiona and told her I'd try to intercede on her behalf with the supervisor.

But first, I called Dr. Drake's office and scheduled a follow-up appointment for the very next day. I called Huck and Finn and asked them to join me for the appointment so I'd have an extra set of ears (or two) to wade through Dr. Drake's medical mumbo jumbo. I ignored two calls from Officer Bruce's number.

The Washington Truth, dated February 14, 2019
Excerpt from the Op Ed piece, by Nate Essuzare

...Did you know there is no specific protocol or procedure set out in either the Constitution or in any laws of our nation that a member of the House of Representatives can't continue to serve if they become incapacitated in some way? Thus, if a Congressman falls ill or suffers a brain injury and can't logically evaluate a proposed bill or its amendments any longer, he can't be forced to leave his position.

This is true even for a newly elected Congressman who is shot in the head just days after taking an Oath of office, and spends months recovering, and has his course of recovery actually kept under close wraps by his wife whose past is not exactly an open book.

There's nothing to prevent this Congressman from continuing to weigh in on very significant legislation and very significant investigations.

There's nothing to keep him—or her—from playing with other people's lives.

Chapter 30

Huck, Finn, Jude, and I all sat together in a small room staring at new CT scan images. Dr. Drake had taken a new set of films. We'd told him we were worried about Jude's brain changing. We wondered what that would really mean for him. In the long term. We wanted to know if there was any way to halt the changes. Dr. Drake said he didn't know what we were asking exactly, and he didn't follow the mouse story very well, but he agreed that follow-up films were medically warranted to check on Jude's prognosis.

I stared again at the coils on the screen in front of us.

"Wow. Look right here. Jude's brain is changing again." Dr. Drake pointed. Huck and Finn nodded, and I did, too, trying to catch up.

"But how is that possible?"

"Remember how I told you, Aby, that I'd never seen a case like Jude's? That's still true. My powers of prediction are lost here. His brain is reshaping and shifting."

"Shifting back?"

"No, not exactly. It's—I don't how to explain it any other way. The overcompensation areas. Those areas that literally made it impossible for him to lie are now devouring other areas of his brain. Areas that would normally be responsible for memory and other sensory processing."

"He's had memory loss."

"It's more than that," Dr. Drake said. "He's collapsing inside himself. Other vocal and speech functions are impaired as well."

Jude sat still in the room. He appeared alert and as if he was listening, but didn't care. He didn't react at all to Dr. Drake's words.

I tried to control my voice from breaking. "Can we stop this, Doctor? And if so, how?"

Dr. Drake looked carefully from Jude back to me. He pointed at the coils in the middle of the screen. "This area of the brain needs to be controlled. Surgery is much too dangerous given the areas impacted. The interesting thing—the promising thing—is this." Dr. Drake traced his finger through the coil down the silhouette of Jude's neck on the films.

"What is that?"

"Well the vagus nerve is involved in this overcompensated area. And in the reshaped area of Jude's brain. There might be—and keep in mind this is a very long shot—a way to reboot Jude's brain."

"Reboot—like a computer?"

"Yes—it's call vagus nerve stimulation—it's a method I've used to treat clinical depression and epilepsy with some positive results."

"That sounds terrible and risky."

"Well—that's the thing—it's not. It involves a simple procedure. I could do it right here in the office."

I looked at Huck and Finn who nodded in unison. I leaned forward to speak for all of us. "We trust you. We do. But please, Dr. Drake. What exactly are the downsides of this procedure?"

"Well, that it works. That Jude's brain reboots itself. That Jude's filter reestablishes itself in the cerebral cortex."

"Dr. Drake, English, please."

Dr. Drake nodded. "Yes, of course. The only real downside, Aby, is that Jude's brain will go back to its pre-shooting state—that he will regain his ability to lie."

I gave the go ahead because I thought it would save Jude. But as I signed the authorizations and kissed Jude's head before the procedure, I couldn't help but think about the offer still on the table (but expiring quickly) from Officer Bruce to help us get away and to protect us from Laila and Suzana. The one I previously thought was moot.

❧

The procedure only took 73 minutes. I started the stop-watch on my phone after Dr. Drake took Jude into his procedure room. He had summoned in a resident to help assist with the procedure and told us that it would take about one to two hours. So I had decided to time him to see if he was telling the truth.

Seventy-three minutes later Dr. Drake emerged with discharge instructions. A pulse generator had been implanted under Jude's skin in his chest. Dr. Drake had programmed it to begin very slow frequency pulses and ordered us to bring Jude in for weekly checkups until further notice.

"It might be a good idea to try to get Jude out and about—beyond his therapy sessions."

"To his Congressional office?" Huck asked. I panicked. I didn't want Jude out in the world yet.

"No. I think it would be good to try to help Jude's brain along in its effort to reprogram itself. It would be a good idea to try to get Jude out to places he loved before the surgery. Try to stimulate his memory and help the reboot along."

I thought about some of our favorite D.C. haunts, like Little Miss Whiskey's and the Cherry Blossom festival, and tried to imagine revisiting some of those places. But then I thought of one place that might work very well.

"Ok, Doctor. We'll try that. And then what?"

"Then, we wait."

⌐

While Jude waited on the dock, patiently doing as he was told, like he was a child, or an elderly man who'd lost his fight, I got on *Front Runner* and shook out the cushions and checked the gas tank and made sure everything was in order. We hadn't been on the boat in months. The Harbor-master had been paid to put the boat back in the water in the spring, and to inspect it and run it occasionally—with enough frequency to ensure that everything was still in working order.

From my cursory inspection, the Harbormaster appeared to have been doing his job. I led Jude onto the boat, and watched as he massaged his chest. I winced thinking about how much Jude had been through in one day.

"Does the new device hurt, Jude?"

Jude kept on massaging but shrugged.

"Jude, you like Dr. Drake, don't you?"

Another shrug. Jude was starting to resemble a petulant teenager.

"Jude, Dr. Drake saved your life. Do you understand why Huck and Finn and I asked him to put that device there? It's not staying forever. But it's going to help your brain. It's going to help your brain heal itself. So you can go back to being the way you were before the shooting. Do you want that, Jude? Do you want things to go back to the way they were before the shooting?"

Another shrug.

I waved Jude to the bed. "Lie down, Jude. Let's get some rest. I'll sleep over here so you can stretch out." I started to pile up blankets on a chaise lounge stored next to the bed in the cramped bedroom.

"No, Aby. Come to bed." Jude pointed to the spot next to him, and even moved over to make room for me. Jude rolled over and closed his eyes, and I took my place by his side, curled up under one of the blankets.

I checked my phone. One more missed call from Officer Bruce. A text from Huck and Finn telling me to call them if I needed anything. A text from the security detail out on the dock letting us know they'd be stationed there all night.

And one more surprising text. From Laila.

I heard about Jude's "condition." If you're finally ready to hear the truth, you should hear it from me.

"Aby."

"Yes?"

"I'm sorry," Jude whispered into the quiet of the night. The water lapped up against the boat hypnotically.

For what, I wondered?

I was afraid to ask. And I wondered if it was the truth speaking or if Jude's brain was rebooting already, allowing him to lie. The rocking boat lulled him to sleep quickly, and I got up and walked up on the deck of the boat staring at the moonlight dancing on the water and the boats nearby. It looked like everything was coated in glitter.

As a child, I had a beloved collection of glittery snow globes scattered around my bedroom, but when my mother built a shelf solely to house the collection, I realized how ugly my treasures really were.

Lined up on the shelf, the globes' ugly unreal scenes mocked me every time I entered my room, until I went down the line, shaking and scattering the confetti pieces to create a row of glittery-coated false landscapes. The pretending only lasted a few moments before the confetti settled to the bottom again, and I'd have to turn my back to them.

I grew to hate those snow globes.

Similarly, I had been trying to shake off the memory of the night of the shooting. All that shaking and pretending was exhausting. Eventually, the confetti settled for good, and I let it. Looking out at the water *Front Runner* was rocking in, I *remembered.*

I had told Monica of *The Washington Truth* where I'd be that night. I had told her where *Jude* would be that night.

I sat down on the deck of the boat, letting my body feel the weight of what I had done.

Monica had called a few times after the swearing in, still trying to get me to introduce her to Jude. But I didn't want to talk about Jude anymore. I wanted to talk about me. I wanted her to tell someone about *me.* About the good work I was doing at Appletreese. When she asked me what I was doing later that night, she seemed interested to hear that I was headed after work to return a lost and valuable football to an 11-year-old boy from the projects. Isaiah Morris. I'd wanted to include his story in marketing materials for the

Foundation, and a spot in *The Washington Truth* seemed like a good place to start.

I once read an article that every good deed releases a chemical from the brain. I blame the chemicals for what came next.

What a nice gesture, Aby. Will you be going right from work?

No we will be going around eight. We have a Capitol Hill cocktail event.

We?

Jude and I.

Even though I said his name on purpose, even though I knew she'd be more interested in a photo opp of Jude than me, I didn't take enough time to dwell on the decision. At that point in my life, I was still only afraid of Laila Rogers and Suzana Treese.

Not the media.

But I'd told them where he'd be that night.

The police concluded that Jude was the victim of a shooting on the wrong side of town. An unsolved crime. A crossfire victim in the hard innards of the "inner city."

But maybe he was none of those things.

And if that was true, I'd put him in the trail of that bullet just as sure as if I'd pulled the trigger myself.

The glitter confetti finally settled once and for all to the bottom of the globe, revealing the ugliness underneath.

I headed back to bed next to Jude, letting the boat rock me to sleep, wondering if I'd been afraid of the wrong people all along.

I thought about Laila's unanswered text. I thought about all that I'd been running away from. I thought about how I'd been afraid to tell Jude about my past. About the lies I'd told and the reasons why. I thought about how I'd been afraid to ask the difficult questions of Jude, because I'd been afraid of learning the answers.

It was time to stop running from the truth.

I decided to go confront Laila on my own.

The Washington Truth, dated March 1, 2019
Excerpt from the Op Ed piece, by Nate Essuzare

Have you ever heard of the Baader-Meinhof phenomenon?

Yes? No?

No worries. You'll be hearing about it again soon. And again.

Baader-Meinhof is the name for that weird thing your brain does when it stumbles upon a piece of random information and then notices it *everywhere.*

You know, when your BFF is all "have you tried the apple cider diet?" and you're all, "that's disgusting." Only, then the next day pretty much everyone you know is drinking apple cider. Actually, maybe that's a bad example, because apple cider is trendy, so of course it's everywhere. Like sleeve cutouts and military hats.

Baader-Meinhof works better when you're talking about obscure things. Not trendy things. And it might even feel a little like coincidence, only there's no such thing as coincidence, of course.

I read an article in one of my high school science classes (I won't tell you exactly how long ago that was) that says that our brains love patterns. They seek them out in fact, sometimes ignoring all the other uninteresting data that comes between a few points of similarity. Our brains, it turns out, are really sort of amazing when you think about it.

Lately there are so many coincidences popping up in my life, but I guess it's just the Baader-Meinhof phenomenon causing my brain to focus on a few key things recently like Jude Birch's winning campaign. And Innovative Media's LessThan, and *Out The Bullies* new rise to the top in defiance of all that Innovative Media is doing. And Jude Birch's beautiful bride at the center of it all—Aby Boyle.

Chapter 31

The next afternoon, after I took Jude home from the boat, I texted Laila for the first time since the shooting. *Where can we meet?*

Three dots and then, *meet me at the campaign office.*

I was shocked that we still had access to it. I thought our short-term lease was up. But of course, Laila was in charge of closing out the office. Jude had trusted her with too many things. I wanted to meet somewhere more public.

No. How about Pete's?

I'm not in a condition to drive anywhere. Sorry. It's here or nowhere.

I could tell I was dealing with drunk, slurring Laila. Even via text.

It wasn't reasonable to assume that because she was drunk, she was harmless, but I didn't really know what else to do. I wanted to know the truth finally.

I went to the campaign office, and I didn't say "hello" or "what did you do?" or "do you know who shot Jude?"

I simply asked, "What did he do to you?"

Laila was sitting alone in the semi-dark office, the dim light reflecting off a Manhattan glass with ice clinking alone at the bottom.

Maybe she's only had one drink so far, and I can still get the truth out of her.

This thought quickly evaporated in the wake of Laila reaching for a near empty bottle of whiskey next to her and rushing the brown liquid over the ice crystals left in the bottom of her glass. The clinking stopped.

I watched Laila sip the liquid strength.

"Do you have any idea what it's like being the only woman working for a family-owned construction company?

The jokes, the innuendoes? I've heard them all. The catcalls, the whistles. Honestly, I *stopped* hearing them after a while. Like background static or white noise. The Treese Company had kept its name out of the financial scandal of the 2000s and had the potential to become the fastest growing construction company in the region. I saw that right away. So I was willing to put up with quite a lot."

I wondered what she was looking for me to say here.

"I have a mind for numbers. For marketing and for strategy. I became sort of valuable. Scratch that, I became sort of *invaluable*, and the stupid, dirty jokes seemed a small price to pay for the kudos I started getting in the weekly staff meetings. The promotions, the pay raises. I could have been the one to take that company over in the end."

Realization washed over me. It wasn't as bad as I thought. She had been ousted by a new influx of men. I volunteered my deduction. "And then Jude and his friends came along."

"What?" Laila's expression turned confused and then indignant.

"Dear God, no. Do you think Jude and the Tom Sawyer twins took my life away just because of some garden variety male chauvinism? Oh no, my dear. I wish. I could have surpassed the clumsy trio on my merit alone. I have no doubt. Sure it would have taken longer, but I could have done it."

"Oh," I said deflated. "So what *did* happen between you all?"

"I had to get cocky. When Dominic Treese decided to run for the Maryland Senate seat, I agreed to run his campaign for him. Could you imagine a dumber idea?"

She hiccupped a laugh.

"But Laila, that's what you do," I said gently. I was feeling nervous for her. I knew I should feel more nervous for *me*.

Laila slammed her drink down. "It is *now*. I have no choice. But back then, I was on track to be the first female CEO of that goddamned company, of Treese Construction. The Board was very impressed with what I was doing. I think

Dominic knew that on some level, and wasn't too happy about it. He hoped I'd run his campaign and it would marginalize my work at the company."

"But Dominic's campaign was over before it started, right? Did he blame you for losing?"

"Is that what you think happened? Dominic Treese dropped out of the campaign because he was losing? Dominic Treese doesn't lose. Believe me, he makes sure of that. I learned that the hard way."

Laila poured the last of the liquid over melted cubes and stared at me. "Treese invited me to a strategy meeting shortly after the Maryland campaign announcement. At the W Hotel. Turns out the only attendees to the meeting were him and me. And the room number he gave me wasn't a conference room—it was a suite covered with rose petals with champagne chilling bedside. That asshole actually thought he was going to wine and dine me. I turned on my heel to leave. But Treese said, 'No, stay. I misunderstood the signals you were giving me. Let's not let that derail us from an actual planning session.'"

"The signals?"

"Yeah, you know, saying 'Hello, Mr. Treese' each morning. Not running for the hills when he talked back to me. Trusting him when he said he wanted me to run his campaign because I was brilliant. He lured me to that meeting with all sorts of promises of huge bonuses and prestige, and insinuations that when I did finally take over the company, and when he'd stepped down from any management type role for his new life in politics, I'd be a lock for any government contracts bids. I was heady with the promise of the future.

"I was prepared to sign on to be his campaign manager right then and there. God, for a smart woman, I was so stupid. The secretaries knew it. The interns knew it. The other workers knew it. Everyone knew it but me. Why do you think there were literally no other women working there? I wasn't special. I was stupid for sticking around. And for thinking he actually wanted to give me a special position in the company.

"And you know who else knew it? Jude Birch and the Tom Sawyer Twins. Still, they let me go on and on at lunch about what an opportunity I was getting. I told them I was going to that strategy session at the W. They looked the other way. Jude told me later he thought I actually wanted to sleep with Treese. *Wanted to*. That's what a fucking asshole your Prince Charming is."

"You got out of that strategy meeting at the W, right?" I asked with a hint of panic in my voice.

"I got out of there all right. But I had to pay a toll to Treese, first. He said after he had put all that work into me, he wasn't going to let me leave without giving him what he had looked forward to all week.

"And then he threatened me that if I ever told anyone, he'd make sure I was ruined in this town."

"Laila, I'm so sorry. This is all news to me, of course. And I'm sure Mena has no idea."

"How can you be so sure?" Laila looked momentarily suspicious but it was fleeting. It was replaced with the same vicious anger she'd been holding in her eyes since the moment I walked in.

A wave of guilty relief cascaded over me. Jude and Laila hadn't had a relationship. Jude had thought Laila wanted to sleep with their boss and she was insulted. That's why she hated Jude all these years? That's the blackmail she was holding over him?

"And so you're still mad at Jude for not warning you about Treese? I completely understand your anger, Laila. It's more than justified." I had already forgiven him before the words came out.

Laila stood up and walked to me. On heels so high, and with a gait so balanced, I couldn't believe she had just finished off a bottle of whiskey. But her breath betrayed her as she stood inches from me. Hissing.

"Aby, Jude didn't just not warn me. He knew exactly what Treese did to me. I told him. I got back to the office, I went directly to Jude's office, closed the door, and told him I was going to report Treese to the Board, and bring the company down with him. Jude asked wasn't I concerned about it being my word against Treese? And I said yes, of course.

"That's why I was begging Jude to get his friends to corroborate my story, knowing what they did about him. But Jude said he wasn't in that room at the W, and that everything he knew about Treese was just rumors. He wasn't getting involved. He'd lose his job and maybe Treese would even destroy his already pending offer at the U.S. Attorney's Office. Treese had written the letter of recommendation to an old buddy at the Department of Justice, and Jude was convinced it had been instrumental in getting him a job. Treese had tentacles everywhere, and Jude didn't want to be part of a scandal. I went to him bruised and broken, but he wouldn't agree to tell the truth, because he didn't want to get involved."

I gasped in physical pain. How could my Jude have done something so horrible? This woman was clearly broken as a result. And it was as much from Jude's actions as Treese's.

"But that's not like Jude—"

Laila retreated back to her chair on legs that looked more shaky now. "Exactly. Jude had been a friend—a good friend— all through law school and up until that very moment, in fact. You expect terrible things from men like Dominic Treese. But not from men like Jude Birch. You expect better from men like that, until they let you down very spectacularly. And then you expect nothing from anyone ever again."

I backed away from Laila with tears streaking down my face.

The truth unmasked.

Jude was a liar. He was nothing but a liar.

He was no better than me.

Maybe it's not the truth that sets us free at all. But the realization that *everyone* is lying.

〜

We stayed silent for a few moments as the truth sunk in.

Laila wasn't to be feared. She was to be pitied.

I still had questions. "But Jude helped you quash Treese's aspirations in 2015, right? When Donald Trump became the presidential candidate?"

Laila looked up at me over the amber drink like she was seeing something in me for the first time.

"You're from rural Pennsylvania, right?"

"Un hunh."

"There's this place there I've always been obsessed with. The Hawk Mountain Sanctuary."

"Oh, I've heard of that place."

"Do you know what used to happen there?"

I shook my head.

"Hunters would come and perch there waiting to kill the migrating hawks as they flew by. They'd shoot them and leave their rotting carcasses there. They believed the hawks were killing off the food supplies. They believed they had no choice other than to kill these beautiful birds of prey.

"Of course what they failed to account for is that Mother Nature takes care of her own. With the birds of prey gone, other animals in the nearby areas began to flourish in unchecked numbers. Killing the birds of prey didn't preserve the weaker species. Indeed, it only served to create larger, unchecked populations of predators. Everything was out of balance."

"I feel like you're trying to tell me something."

"You know who saved the whole thing at Hawk Mountain?"

"Let me guess. Some genius of a man?"

"No. A woman."

"Who was she?"

"A very rich woman who gave a damn. She took pictures of all the carcasses and then she took the photos back to New York City and got some other people to give a damn And then she bought the whole damn park and had signs posted so no one could shoot hawks anymore.

"Politicians can only do so much, Aby. But money? Money can do a great deal more. And smart, rich women can do the most."

"I'm not following."

"Aby, I asked Jude to introduce me to Suzana Treese, which he did. An apology gesture of sorts, I guess. He'd met her once or twice when he worked for her husband. Once I told Suzana everything, she wanted to destroy her husband just as much as I did."

"She helped you quash the Presidential bid?"

"Oh she did more than that, Aby. She invested in a corporate competitor, and set out to destroy all his investments. She's currently the primary shareholder—calling all the shots—in a little company known as *Out The Bullies.*"

Everything I thought I knew was unraveling.

"It all makes sense now. Suzana helped you quash Treese's campaign aspirations and then she helped Jude win. All so that her husband would lose. Politically and financially. She knew with Jude in power, her husband's investments wouldn't be so secure in this city. She helped you get revenge by hitting him directly in the pocket."

Laila nodded her drink in my direction like I was finally getting it.

"I wanted to expose him. What he did to me. To others. But Suzana kept pointing to that poor girl, Monica Lewinsky. She was destroyed by Bill Clinton. Just for telling the truth. Suzana said she didn't want that to happen to me. She had another plan. A better plan, she promised."

"She's right, you know. He would have dragged you down with him."

Laila shrugged.

"And *The Washington Truth*? You and Suzana were feeding them information all throughout the campaign?"

Laila chuckled. "Something like that."

My fears that Monica actually had something to do with Jude's shooting reared up again.

"So now what?"

"Well, it hasn't been as satisfying as I'd hoped. We beat Kylie Rutter and Innovative Media very publicly. Their shares are practically worthless. But I still feel like shit, and Dominic Treese is still running free. So you know, cheers." Laila raised her glass in my direction.

My eyes burned. I thought about all the time I'd wasted being jealous of Laila. And all the time I'd wasted thinking Laila was a threat to all of us.

I remembered my mother's painful last words. Whether it was the morphine, exhaustion, or delirium, she hadn't been outraged. She hadn't been indignant. She hadn't stuck up for me, or told me to go press charges. She'd told me what she thought was the best advice she could give me in those final moments—*move on. Just move on.*

I knew how Laila felt. Dismissed. But I also had come to understand that my mother was right. Had I stayed in town and fed my bitterness against Rafe Wilson and the system, it would have only destroyed me. I moved on. I created a new life. New love. Healthy love.

But Laila? She'd been feeding this hatred for years. She had been hurt irreparably by Dominic Treese and she blamed Jude—maybe only somewhat irrationally—for contributing to the pain she was still feeling. For dismissing it. For failing to give it a name or a spotlight.

Laila was angry and bitter, but she wasn't a murderer. I'd tell Officer Bruce only that much. We'd have to all move on. Maybe it *was* a gang-related shooting, and nothing else. Maybe I told Monica where Jude and I were going to be that night, but so what? There was a roadblock a few blocks away investigating gunshots in the area that night.

I needed to quash the seeds of doubt Dominic Treese was still trying to nurture in me.

"Dominic Treese is still trying to convince people that Jude's shooting was not accidental." I blurted out.

Laila murmured, "Asshole."

At that curbside visit, I'd been face to face with evil and not even realized it.

I stared out the window of our old campaign strategy room. *Where everything happens.*

And what about Mena?

I asked the question out loud. "How much does Mena know about Dominic, Laila?"

Laila gave a hearty, sad laugh. "According to Suzana, nothing. She protected her all these years. Mena Treese is so delusional that she actually thinks I'm the bad guy here. But then again, she disavowed her fortune. Her legacy. I believe on some level, she's always known. Known that her father was capable of doing bad things, and that she wanted a safe distance from him."

"Laila, I'm sorry. I really am." I took a step toward her. "I don't know where we go from here."

Laila put her hand up to stop me.

"You don't know. You don't know how it is to be broken at a time in your life when everything is just starting. Your confidence, your hope. Your sense of self. You don't understand."

And then I pulled up a seat and told Laila Rogers that I absolutely did know exactly what that was like.

⌒

"What did you do? To get past it all?" Laila asked when I was done.

"Lots of therapy and some medication and lots of self-help books. I moved here and threw myself into my work."

"And it's all helped?"

"It's *helping*. Present tense. It's an ongoing battle. An ongoing struggle. I still take it one day at a time. Outing him through my writing on the *Out The Bullies* app helped a lot. It helped to put it in words. I even wrote his initials when I'd write about him. R.W."

Laila nodded. "Yeah. I think I've seen that. Well, maybe I'll join *Out The Bullies,* too. Who knows? Listen, I feel like I need to be alone right now, ok?"

"Can I drive you somewhere? Home maybe?"

Laila stood up shakily, "Sure."

I drove Laila home in mostly silence and dropped her off without getting out. I watched her walk up to her door and get into the house like I was dropping her off for curfew. She gave a short backhanded wave and disappeared inside, leaving me alone to drive home to confront Jude.

When I got home, the lights were on in the living room, shining like little spotlights on the flamingoes and the picture of *Front Runner*, and the day's edition of *The Washington Truth* on the coffee table. I turned them all off and headed to the master bedroom.

"Jude," I whispered.

"Hmm."

"How does your chest feel?"

"Ok. Where were you? I tried to call you."

"I'm sorry. I didn't—" I reached instinctively for my phone, and realized I didn't have it and didn't remember having it the whole time I talked to Laila. I wasn't even trying to tape her. I was just listening to her. My phone was probably still in the car plugged into the car charger.

"Hold on." I walked out to the curb to retrieve my phone and as I ducked my head into the car, I was overwhelmed. The almond scent Laila had left behind in the passenger seat helped me put the final pieces inside the puzzle.

I was wrong about the shooting. Monica didn't have anything to do with it. And it wasn't a gang-related shooting either.

I stumbled back into the house to ask Jude if he remembered, too. And for the first time since the shooting, I was hoping he could still tell only the truth.

Chapter 32

We were headed back from a political event. The kind of event where Jude was masterful. Champagne flowed like lava and the conversation was stuffy and meaningless. Jude was making promises to everyone in the room. Including me. He promised me we could swing by Isaiah's house on the way home and give him the football he'd left behind at the Foundation. I even heard him bragging about the promised errand to a few people at the event.

I'd escaped to the bathroom at one point of the evening. I was tired and stressed. I was dodging calls from Officer Bruce and trying to figure out how to convince Jude we should leave all this behind. I'd spotted Laila at the event, and I'd been avoiding her. I'd noticed Jude had been avoiding her, too. I jotted a new entry on *Out The Bullies*. I probably left the app open carelessly; even though Officer Bruce had mentioned that geofilter, I don't think I believed him until all the pieces came together for me. Someone would have been able to use that app to track me and Jude to Anacostia. If they had connections to *Out The Bullies*. And if they were hoping to track Jude to a place where stray gunshots might not raise too many eyebrows.

I knew Isaiah would be missing his football. And it was important to me that he knew he could count on me. I knew he'd be so surprised and happy at the small sacrifice of bringing it by his foster home on a weekend, so I made Jude promise that we would not go home without dropping it off.

After the event, I drove. It was only about 7 pm, just starting to get dark on that January evening. Jude had had a few glasses of champagne, and I'd only had tonic water because I was getting up early the next day. Plus Jude didn't know where we going. Anacostia was as foreign to him as Serbia. I knew Isaiah's neighborhood. I'd been there before plenty of times.

There was a roadblock as we approached Isaiah's street. A police car stopped in the road lengthwise. You could get around him if you wanted to. Which I sort of did at the time. But his lights were on, and I could tell we were supposed to stop and probably turn around. Isaiah's street was the next one over. I didn't really know how to detour. I rolled my window down and called out to him.

"Excuse me! Excuse me!"

His windows were up, though.

I flashed my lights briefly. His door swung open and he arrived at my car wearing his hat and authority.

"Can I help you?"

"I'm trying to get to the other side of you. I need to drop something off."

"You need to drop something off?"

"Yes."

"And it can't wait?"

"No. A boy who comes to my afterschool program left his football. I want to return it tonight. It means a lot to him."

The cop looked down at me like I was lying. Or was crazy. "Well, I highly recommend you put that trip off for another day. I'm here because of a report of gunshots in the area. You should probably turn around and head home and worry about the football on another day."

City life had desensitized me. Gunshots were news fodder every day. It didn't startle me that there had been gunshots, and something in my mind deluded me that they had nothing to do with me. Just as they had never had anything to do with me. I forgot that when gunshots had little to do with me it was because I lived in my gentrified neighborhood a few miles away where the drugs and violence lived but hid deeply inside, rarely spilling out into the street the way it did in more honest and transparent neighbor-hoods.

"But please. I don't want to disappoint Isaiah."

"Isaiah Morris?"

"Yes," I was relieved. This cop knew him.

"Isaiah's my nephew. Why don't you give it to me? I'll see that he gets it."

"Oh." I sunk. I didn't want this cop to take the credit for returning it. I wanted to return it. I wanted to see Isaiah's face when he knew what I had done. I wanted all the credit. In an instant it became about me and not Isaiah at all.

Jude reached under the seat for the football about to hand it over to the officer. "Great," he replied.

I waved him down. "No, no. I can't give it to you. Isaiah accidentally took another kid's football. A white kid at the program. And the mom is sort of going ballistic. Apparently it was signed by some rookie or something and the kid wasn't supposed to bring it at all. So I need to trade Isaiah for the ball and smooth this whole thing over. You understand, don't you?"

I felt Jude staring and smirking from the front seat but I ignored him.

The hulking cop sighed. I knew it was the fact that it was a white kid in my story that would persuade him. He would want to help Isaiah avoid grief and racism that was between the lines of my made-up story.

"Ok, but listen. You gotta drop it off and get out of here. No one is supposed to be out. There's sort of an unofficial curfew at this point. By 8 pm, I have to make sure everyone is off the streets who isn't supposed to be out here. And no one is supposed to be out here. You got it?"

"Yes." I put my window up and hurried around his road-block of a car before he or I changed my mind.

"There's no rookie-signed football, is there?" Jude asked sleepily from his seat. "No, but I'm not going to let that cop take all the credit for my good deed. I want Isaiah to see it come from me. Call me selfish."

"You're selfish," Jude laughed. "But also beautiful." He winked at me, which I caught out of the corner of my eye as I spotted Isaiah's house up ahead and pulled to a stop in front of it. Jude stayed in the car and I went up to the front door to tap a loud buzzer that sounded more like a snore than a doorbell. I tapped a few times without response and then heard Jude behind me.

He'd rolled down the window, and I turned to look at him. "Hey babe, he's not home. You're going to have to read all these signs to mean this isn't going to happen today. Either leave the football at the door, or bring it back to the car."

I stood there stubbornly for an extra beat as I tried to decide what to do. I put a finger up to him to say I'd be back in a minute, and I ran around to the back of the house to see if there was a back door that someone would answer instead. Still no answer, and as I came back around to the front of the house, I heard a car backfire nearby.

I startled, and moved more quickly to the front of the house where I could see the car on the curb. I saw Jude slumped over onto the dashboard with a dark stain spreading beneath his head. It took a moment to realize it wasn't a car backfire at all, but by then I had hopped back into the car, and was headed to the hospital on auto-drive. I had dropped the football in the yard, and I never did find out if Isaiah got it back.

There was no police roadblock as I sped away from Isaiah's house. There was only the sound of more gunshots and police sirens, a cascade of forces that became a distant memory. Until now.

As I drove Jude to the emergency room that night, and prayed he'd be ok, I'd inhaled the almond scent in the air. It was lingering on the night, even piercing the metallic smell of blood in the car.

Her perfume. She had been there.

In the bloody mess of the night, I had forgotten, but

now I remembered the scent of her.

Laila had been there.

Chapter 33

"Jude," I sat on the edge of our bed and asked the question I hadn't wanted to ask.

"It was Laila, wasn't it? She shot you?"

Jude sat up and clicked on the nightlight by our bed. He looked mussed and sad. He rubbed his chest gently.

And then he nodded.

"Yes, but—"

"I saw her tonight. She didn't admit the shooting, but she told me what Dominic Treese did to her. And what you refused to do."

Jude looked up at the ceiling. "I thought I was helping her. She would have been ruined in this town. She wouldn't have worked again. He would have ruined her. It would have been Bill Clinton and Monica Lewinsky all over again."

"She told me Suzana had that same theory."

Jude laughed wryly. "She conveniently forgets that I'm the one who told her that first. She thinks of Suzana as her savior, and I get it. Suzana has hit him where it counts. She's a strong amazing woman. As is Laila, and I have been trying to encourage her to get the help she needs."

"She tried to kill you?"

"No, she was crazed that night. She drank too much at the event, and then she must have followed us out to Anacostia. When you got out of the car, she showed up at my window with the gun and was threatening to kill herself. I was trying to talk her down; I was about to get out of the car, and then I don't know what happened next."

"We have to turn her in, Jude. We can't let her get away with this."

"With what? She hasn't gotten away with anything. She's sad and terrorized. She's despondent. Huck and Finn have seen her a few times and said she's drinking all the time, and spiraling out of control."

I thought about the broken woman I'd seen at the empty campaign office. Jude read my thoughts.

"You saw her tonight. Did she look dangerous?"

I shrugged. I wasn't sure, frankly. "She looks broken."

"She is. Dominic Treese broke her a long time ago and she tried to hurt herself, and I got shot in the process. It's tragic, but I'm not sure she should be punished for the rest of her life." Jude took my hands. "Aby, you're so strong. You might not understand that broken people can do crazy things. But they shouldn't be punished forever for them."

"Jude," I gasped, as I stared at his forgiving face. "Do you mean that?"

"Of course I do."

I'd been waiting for someone to tell me that my whole life.

The dam broke wide open, and I told Jude about every single lie I'd ever uttered.

And most importantly, I told him ... why.

Epilogue

The Washington Truth, dated June 1, 2019
Op Ed piece, by Suzana Luric Treese.

Dear Readers, *The Washington Truth* has been kind enough to let me write under a pen name for several years now. You know me as Nate Essuzare. But in fact, I am Suzana Treese, using an anagram of my name as my alias. Do not punish *The Washington Truth*, if you disagree with my use of an alias. It was at my insistence, and I always planned on revealing my identity to you. Thank you for your indulgence as I have written about the truths in this town and the lies. My work here was in large part a social experiment to see how much truth you as readers wanted. Just how much you were willing to overlook.

I think I now have my answer.

My soon to be ex-husband, Dominic Treese, has been a respected man in this town for some time. But there is much you don't know about him. I think it's time we shine a light on the truth here. Below you will find a letter, published in its entirety by a Ms. Laila Rogers. The letter and its raw contents reveal events that occurred on the evening of March 15, 2013. She has long kept these truths secret, fearing that no one would believe her, and worse, that no one would care even if they did.

I believe her.

I care.

Dear Readers, I hope you will, too.

It's time.

ACKNOWLEDGEMENTS

As I sit down to write this—my fifth Acknowledgement section—I am overwhelmed by gratitude to Nancy Cleary of Wyatt-MacKenzie Publishing. I am so honored to be on this journey with you. You have been an amazing champion of my work for five wonderful years now. I will never stop being grateful about the care you take with my words and stories. From the bottom of my heart—THANK YOU.

To my agent, Bob Diforio, for your zealous representation—thank you so much.

To my sisters and early reviewers, Megan and Katie, for the kind and honest feedback, and for always having my back, cheers to you both!

To Ann, Kelly, Katie, Katie Rose, and my Tall Poppy sisterhood, my amazing tribe. I have no idea where I'd be on this writing journey without all of you. I never want to know. Ditto for all you amazing readers in the BLOOM community (www.areyouinbloom.com) who have supported the Tall Poppy Writers, and me personally. Writing is such a raw and humbling experience, I can think of no greater reason to take the risk other than the reward of incredible connection. Through the connection with all of you, I have received that reward in big beautiful doses. Thank you for believing in the mission of the Tall Poppy Writers. Thank you for believing in US.

This story takes place in one of my favorite cities, Washington D.C.—the place where I started my legal career; so I have to thank my early legal mentors: my fabulous peers and professors at George Washington National Law Center, the smart and creative attorneys in the General Counsel's office of The American Petroleum Institute, and my colleagues at the Special Masters Office in the U.S. Court of Federal Claims, with a special debt of gratitude to Chief Special Master Gary Golkiewicz. The years I spent at the Court of Federal Claims were some of the most interesting, challenging, fun years of my legal career. The hours spent debating cases and policy with the Chief Special Master before setting pen to paper to write pioneering and pivotal legal decisions in cases pending all over the country, helped me understand that I was a litigator at heart—and would always be at home in any courtroom in any city.

Thank you to my dear friend, Stephanie Shipley, who introduced me to Talbot County, Maryland, and St. Michaels, a place that stole my heart from the very first moment.

To Paul for the all the good memories on the Hudson River, the Long Island Sound, and even the Atlantic Ocean, on our first boat, *Kokomo*, that inspired Aby and Jude's escapes on *Front Runner.* I'm glad you convinced me to sink so much of my hard-earned cash into that beautiful Sea Ray Sundancer. We weathered a lot of storms on that boat.

To my dearest friends, especially Kelly Wasielevski and Paula Tziavragos, who support me in writing and life and motherhood the way few others do.

Thank you to Francis Ford Coppola and the team at Coppola Winery for supporting me in a special way through your Books & Bottles program. Thank you to all the book communities, bookgrammers, book bloggers, reviewers, Facebook and Goodreads groups that have featured my books. It is increasingly hard for authors to get their works noticed in the crowd these days, and I would never succeed in that mission alone, which is why I'm so thankful to Barbara Bos, Leslie Lindsay, Andrea Peskind Katz, the Ninja Reviewers, Tamara Welch, Jenny O'Regan, Holly's Little Book Reviews, Liz Fenton & Lisa Steinke, Novel Gossip, The Literary Connoisseur, Dee's Rad Reads, Marisa Gothie, Readers' Coffeehouse, Bookworms Anonymous, Kristy Bee, Susan Walters Peterson, Nalana Lillie, the group at WFWA, and the many, many more who have helped LIFT my books onto the top of so many readers' To Be Read piles.

Which brings me to you, dear readers. Thank you for

coming on this journey with me. For picking my book for your Book Clubs, for inviting me to your Book Clubs, for asking your libraries to order my books, for buying copies for your friends as gifts, for reaching out to say "Your book resonated with me. Here's why." I am grateful for every single one of you; I still pinch myself at being so very lucky to be writing my FIFTH acknowledgment section right now. To be *heard* through my writing has been one of the greatest gifts I've received in the last decade. (A special warm and exuberant hug to the readers who have been with me since my debut, *Lemongrass Hope*. Stay tuned for a special announcement regarding my next book—a love letter to *you*.)

And last, but not least, to my amazing, creative, interesting, hard-working, totally persistent, maybe just a little bit stubborn, children: Paul, Luke, and Grace. Each of you is honestly my favorite.

And you each know why.

BOOK CLUB DISCUSSION GUIDE

Dear Book Clubs,

If your Book Club is anything like the dozens of Clubs I've been invited to over the years, the book you choose is often just the backdrop for much bigger discussions about love and life (and yes, even politics). Here's hoping the characters and twists and turns in *Why We Lie* provide the perfect jumping off point to some robust discussions from both sides of the aisle. I hope you'll share your Book Club's thoughts (and photos!) with me. Get in touch at amy@amyimpellizzeri.com.

Xo
Amy

P.S. I hope you won't think I'm rude, but I'd love to invite myself to your Book Club, either live or via FaceTime. Use the subject line "My Book Club is reading *Why We Lie*" when you email me and I'll be sure to get back to you ASAP!

～

1. "We're just here to get the bad guys." Officer Bruce of the Capitol Police delivers this line to Aby during a key point of the novel. By the end of the novel, can you list for certain the "bad guys" versus the good guys? Which column do these characters fall on your list: Monica Landsberry, Officer Bruce, Laila Rogers, Gary from The Watchdog Group, Philomena Treese, Dominic Treese, Suzana Treese, Aby Boyle, Jude Birch, Madelyn Boyle, Demi Poole, Rafe Wilson, the "Tom Sawyer twins"?

Is your list the same as the Book Club member sitting next to you?

2. Go back and count all the lies in this novel. Just kidding! Even I don't know exactly how many there are – suffice to say, a lot. That the characters are lying and have lied is not a plot twist in this book, but the reasons why provide the real surprises. Aby refers to the lie she is "most ashamed of" before it is actually revealed. Did you pick up on which lie she's referring to? Do you think she is right to be most ashamed of this lie?

3. In this novel, the timeline fluctuates a bit. Did you notice, however, that the excerpts of *The Washington Truth* are laid out end to end in chronological order from 2014 through 2019 as a device to ground the narrative's chronology? What do you think of this device? Does it work to make the timeline more understandable?

4. Speaking of *The Washington Truth*, a big theme in this story is that of politics versus the media. The July 1, 2018 Op Ed piece reads:

"Political correctness, they call it. And it's advocated for. What an odd turn of events. Since when did politics become the barometer for what is true, for what is correct? Since when did the media become the enemy?"

Do you think this a fair reflection of the tension between politics and media in contemporary times?

If so, how did this tension evolve? Or, has it always been this way? If not, why not?

5. Let's talk about LessThan and Out The Bullies. Both are completely fictional companies/apps. Do you think these

are realistic portrayals of companies that could exist (and indeed flourish) in this day and age? Could you imagine yourself (or someone you know) who would withdraw money from their kids' 529 fund to finance a virtual status symbol? Or did I go too far? (By the way, is it hypocritical of Aby (who purchased red-soled Louboutin shoes to wear to Jude's campaign announcement) or Jude (who purchased a $50,000 boat to use on weekends only) to judge parents who got swept up in the LessThan craze to help their kids get into college?)

6. Assuming they would be perfectly fine, except they couldn't lie (as Aby believed about Jude in the beginning of the novel), who is the person in your life you might like to see wake up tomorrow and be unable to lie?

7. On the very last pages before the Epilogue—there is a (hopefully!) surprising reveal and a decision by Jude. Do you agree with his decision? Why or why not?

8. There is a very poignant and heartbreaking letter referred to in the Epilogue. Do you think it was a good idea or not for the author of that letter to agree to it being published? Why or why not?

6/19

F IMP
Impellizzeri, Amy
Why we lie